Twins of the Twenties

Bright, young bachelors find love in New York

Brothers Patrick and Connor McCormick aren't alike in just looks—their rebellious spirits mean they've both left the prestigious family business behind to forge their own paths in life...

New York cop Patrick devotes his life to helping others, but the one woman who can help *him* overcome his demons is on the wrong side of the law!

Businessman Connor's playboy reputation precedes him and there's not a woman in New York who can tempt him to settle down... until his high school sweetheart returns!

Join these bachelors of the Roaring Twenties as they take New York by storm in

Scandal at the Speakeasy

and

A Proposal for the Unwed Mother

Both available now!

D1413787

Author Note

Welcome to the second book of the Twins of the Twenties duet. *A Proposal for the Unwed Mother* is Connor and his high school sweetheart Jenny's story. The two of them need to figure out what went wrong in the past so they can focus on their happily-ever-after.

I hope you enjoy Connor and Jenny's story!

LAURI ROBINSON

—

A Proposal for the Unwed Mother

HARLEQUIN

HISTORICAL

HARLEQUIN®
HISTORICAL™

Recycling programs
for this product may
not exist in your area.

ISBN-13: 978-1-335-50622-1

A Proposal for the Unwed Mother

Copyright © 2021 by Lauri Robinson

This edition published by arrangement with Harlequin Books S.A.

For questions and comments about the quality of this book,
please contact us at CustomerService@Harlequin.com.

Harlequin Enterprises ULC
22 Adelaide St. West, 40th Floor
Toronto, Ontario M5H 4E3, Canada
www.Harlequin.com

Printed in U.S.A.

A lover of fairy tales and history, **Lauri Robinson** can't imagine a better profession than penning happily-ever-after stories about men and women in days gone past. Her favorite settings include World War II, the Roaring Twenties and the Old West. Lauri and her husband raised three sons in their rural Minnesota home and are now getting their just rewards by spoiling their grandchildren. Visit her at laurirobinson.blogspot.com, Facebook.com/lauri.robinson1 or Twitter.com/laurir.

Books by Lauri Robinson

Harlequin Historical

Diary of a War Bride
A Family for the Titanic Survivor

Twins of the Twenties

Scandal at the Speakeasy
A Proposal for the Unwed Mother

Sisters of the Roaring Twenties

The Flapper's Fake Fiancé
The Flapper's Baby Scandal
The Flapper's Scandalous Elopement

Brides of the Roaring Twenties

Baby on His Hollywood Doorstep
Stolen Kiss with the Hollywood Starlet

Oak Grove

Mail-Order Brides of Oak Grove
"Surprise Bride for the Cowboy"
Winning the Mail-Order Bride
In the Sheriff's Protection

Visit the Author Profile page
at Harlequin.com for more titles.

Dedicated to my sister-in-law, Jeannette—
because she's amazing. Love you!

Chapter One

1927

Connor McCormick let out a curse and wiped the sweat off his brow with the back of one hand before he turned around, needing more pushing power. He grasped ahold of the bumper, braced his legs, and put his back up against his car. A Packard Phaeton, red and black, without a scratch on her. That was about to change if he couldn't get the damn thing off the tracks before that train whistle got any closer!

The long, low-riding chassis of the four-door sports model had become high centered on the railroad tracks, in the middle of nowhere. There were plenty of places like this in upstate New York, where the farms were miles upon miles apart, nearly cut off from the rest of the world by rutted and narrow gravel roads. That's why he was here, to bring these people a connection to family, friends and the world via his phone company. He'd already sold lines to three farms, and needed to sell at least a dozen more to make stringing the lines profitable, and he needed his car in order to do that!

He would call about this crossing as soon as possible. Tell the county that the spring rains had washed away most of the gravel, leaving the tracks exposed for any car to get stuck on. People could get killed!

The train blew its horn again. He couldn't see it coming around the bend, but the ground beneath his feet was vibrating. He dug his heels deep into the gravel, drew in a deep breath that was full of the scents of the white pines and Norway spruce trees blocking his view of the oncoming train and pushed against the car so hard he growled at the exertion.

With a scraping of metal on metal, the car rolled, just an inch, but it was all he needed. Heaving in a fortifying breath, he put everything he had into giving the car another hard push.

More metal-on-metal scraping sounded. So did another grunt, and just as he was about to give in long enough to suck in more air, the car broke loose and rolled over the tracks.

"Yes!" He ran, jumped in the open door, engaged the clutch and hit the ignition. The engine roared to life and he laid his foot on the gas. The tires kicked up gravel as the car shot forward, just as the train horn blared again and the locomotive rounded the curve at full speed, a mere five yards behind him.

The car's top was down, and Connor kept his foot on the gas pedal to outrun the cloud of dust caused by his tires and the train. Exhilaration filled him. Life was full of challenges, and he thrived on them. Even being high centered on the railroad tracks.

Slapping the wheel, thrilled he'd won against that could-be disaster, he steered, along the winding road that would lead him to more houses where he would convince people they needed a telephone from the Rural Rochester Telephone Company.

The very company he'd started several years ago, and continued to grow each and every year since then.

He loved his life, he loved his automobile, he loved his family and friends, and the list of dolls who were always ready and willing to spend an evening of fun with him, but most of all, he loved his phone company. He'd been enthralled with phones from the time he'd been a small child, and wouldn't change anything about his life. It was downright perfect.

The sun was shining, the sky bright blue, and whistling a tune, Connor drove the Phaeton along the dirt road, looking for the next driveway, the next farm that he'd convince they needed a phone line, one he'd gladly provide. For pennies on the dollar.

That was the best part. Unlike other companies, his phone lines were affordable, and the profit he made provided him a good living. The larger, more expensive companies had a monopoly on the city markets, had for years, that's why, right from the get-go, he'd focused on the rural areas.

It had paid off; every year he'd expanded lines, expanded his business, farther outside of Rochester, and his goal this year was to run lines all the way to Syracuse. It was a hundred miles, and there were enough farms along the way that needed phones to make it profitable, even if he just signed up half of the farms. He'd already expanded lines that far in all other directions from Rochester, and was confident in his ability to complete this route.

He'd gotten a later start in searching out new customers than he'd intended, but only by a couple of weeks. It was still April, giving him plenty of time to get people signed up and all the lines run long before the ground froze again next winter. His brother Mick had asked him to hang around Rochester in case their mother needed anything while Mick had gone to Missouri. That still seemed odd to Connor. How Mick had taken it upon himself to travel across the nation to haul home a girl to see her dying father.

He and Mick were twins, but they certainly weren't two peas in a pod. The two of them were more like corn and beans. Mick being the beans. He was a good guy, but hard to crack. The reason. Because he was the oldest. Older by fifteen minutes, but those fifteen minutes had defined both of their lives. Mick's role of the oldest meant he had to follow in their father's footsteps. Their father had been a hard shell, too. It was a McCormick trait, or curse.

Connor had often felt bad because he'd been allowed to spend summers as he'd pleased, play with friends after school, go to parties on weekends when they got older, date girls, while Mick had been expected to work at the family business every summer and on weekends, all in preparation to take over the helm someday.

That someday hadn't happened. Their father had died while they'd been seniors in high school, and the *family*, namely their uncles, had declared Mick wasn't old enough to run the company.

Mick, being Mick, had found a way to still be active in the business, while continuing his own goal of becoming a police officer. He was now a detective, one of the best, if not the best in Rochester, and Connor couldn't be happier for his brother. Or more proud of Mick. They both wished their father hadn't died, but if he hadn't, Mick's life would have been a lot different.

Connor's wouldn't have been all that different. He'd been able to pursue his dream from day one—that of owning a phone company.

The only thing that would have changed his life was a girl. Jenny Sommers. She'd been the prettiest girl in school, with dark brown hair and big coffee-colored eyes. Hardly a day went by that he didn't wonder what had happened, where she'd ended up, how she was doing.

He tried not to think about her, but Jenny was always at the back of his mind. Which was why he preferred to think about Mick, or his friends, or the dolls he knew, or his phone company. Anything but Jenny.

It had been seven years, so not thinking about her should be possible.

The mailbox that came into view as he drove around a curve brought his attention back to where it should be. He downshifted and applied the brakes enough to turn into the driveway. Just like they'd lined the curving road, long-needled white pines and big Norway spruce trees, with their huge boughs creating a canopy for shorter vegetation of weeds and shrubbery, were on both sides of the driveway.

No house was in view because the driveway curved to the left and Connor kept his speed low. Prohibition was in full force, and while selling his phone lines, he'd been met by more than one shotgun-wielding homeowner who was diligent in keeping federal agents off their land.

So far, he hadn't been shot at, and he wanted to keep it that way.

The road widened out after the curve. A large farm-house, painted red with a green shingled roof, wide shutters and a lengthy front porch, was surrounded by several flower beds, hosting an array of colorful spring flowers like he'd never seen. There were also two large sheds and an older-model truck with a wooden box parked in the shade of two large cedar trees.

Connor didn't see any movement, other than the clothes flapping in the wind on the clothesline near the far side of the house.

He pulled his car up to where the gravel stopped and the grass started and shut off the engine, while scanning the entire area closely for a shotgun-wielding homeowner.

None came into view, but he still used caution as he opened the door and slowly made his way up to the house. The entire area was clean and orderly. That, along with the clothes hanging off the lines stretched between two poles, told him there was definitely a woman in residence. They often took to the idea of a telephone more quickly than men. Or maybe they were just more likely to fall for his charm. He'd never had an issue of turning it on when the need arose.

With his telephone spiel well memorized, he pulled up a dazzling smile and knocked on the screen door.

A moment later, the house door was opened by a young woman.

"Good afterrrnoooon," the word stretched out as his breath slowly left him. Stunned and questioning if he was seeing things, he pulled open the screen door. Was his mind playing tricks on him because he'd just been thinking about her, or was it really her? "Jenny?"

The house door slammed shut so fast there wasn't time to react.

Other than to realize it had been her! Jenny Sommers.

He hadn't seen her in seven years, but even after a hundred years, he'd know her face. She'd looked as shocked as a deer bounding onto a road with oncoming traffic, and had responded just as quickly.

Grasping the doorknob, he tried turning it. "Jenny! Jenny! It's Connor. Connor McCormick!"

The door was locked.

Locked or not, he kept trying to twist the knob with one hand and he knocked on the door with the other.

Again, and again, until he was pounding on the door as hard as his heart pounded inside his chest. "Jenny! Jenny!"

He'd never admit that his heart had been broken, because he was the fun-loving, always happy, Connor McCormick, but the closest it had ever come had been when Jenny had left town. Vanished without a word. He'd questioned her mother, who had merely said that Jenny had moved away, to live with family. Despite his attempts to find out more, he'd failed.

Failed for months.

Then his father had died, which had been another crushing blow, but life had gone on. Had to. He'd had to go on, without looking back.

He had gone on. For a long time.

He pounded harder on the door.

His heart nearly stopped when he heard a click and felt the knob turn. "Jen…" He paused, stared at the older woman who'd pulled open the door.

"What is it you need?" she asked.

Other than her long brown hair braided and hanging over one shoulder, the woman was built as close to a man as he'd ever seen. She looked about as friendly as a shotgun-wielding landowner, too.

Connor shifted to look over her shoulder. "The other woman, the one who opened the door a moment ago—"

"I am the homeowner." The woman's green eyes narrowed as her pointed chin stuck out a bit farther. "State your business."

There was no one behind the woman, nothing to see except a living room. "I'm with the Rural Rochester Telephone Company and…" Connor's thoughts stalled. Whether it was the unfriendliness of the woman, or knowing that Jenny was in that house, his often used and well-known spiel escaped him.

"I don't have a telephone," the woman said.

"I know, I'm here to uh—" He shook his head. It was no use trying. His mind couldn't focus on phones. "The other woman, the one who first opened the door, her name is Jenny, isn't it?"

"Good day." Stepping back, she swung the door.

Connor stuck his foot in before the door slammed shut. "A telephone line will be run past your property in the near future and I can offer you—"

"No, thank you."

"Having a telephone installed could—"

"I said, no thank you, now kindly remove your foot or I will use Old Bess." While speaking, she reached over and picked up a double-barrel shotgun that must have a permanent spot next to the front door.

Connor had no doubt the woman would use it. Stout and stern, she'd probably used the gun before—on man and beast. He pulled his foot away from the door, but held it open with one hand long enough to say, "Would you please tell Jenny that I've always hoped to see her again."

The woman provided no response, other than to shut the door.

Connor stepped back and closed the screen door, his mind racing. He'd never understood why Jenny had left, and certainly didn't understand why she wouldn't see him now.

He wasn't going to give up this time. Not by a long shot. She owed him an explanation for leaving town without a word, and he was going to get it.

The curtain next to the door fluttered, and he saw the older woman peering out of it, directly at him.

With a tip of his flat-brimmed leather newsboy hat, he pivoted and walked down the steps. He kept walking, straight to his car and climbed in it. After starting the car, he backed up and then drove away, down the tree-lined driveway. The entire time, he kept seeing Jenny's face. Determination to have answers grew inside him, and by the time he arrived at the mailbox, he'd started a countdown of when he'd see her again and get those answers.

Holding her breath and both hands over her pounding heart, Jenny Sommers watched from behind the curtain of the upstairs window as Connor drove away. Connor McCormick.

The Connor McCormick.

Good Lord, but he was as handsome as she remembered. He might be a bit taller, a bit broader at the shoulders, but the rest of him... A tiny groan rumbled in her throat. From the top of that leather hat covering his brown hair to the very soles of his feet inside shiny black shoes, he was the perfect specimen of the male species. Always had been.

Her eyes stung as his black-and-red car completely

disappeared around the curve in the driveway. Despite all she'd gone through since leaving Rochester seven years ago, barely a day had gone by when she hadn't thought of him.

Some days she even blamed him for how her life had turned out, even though he had no idea what had happened after he'd lied to her.

Or did he?

Was that why he'd shown up here today?

No. He couldn't know. Most likely didn't care. Their romance—if it could be called that—had been short lived; he probably didn't even remember it. He'd been the one to end it. She'd been the one to let it break her heart.

She was older now. Wiser. Stronger. A heavy sigh left her lungs as she turned away from the window.

Gretchen stood in the open doorway.

As tall as some men, and nearly as broad shouldered, Gretchen Olsen had saved her life, and Emily's, almost seven years ago, and had saved her again today, because in the moment she'd seen Connor, she hadn't been as strong as she needed to be.

"He'll be back," Gretchen said, leaning a shoulder covered in a red-and-black flannel shirt against the door frame.

Red and black, the same as Connor's car.

Stop it! Jenny told herself. If only she could! She'd tried so hard to forget Connor. For years. Now, the forgetting would have to start all over again, and would be even harder.

"As sure as the sun will come up tomorrow," Gretchen said, "he'll be back."

Pushing down a wave of hope that did nothing but make her angry, Jenny asked, "Did he say so?"

"He told me to tell you that he'd always hoped to see you again," Gretchen answered.

Jenny took two steps, but her legs didn't want to co-operate. They were trembling again. Like the rest of her. She eased herself onto the bed and focused on ignoring the little joyous leap her heart had taken at Gretchen's words.

"He's not Emily's father," Gretchen then said, her tone somber.

It hadn't been a question, yet Jenny shook her head. "No, if Connor McCormick had been Emily's father…" Her throat plugged as heaviness filled her, making it impossible to speak, to breathe. Jenny loved her daughter with all of her heart. Had since before she'd been born. It didn't matter who fathered her; she was her daughter.

She considered it a blessing that Donald Forsythe knew nothing about Emily, and if Jenny had her way, he never would. Having Connor find her could change that. Change it as quickly as a hummingbird flaps its wings.

"I haven't questioned you about her father in six and a half years, and won't start now, but that young man will be back, and he will question you. I'll do what I can, but…" Gretchen let her shrug finish her sentence.

Jenny nodded. She'd always feared that someday her past would catch up with her. Blinking hard and fast didn't help. Hot tears still worked their way forward. She bit her bottom lip, fighting harder to hold the tears at bay, keep them from falling down her cheeks.

The bed sank beside her and Gretchen's calloused hand took hold of hers. "Who is this young man? This Connor McCormick? Is he one of the McCormicks?"

The McCormick name was well known because of the large family textile business that had been in Rochester for years. "Yes. And the reason I became pregnant," Jenny replied. As soon as the words were out, regret struck. It wasn't fair to blame Connor, but somehow, doing so had eased her own guilt of what she'd done. She'd wanted to hurt him that night, as badly as he'd hurt her. Her own foolishness had backfired on her, and she alone had been the one to face the consequences.

"How so?"

Long-ago buried yearnings rose up inside Jenny. "I was young. Stupid. Thought I was in love with him." Her story was much the same as many of the girls who had lived with Gretchen, and her, over the years. She felt sympathy for them, but only anger for herself. Connor had been dashing, handsome, gallant. Everything that would kick a young girl's heart out of control. "He was two years older than me and though I'd worshipped him from afar, he hadn't even known I was alive until the school play. I'd been given the job of painting scenery boards." She'd begged for the job. Would have done anything to be in the same room as Connor. "His role was Captain Trevor in the play, a dashing charmer who would stop at nothing to win the heart of the female lead. He'd been perfect for the part. Even Mrs. Ellis, the director, had said he was the best actor on the stage, and she never gave out compliments—to anyone. His charm had won her over and literally stole the show."

"And your heart."

Jenny couldn't stop how her heart warmed at the memories. "Yes, completely." Gretchen already knew so much, there was no reason to not tell her the rest. "Just like nearly every other girl in school. Connor McCormick was the one subject that was guaranteed to come up at every lunch hour, every walk home and every slumber party." Those carefree days of giggling with friends and secretly gossiping had all disappeared the night she'd been driven to Albany.

Even with pain, disgrace, working its way into her heart, Jenny couldn't stop a smile from forming as she pushed that night out of her mind and focused on the play again. "During a rehearsal, a dancer lost her footing and stumbled into the scenery board I was painting. The board toppled and paint splattered everywhere. Connor was who helped me off the floor, and everyone claimed the board was ruined, including Mrs. Ellis, but not Connor. He said it wouldn't take long to fix, and that he knew I could do it. Fix it. He stayed and helped me, and from then on, we were nearly inseparable. All the girls wanted to be me. It was the best month of my life. Then summer arrived, and Connor said he was going to New York City, to work at a phone company there." Her throat burned. "But he didn't. He'd only used that as an excuse to break up with me."

"How do you know that?"

"Because I saw him two weeks later, and..." She'd accepted what had happened long ago. "And I decided to forget all about him. Another boy asked me out and I went."

"Emily's father?"

"Yes." Jenny stood and thrust the bitterness inside her toward Connor. Toward every memory she had of him. "He won't be back."

"He told me he was with the Rural Rochester Telephone Company," Gretchen said. "That they were running a phone line past our place."

Jenny's insides quivered. "He did?" That had been his dream, the reason he'd supposedly been going to New

York, to work at a company there, learn all he could so that when he graduated, he could start his own company. Not work for the family business.

"Yes, he did," Gretchen said.

It was unfortunate how deeply Connor could still affect her, but it was also true. "We don't need a phone. I'd just as soon pack up Emily and leave than let Connor McCormick set foot in this house."

Chapter Two

Connor had never been overly patient, and not driving up Jenny's driveway again, demanding that she speak to him, was the hardest thing he'd ever had to keep himself from doing, yet he did it. He didn't drive up her driveway.

For two days.

He'd been busy every one of those forty-eight hours—less a few hours of sleeping which he'd done in a small inn five miles up the road from Jenny's house. Syracuse was only fifteen miles away, but he didn't want to travel that far, especially just for a comfortable bed. A small town, Twin Pines was made up of a school, post office, grocer, gas station, diner and the inn where he'd booked a room for the length of his stay.

The end date of his stay was unknown because he wasn't going anywhere until he'd talked to Jenny and got some answers to questions that just kept mounting.

With a population of twenty-four, of which each and every person was excited at the idea of a telephone line being hung throughout the town, Twin Pines had welcomed him. They were also glad that he'd called the county and had the gravel on the railroad tracks replaced up the road, and had told him plenty about Gretchen Olsen, the owner of the house where Jenny lived.

Gretchen raised flowers and sold them to shops in Syracuse and Albany, and often hired young women to help her. In the winter time, she grew the flowers in her sheds, that he'd have to take a closer look at on his next visit. It was reported that the sheds were made of glass, not wood. To his disappointment, no one was overly talkative about any of the young women Gretchen hired, including Jenny. It was almost as if that was a town secret that everyone had sworn an oath to protect.

One of the things he had learned was that this time of year, Gretchen delivered flowers to Syracuse a few days a week. During the summer months, she delivered them more often. He'd never thought much about the flower business, but it appeared that Gretchen Olsen had been growing her flowers for years, and made a good living doing so. The town people insisted the roses she grew were highly sought after, and that the winter plants, poinsettias and such, were even more sought after during the holiday season.

With his car well-hidden behind the small inn, he'd watched Gretchen roll through town, and after a short while, of which every minute felt like an hour, he was convinced she wouldn't be returning to the farm for hours.

There had been a woman in the passenger seat of Gretchen's truck, but she'd had red hair, not brown.

He climbed in his car and drove to the flower farm, but rather than drive up the curved driveway, he pulled his car off the road near the mailbox, and left it there, choosing to walk up the driveway so Jenny wouldn't be warned of his arrival by the sound of the engine.

He stayed hidden within the tall pines and cedars. There were other leafed trees and plenty of spring brush to keep him from being seen.

Exiting the trees near the sheds, he stepped closer to examine them. They both had what appeared to be wooden shutters that reached from near the ground to the roof line, and today they were pulled open, exposing rows of windows that ran the length of the sheds, on three sides. The fronts didn't have windows, just large doors. Greenhouses in order to grow flowers in winter. A peek inside a window showed long, raised beds of plants, some flowering, some not, as well as large heaters near the front, to keep the sheds warm during the cold months.

He was impressed, but didn't spend a lengthy amount of time at the sheds, instead, he worked his way around them and paused to scan the house and yard.

A bolt of excitement shot through him as strongly as two electrical lines meeting when his gaze settled on a woman hanging clothes on the clothesline. It was Jenny. Her long, glistening brown hair hung down her back, just like he remembered. He could recall how it had always smelled as sweet as honeysuckle. It had driven him crazy, and every time he'd caught a whiff of honeysuckle over the years, a deep and powerful yearning had put Jenny in his mind.

He'd tried hard to get over her as time had gone by, but there had never been another woman who had been able to do that. And there had been plenty. After she'd disappeared, he'd dated a lot of females, but he'd never put his heart on his sleeve again, not like he had with her.

Because not a single woman he'd met in the past seven years had leveled up to Jenny. He understood he'd put her on a pedestal in his mind, making it impossible for anyone to reach that high, and had come to accept that. How she'd been one of a kind.

The one who'd gotten away.

She'd also been the one to break his heart, and he wanted to know why. Deserved to know why.

Her back was to him. The pink-and-blue-paisley-print dress was loose-fitting, but still highlighted her shape, the curve of her small waist and trim hips. The hem ended near her shins, showing the creaminess of her skin above her rolled-down stockings. The dress was short-sleeved, exposing the slenderness of her arms.

He watched as she bent, picked up another item out of the wicker basket, snapped it open and then stretched to hook it on the line with the wooden pins. A hint of a shiver rippled down his spine as he stared at the items she'd already hung on the lines. They weren't clothes, as in dresses, shirts, pants or underthings. They were simple rectangular pieces of bleached white cloth.

That's when he noticed something else.

Actually, someone else.

A small child sitting on the grass.

Diapers!

She was hanging up diapers.

His heart took a nosedive all the way to his toes.

She was married.

With a baby. A boy from the looks of his clothing.

The crushing sensation that hit had happened twice before in his life. When Jenny had disappeared, and at the death of his father. He'd never wanted to feel that again. Ever. That's why he'd put her on a pedestal, an impossible place for anyone else to reach, just so no one else could come close to crushing him all over again.

For a brief second, Connor considered leaving and this time truly forgetting that Jenny existed.

He should be glad that she'd gone on with her life, but something deep inside his very soul said no. He wasn't glad. He was mad. Mad that she had gone on with her life without a thought as to what her leaving had done to him.

He wasn't going anywhere, either, because this time, by God, he was going to get answers to the questions that had haunted him for years.

A shiver rippled over Jenny at the same time her heart leaped into her throat. She whirled around, ignoring the diaper that slipped from her fingers and floated to the ground.

Connor stood not five feet away and the anger in his eyes made her tremble as if the earth beneath her was shaking, rumbling, and the air was so charged, it felt as if lightning was about to strike.

When he hadn't returned two days ago, she'd figured she'd been right. That he wouldn't be back, because the Connor she remembered hadn't been patient. His spontaneous actions had been one of the things she'd loved the most. He'd always been the first to jump in and take action.

Running was all she could think to do. Run fast and far. As the thought found execution, she glanced at William at the same time a hand grasped her arm firmly. She hadn't even had a chance to take a step toward the baby.

Connor didn't say a word. Just stared at her. There was more than anger in his eyes. The only thing she could compare to what she saw glistening in those sky-blue eyes was agony, because that's what she felt, too. Along with a powerful bout of regret for what she'd done all those years ago.

Blame came next, as usual. If he had acknowledged her that night, she wouldn't have done what she'd done.

Her throat was on fire, so were her lungs and her arm where he held on to it. Then she remembered. She was older. Wiser. Stronger. "You need to leave," she said, not sounding like herself.

His laugh was bitter. "Not on your life."

It wasn't her life she was most worried about. Others lived here. Joyce and little William, Rachel and Lora. Not to mention Gretchen and all the others who needed the sanctuary that Gretchen provided. If it wasn't for Gretchen, only the Good Lord knew what would have happened to Emily. Her daughter was the one thing that meant the very most to Jenny, and was the one thing she would protect above and beyond all else.

The bang of the screen door on the back porch echoed through the silence filling the air between her and Connor. Rachel most likely, with more laundry to hang. "Go back inside!" Jenny shouted, not wanting Connor to catch a glimpse of the other woman. Young girl, actually. Rachel was only seventeen. The same age she'd been when she'd given birth to Emily.

"Are you all right?"

"Yes!" Jenny answered Rachel's question. "Go back inside. I'll be there in a moment."

"No, you won't," Connor said as the door banged again. "We need to talk, and I'm not leaving until that happens. Neither are you."

She lifted her chin and prayed that he wouldn't notice how it trembled. "We don't need a telephone."

His eyes narrowed.

"This isn't about a telephone," he growled. "And you damn well know it."

Breathing through the trembling of her body, the burning of her throat, she held his gaze. It took every ounce of her strength, and some, to not consider running again. "I need to take William inside."

He glanced toward the baby sitting near her feet, playing with a rag ball.

Wearing a pair of blue overalls and red shirt, William looked up and offered a huge grin, showing off his two bottom teeth. He would soon turn a year old, and though he was standing with help, had yet to take his first steps. With a babble, he held up both of his hands toward her, an act that never failed to melt her heart.

Connor released her arm.

She knelt down, scooped up William and balanced him on her hip while brushing a kiss on his fuzzy head of golden curls.

"Is he yours?" Connor asked, his gaze going to her hands.

Looking for a wedding ring. He wouldn't find one. Not on her finger. She bit her lips together and tucked William's head beneath her chin. "No. He's not mine."

"Where is his mother?"

"She is with Gretchen."

He nodded and glanced toward the greenhouses. "Delivering flowers."

That would have been easy enough for him to figure out, especially if he'd spoken to anyone in Twin Pines. "Yes."

"Who is in the house?" he asked, looking that way.

"No one of your concern."

His movements were slow, nothing more than his head

turning toward her, and his eyes capturing hers. "You're wrong. It is of my concern, because I'm making it my concern." Arms folded across his chest, he asked, "Front door, or back door?"

"Front." There were chairs there, where he could wait while she carried William inside for Rachel and Lora to keep an eye on until she could convince Connor to leave.

And never return.

He walked beside her, arms at his sides as if ready to grab her if she attempted to bolt, around the house, past the big flower bed, up the front steps, all the way to the door.

"Would you care for anything to drink?" she asked, only to show him that he didn't intimidate her.

"No, I'm fine, thank you." He pulled open the screen door.

She grasped the knob of the front door before he could. "You can wait here—I'll be right back."

He looked at her, at William, at the front door, more than once before he huffed out a breath long and slow.

She'd been holding her breath so long, she was growing dizzy, but didn't dare empty her lungs. Not yet. She couldn't let him in the house. Couldn't let him see Lora or Rachel. He'd have even more questions then. Questions she couldn't answer. Too many lives depended on secrecy.

"Keep the door open," he said. "I watched you disappear into this house once, and won't do it again."

The air eased out of her, slowly, completely, and she couldn't stop from saying, "I didn't disappear."

His eyes hardened.

"I'll be right back." She opened the door and stepped inside the house. Leaving the door partially opened, she gestured for Rachel to come take William. "Take him upstairs, and stay there," she whispered while nodding at Lora who stood in the doorway leading to the kitchen. "You, too."

Rachel took William and carried him into the kitchen. Upon hearing their footsteps on the stairs, which never failed to creak, Jenny glanced at the clock on the mantel. She had less than an hour to get rid of Connor before Emily returned home from school.

Huffing out a breath, she squared her shoulders, only to feel them slump. She had no idea what she needed right now, but hoped the Good Lord did and gave her whatever it might be, along with the strength she needed.

Connor still had hold of the screen door and slowly closed it after she'd stepped past him and walked over to the set of white wicker furniture that she'd sewn new cushions for during the long winter hours. Blue-and-white-striped cushions for both of the armchairs, the rocking chair, and one long cushion and two arm pillows for the small sofa. The furniture had been repainted, white, over the winter, as well. She'd also sewn small tablecloths for the two round tables that completed the set.

She'd done all that, along with hundreds of other things over the years because this was her and Emily's home. Where they belonged. "Are you sure you wouldn't care for something to drink?" she asked while sitting down in one of the armchairs, feeling the strength she'd acquired years ago. She was no longer that young, foolish girl Connor had lied to.

"I'm not thirsty." He sat in the chair facing her. "But thanks."

"Have you sold any telephones in this area?" she asked, not giving him the opportunity to bring up the topic he was sure to bring up. Her. What she was doing here. Why she'd never returned to Rochester.

He leaned back and rested one ankle on his opposite knee. "Yes, several. The line will run all the way to Syracuse."

"That's nice. I'm glad—"

"What are you doing here, Jenny? How long have you been here?"

So much for avoiding that topic. Jenny willed herself to not react to his sincerity and concern. Those were just two of the things that had always made him endearing. She threaded her fingers together, squeezing them as they threatened to tremble, and set her hands in her lap. "I can't tell you that, Connor."

Anger once again snapped in his eyes. "Why not? What the hell is going on? Are you being held here against your will?"

"No."

Clear disbelief shone in his eyes.

There was a sense of panic in her insides, but she managed to tamp it down a mite. "This is my home," she said. "Has been for years. I love it here. I love the flowers and the—" She snapped her mouth shut before saying the girls. "The quietness."

Connor dropped his foot to the floor and leaned forward, his elbows on his knees and his gaze locked on her. "Jenny," he said softly. "I'm here for the truth. All of it. If you need help, I'm here for that, too."

At that moment, Jenny was amazed at how deeply her feelings went for Connor. Even after all these years. She'd tried so hard to forget him, but couldn't. The only thing she could do was blame him, and had to do that again now, because it was his fault. If he hadn't broken up with her in such an underhanded way, she never would have ended up pregnant. When she'd first been sequestered at the home for unwed mothers, she'd dreamed of him arriving there, saying those exact words, and of course that dream had also included him taking her away, loving her. Living happily-ever-after.

Those dreams had been foolish, because she'd still been young and foolish then. She wasn't now. She'd saved herself, and Emily, with the help of Gretchen, and was now helping Gretchen save other girls. "I don't need your help, Connor. I don't need anyone's help. I have a wonderful life here. I wouldn't change anything about it."

He leaned back in his chair again, stared at her thoughtfully. "Where are your parents?"

Her spine stiffened. "Why?"

"Just curious. After the camera company burned, they moved, and I never heard where."

She kept her chin up, her insides calm, and was amazed at how easy that was. She'd heard at some point that her stepfather's company had burned, nearly to the ground, but she hadn't cared, and still didn't. They'd disowned her the night they'd delivered her to Albany. "South," she said. It was as good of a guess as any. Then, taking advantage of the subject, she asked, "How is your family?"

He remained silent, staring at her, then shook his head. "Good."

Jenny couldn't really expand on that. She had only met his parents a couple of times. The time she and Connor had spent together had been all about each other, not their families. He had a twin brother, Patrick. They looked similar, but were as opposite as day and night. The Rochester school had been large, with well over a hundred students in every class, and his brother hadn't been involved in school activities like Connor had been. He'd been on the baseball team, the hockey team, the tennis team and dramatics and music. He'd called his brother Mick rather than Patrick, and had said that Mick was always working with their father, at the family business, a large food company. Connor had been glad that he didn't have to, and could pursue his dream of creating a phone company.

He'd always said that there wasn't room for both him and Mick at the family business, and that telephones were the wave of the future, but the McCormicks' textile company was very large. "Do you really work for the Rural Rochester Phone Company?" she asked.

A flicker of something flashed in his eyes before he answered. "Yes, I do. Ever since it opened. Lines are being extended all the way to Syracuse this year."

"Are they?"

"Yes, they are."

An awkward silence ensued, as if neither of them knew what to say. At least she didn't. He looked much the same, but had obviously grown into a man over the years, just as she'd grown into a woman. That was as natural a process as it was complex. She'd discovered that long ago.

"Do you remember Wilbur Cook?" he asked.

She hadn't thought of others from school for ages—for several reasons—yet at the sound of the name, a memory of a gangly figure formed in her mind, with curly red hair and crooked teeth, who had been a close friend of Connor's. "He played in the band with you, didn't he?"

"Yes, he did. He's with the philharmonic orchestra in

New York now. Did you know he married your friend Marjorie Conklin?"

Instantly transported back to her bedroom years ago, laughing with her best friend, Jenny slapped a hand to her chest as her heart filled with warmth. "Marjorie? No?"

"Yes. They live in New York City, obviously, and have two kids."

Jenny's heart nearly doubled in size, knowing that Marjorie would be a wonderful mother. She'd been the one person Jenny had ached to tell what had happened, needing someone to confide in, but her mother had asked if she was pregnant, even before Jenny had thought of that consequence, and she'd been banished. Hauled away and disowned.

She'd often wondered what her mother had told Marjorie, sure her friend would have been curious, and concerned.

"And that other friend of yours, the one with black, curly hair. She married Seth O'Brien. He works with me at the phone company."

"Frances Dowling?" Jenny asked, glad to chase away the bad memories floating forward. Franny had lived just up the street from her, and was older than her, the same age as Connor, but they had walked to and from school together every day. Franny had made those journeys fun, whether it had been warm and sunny or cold and blustery.

"Yes. Franny." He grinned. "They have four kids. Just had the fourth one last month. A girl."

Franny, too, would be a wonderful mother, and Jenny couldn't help but wonder if Franny's children were as outgoing as their mother. "Do they live in Rochester?"

"Yes, they do, over on Fourth Avenue."

"What about Ruth Isler or Helen Kane?" she asked, growing curious about more names and images popping into her head.

"I don't believe I knew them," he said, with a thoughtful frown. "The names aren't ringing any bells."

"You may not have known them. They were younger than me and lived in my neighborhood. What about Gina Rivers?"

He laughed. "You aren't going to believe it, but she ran off with a circus that came to town. Fell in love with the lion tamer. Last I heard, she's riding elephants and swinging on trapeze ropes."

She laughed aloud. "Baloney!"

"I kid you not!" Connor said, fully captured by her laughter. In that moment he saw the Jenny he used to know. The one with a spirit so bright, so bold, she'd made every part of him come alive the first time he'd laid eyes on her. Wanting that Jenny to return, fully, he kept talking about other people they both had known in school. It had been that way right from the start between the two of them, the way they could talk, about anything.

They both laughed several times while discussing other people they'd known back then. It appeared as if she hadn't kept in touch with anyone. He kept bringing up names until he couldn't think of any more.

He had memories he could bring up, many of the two of them, but his instincts said if he did so, she'd clam up. There was a lot going on here, more than what met the eye. She wasn't going to willingly tell him, not yet anyway. The patience that he'd gotten a taste of the past couple of days was going to have to be something he got used to for a while longer.

Connor had purposefully brought up Franny earlier, knowing that her friend hadn't heard from Jenny since she'd left all those years ago, to live with family. That's all her mother had ever told anyone. That Jenny had gone to live with family out of state and wouldn't return to Rochester.

Nodding toward the house, he asked, "How are you related to Gretchen?"

"Related?"

His question had caught her off guard, the way her eyes had widened and her hesitancy made that clear. "That's what your mother said, that you went to live with family. Out of state."

She pinched her lips together and looked everywhere but at him before finally saying, "I'm not related to Gretchen, by blood, but we are family, and I have a lot to do before she returns today."

Connor wanted to push for more, but like when dealing with potential customers, he knew when to back off. He would have to gain her trust—that would be the only way he'd get the truth. The entire truth. "It's good seeing you, Jenny. I've missed you."

She stood, and once again avoided any eye contact. "Yes, well, I hope you sell a lot of telephones."

He stood and took a hold of her hand, which trembled. His thumb caressed the inside of her wrist, where her pulse raced, despite how calm she pretended to appear. A smile formed inside him, and he let it rise onto his lips as he gave her hand a gentle squeeze. She wasn't as unaffected by him as she was pretending, which gave him hope. Without another word, he turned to walk down the steps.

He hadn't gotten the answers he'd been searching for when he'd arrived, but he did gain insight, and that insight said Jenny wasn't nearly as happy as she'd tried to make him believe.

Each step Connor took toward his car became more difficult to take. He'd never let anyone know how deeply Jenny's disappearance had affected him. They'd only been dating for a short time when summer had arrived and a phone company that had been interested in two models of telephones that he'd invented had invited him to spend the summer in New York City, working for them. He'd been torn about going, about leaving her even for almost three months. He'd had to go, though. It had been his opportunity to show his father that he might not have been the oldest, the one destined for greatness, but that he too was going to be a success. All on his own. Without the help of the McCormick name. That had been another thing he'd always kept hidden. Being the second best.

He hadn't told Jenny that, or that he was leaving until the night before he left, because he'd been afraid. If she'd have asked him not to go, he wouldn't have gone. He'd been that infatuated with her. In fact, she'd made him want to go, want to succeed, even more. For their future. He'd already been dreaming about that.

Arriving home and finding her gone had been devastating. He'd still been looking for answers as to where she could have gone and why, when the rest of his world went haywire. His father had died in an automobile accident.

Chapter Three

Connor arrived at his car and climbed inside, pulled the door closed. He didn't start the engine. Life had changed so much after his father's death. Loss became a norm. One he'd had to learn to accept. That's what had happened. He'd had to accept his father's death, and accept that Jenny was gone, too.

One had been as hard as the other.

His senior year in high school was little more than a blur of memories. On the outside, he'd gone on being the Connor he'd always been. The happy-go-lucky guy who never let anything get him down, while inside he'd been in the darkest place he'd ever been.

The summer after graduation, he'd started his phone company. By then, that dream had become the only one he'd had left. It had helped. Focusing on anything would have helped. For him, the focus had proven successful; within in a year, he'd patented two other telephone models, which had given him the capital to run his first telephone lines. It had all been smooth sailing since then.

As far as business was concerned.

His personal life hadn't been quite as successful. He'd

pushed on, despite the emptiness inside him. An emptiness he hadn't let show, but it had been there. A void left by Jenny's disappearance as much as by his father's death.

Death was easier to come to grips with. Though tragic, death was a natural process of life.

Jenny's leaving had just been tragic.

The void that had left didn't feel as large now, and he anticipated that it would shrink a little bit each time he saw her, until all was resolved. He didn't dare dream as to what that resolution might all entail. Not yet. But couldn't deny he was glad to have found her.

A plume of dust appeared on the road ahead of where his car was parked, and a moment later, he recognized it as a Ford school bus. Made mostly of wood and painted yellow, the bus slowed and then stopped near the end of Jenny's driveway.

Curious to see how many other children, besides the baby, lived at the house, he watched and waited.

After some time, a little girl jumped out of the back of the bus and walked around it, a mere few feet away from his car.

Connor's skin turned cold at the girl's long, dark brown hair. It was more than her hair. Her features, her movements. She was a miniature Jenny. An exact replica. Just much smaller, younger. Maybe six or so.

Six.

Yes, that's how old children were when they started school.

Six.

He shook his head, trying hard to dispel the direction his mind was going. That's where it went, though. To Jenny having a six-year-old daughter as his gaze followed the little girl all the way to where Jenny was standing, arms open.

The girl and Jenny embraced, briefly, before Jenny noticed his car partially hidden by the shrubbery. She then grasped the girl's hand and hurried up the driveway.

A deep, sickening, sinking feeling overcame him.

The baby may not have been hers, but this little girl was Jenny's. His gut, his mind, said there was no doubt. She must have given birth within the year after she'd left Rochester.

There was no way it could be his child. Their relationship hadn't gone to that level. But it had gone to that level with someone else. Shortly after he'd gone to New York City. No wonder she'd left without saying a word.

His throat burned as if it was full of shards of glass, and his heart felt like someone had just stomped on it. Just like years ago.

Locking his jaw as anger began to rise inside him, Connor started his car and hit the gas so hard gravel spewed from beneath the tires.

Jenny flinched as the car spun away. There was a limit to her endurance, and she feared hers was close. That couldn't happen. After all she'd been through, Connor McCormick would not be the cause of her to break down. Not again. She'd hit a breaking point once because of him, and wouldn't—absolutely would not—do that again.

Why couldn't he have just left? The second she'd seen his car on the side of the road she'd known what had happened.

He'd seen Emily.

Her heart felt as if a huge fist was squeezing the blood right out of it.

"Mommy? Why are we running?" Emily asked.

Jenny forced her footsteps to slow and eased the grip she had on her daughter's hand. "Because I have chores to finish." That was an excuse, and very unfair. Stopping, she knelt down, took Jenny's lunch box and kissed her forehead. "But I am sorry. I didn't mean to make you run. How was school today?"

"Teddy Wright found a frog and put it in his pocket." Emily's brown eyes glowed with golden highlights as they did when she was excited. "And it kept croaking to get out!" Her giggle filled the air. "It made everyone laugh."

"I'm sure it did." After another peck on Emily's forehead, Jenny stood, and holding Emily's hand softly, walked slowly toward the house. "What happened then?"

"Mrs. Whipple made him take it outside." Emily sighed. "That made Teddy sad."

"Poor Teddy, but frogs don't belong in school," Jenny said, smiling down at her daughter.

Emily nodded, but was still smiling. "That's what Mrs. Whipple said, too, but Teddy wasn't sad when he got on the bus."

"Oh, why is that?"

"Because he found the frog again!"

Jenny giggled along with her daughter. She couldn't help but think about all the names Connor had brought up. Some of those people she hadn't thought about in years. Others, mainly him, she'd thought about many times and had wondered how and what they were doing now.

The small school in Twin Pines was so different from

the one she'd attended in Rochester. There were only sixteen children in Emily's school. Mr. Whipple drove the bus, and was the school principal, while his wife, Mrs. Whipple, taught all six grades, from first through sixth. Children attending higher grades were transported to Syracuse. Some stayed all week with families in Syracuse, returning home only on weekends. She couldn't imagine being separated from Emily like that, seeing her only on weekends.

The Whipples also managed the post office and delivered the mail. Often sending it home with the children. Jenny didn't need to ask if there was any mail. When that happened, Emily was always waving it as she climbed off the bus.

"What did Mr. Whipple think about Teddy's frog?" Jenny asked as they arrived at the house.

"Mr. Whipple doesn't know about the frog," Emily said. "The bus was too noisy for him to hear it croaking. He really is a nice frog, Mommy. Teddy let me pet him."

"He did?"

"Yep."

Certain Teddy's mother would insist that Teddy let the frog go once he arrived home, Jenny changed the subject. "Well, let's go get your clothes changed and then you can help me hang clothes on the line," she said, not mentioning the handwashing that would happen first. Teddy was the only other first grader. Therefore, he and Emily had become fast friends. Jenny did wish that Emily could have other friends, especially some that lived nearby so they could play together outside school. There were a lot of things she wished. Things that just couldn't be.

They had a good life here, with everything they needed. A solid home, food, clothing. She couldn't complain. Nor would she. She was extremely thankful for the life she and Emily had here with Gretchen. It was fulfilling, too. Helping other girls who were caught in the same situation she had been.

With an apron covering her rounded stomach, Rachel was in the kitchen. William was sitting in the highchair, munching on a cookie, and a plate holding two cookies and a glass of milk awaited Emily at the table. "Lora is hanging up the rest of the laundry," Rachel said, quietly.

Jenny nodded as she led her daughter to the sink and helped her wash her hands thoroughly. "Eat your cookies then go change your clothes." As Emily skipped to the table, Jenny patted Rachel's shoulder. "Thank you."

Petite, with a host of curly blond hair and big green eyes, Rachel was showing signs that her time of delivery could happen any day. Jenny had come to recognize even the most subtle of changes, from how they carried the baby lower, to a burst of energy that often happened right before labor would set in.

Lora's time was fast approaching, too.

Both girls had been with them for several months, and Joyce had been with them for over a year. Her baby, William, had been born just weeks after Joyce had arrived. No one was ever asked to leave, or to stay. Those were decisions they made on their own.

For the briefest of moments, Jenny thought about a telephone, and how beneficial that could be to some of the girls.

Resigned to not think about Connor in any way, Jenny shook her head to dispel all thoughts, including those of telephones, and walked to the back door. After the clothes were hung, and others that were dry were carried in and put away, she spent a few hours in the greenhouses, snipping and pruning the carnation plants that would soon be transplanted into the ground behind the house. Carnations were one of Gretchen's bestsellers, and once planted outside, they grew quickly, providing dozens upon dozens of lush, big and colorful flowers to be shipped regularly to the shops in Syracuse and Albany.

May was a tricky month. There were days like today, where the sun was shining and so warm it felt as if summer was right around the corner, however, there was no guarantee that the overnight temperatures wouldn't reach freezing levels. Therefore, the transferring of plants from inside the greenhouses to the fields behind the sheds wouldn't come until closer to June.

Jenny hadn't known anything about growing flowers before coming here. Her mother hadn't grown so much as a vegetable garden. She would soon be planting one of those, too. On the west side of the house, and once it started producing, she'd be busy canning vegetables to fill the pantry for winter.

Looking back, she had to admit that she didn't know much about anything when she'd arrived here. At that point in her life, it had been about saving her baby, Emily, from adoption, or worse.

They'd tried to make her sign those papers, even promised she could go back to her family if she did. That had been the last place she'd have returned to, still was. Her mother and stepfather had disowned her, and she'd disowned them.

Jenny was still in the greenhouse when she heard the rumble of a truck coming up the driveway. The flowers Gretchen and Joyce had delivered today had been mostly tulips and lilies of the valley. The tiny lilies were her favorite. They smelled so wonderful and their precious little white bell-shaped flowers were so pretty. She loved walking outside in the morning and catching a whiff of them. Very seasonal, the flowers didn't last long. Soon the large beds of them surrounding the house would be nothing but lush, green leaves. At that point, they'd dig up clumps and sell them as starters for those looking to start their own flowerbeds.

"How did everything go?" she asked as the truck pulled up next to the greenhouse.

"Better than expected!" Gretchen climbed out and shut the truck door.

Joyce's red hair bobbed as she climbed out of the passenger door, grinning brightly. "Willingham's Floral bought the entire truck load. They needed them for several weddings this weekend, so our timing was perfect."

"Wonderful!" Jenny was truly pleased. Although several shops purchased flowers regularly, there were still times that Gretchen would take to selling flowers along the side of the road in order to return home with an empty truck. That tended to happen more during the summer months, when flowers were more plentiful.

"Yes, it was," Gretchen agreed, walking to the back of the truck.

"There are enough tulips and lilies for another trip tomorrow." Jenny grabbed two wooden crates out of the back of the truck.

Gretchen nodded while taking more crates. "I promised Wells Hansen I'd be there first thing in the morning. Of course, he wants glads, but I told him they won't be ready for a month or more."

Wells was the funeral director in Syracuse, and preferred gladioli for funeral arrangements.

"He'll be happy when they do start blooming." Jenny

had planted several rows of the bulbs earlier in the month, and was watching them carefully because the deer and rabbits didn't mind eating the tender leaves as soon as they popped out of the ground. She would continue planting the bulbs for months, so they would have fresh gladioli until fall.

The three of them talked about flowers as they unloaded and carried all of the empty crates into the greenhouses, and then Joyce excused herself, anxious to see her son, and walked over to where William and Emily were sitting on the ground, playing with a ball.

"How did things go around here today?" Gretchen asked.

"Fine." Jenny kept her gaze on Joyce and the children.

"No visitors?"

Jenny's spine shivered even as a heat flushed her face. "Yes, he was here."

"He's been staying at the Bird's Inn."

"Selling telephone lines."

"Is that what he said?"

Jenny's throat grew thick as she turned, looked at Gretchen. "That's why he's in the area."

Gretchen nodded. "Until he'd found you."

"He won't be back."

Gretchen had the grace to not laugh out loud, but the challenge in her smile said she didn't believe Connor wouldn't be back.

Jenny did. He'd seen Emily.

Holding on to that thought like it was a lifeline, the only thing saving her from drowning in a raging flood, Jenny forged forward, day after day. Each night, she'd say a prayer of thanks that Connor hadn't returned, and then fight against the tears she refused to let flow because he hadn't.

Over the years, she'd felt every emotion possible for Connor. From love to hate. And was going through each one all over again as she lay in bed, staring out the window at a sky full of stars.

It had been over a week since his last visit, and Gretchen had said he'd checked out of the Bird's Inn. She should be happy about that. He had no right to come back into her life. Making her laugh just like he had years ago. It had been so easy, laughing, while they'd been talking about people she used to know, while he'd told her what those people were doing now, how they'd married, had children.

She had a child, and had never been married. Emily asked about that, about her father, especially since starting school. Jenny had told her the truth. That she didn't know where he was, but that it didn't matter because they had each other.

There was more truth to it than that and the thoughts swirling in her mind, of how young and foolish she'd been, made her throat burn and her eyes sting.

Still, she refused to cry. She'd cried enough years ago and those tears hadn't changed anything. If only Connor hadn't lied to her about going to New York. She would never have agreed to go out with Donald. Would never have tried so hard to forget Connor.

Connor and Donald had not been friends. More like enemies. Connor had never said much about Donald, who had been a year older than him, three years older than her, but Donald had said plenty about Connor. Especially after the play. Donald had been the leading man in the play, and had been very mad that Connor had stolen the show.

She threw back the covers and leaped out of bed before any more memories could form. With her mind not full of thoughts, her hearing kicked in, and she went to the door, pulled it open.

Long black hair glistened in the moonlight near the top of the stairway.

"Lora?" Jenny asked, stepping into the hallway.

Holding on to the rail post, Lora slowly turned. "I'm sorry. I didn't mean to wake you."

"You didn't wake me." Jenny moved closer. "Are you all right?"

"Yes, just hungry."

Jenny grinned. "Thinking of that chocolate cake Rachel made?"

Lora covered her mouth with one hand and nodded shyly.

"Me, too." Jenny hadn't been thinking about the cake, but stepped forward and took hold of Lora's arm to guide her down the steps. "When I was expecting Emily, I ate nearly an entire cake, all by myself."

"I could do that tonight." Lora rested a hand on her stomach. "I'm starving and supper was only a few hours ago."

"That has a little to do with cravings," Jenny assured. "And it's best to feed those cravings, otherwise you'd lie awake half the night, thinking about how delicious that cake will taste."

"I am sorry for disturbing you."

Jenny continued to hold on to Lora's arm as they stepped off the stairway that led into the kitchen, where the light was on. "You didn't disturb me, but we might be disturbing someone else."

"Just me," Rachel said from the kitchen. "I had a craving for cake and milk."

Laughing as she and Lora walked around the corner, Jenny said, "Us, too. Is there any left?"

"Right now, there is," Rachel replied. "I can't say that will be true in a few minutes."

"You sit down," Jenny told Lora. "I'll get us some plates before it's all gone."

The house was quiet, except for the three of them, eating the delectable and moist chocolate cake, heavily slathered with a rich chocolate frosting, and taking sips of cold, creamy milk.

"I do hope you are willing to share this recipe," Jenny told Rachel. "It's sinfully delicious."

"I'll try and write it down," Rachel answered, beaming at the praise. "I don't measure anything, just sort of dump in amounts that look right."

"It's right, that's for sure," Lora said, scooping up a second piece of cake from the platter in the center of the table. "I've been thinking about a second piece since eating one for dessert after supper. I just couldn't stand it any longer."

"Me, too," Rachel said, her green eyes still shimmering. "And I'm glad it turned out exactly as I remembered."

"Is it another cake your grandmother who owned the bakery in Queens made?" Lora asked.

"Yes," Rachel replied. "Grandma Nina. We lived with her until after my father died, up until my mother remarried. That was four years ago. I haven't seen my grandmother since then." She sat back in her chair and placed a hand on her stomach. "I'm going to write to her, after my baby is born, and if she agrees, go live with her."

Through discussions they'd had since Rachel had arrived several months ago, Jenny was aware of Rachel's plans, and once again thought about how nice a telephone would be for Rachel to call her grandmother.

Lora huffed out a long breath. "I still don't know what I'm going to do after my baby is born. My family disowned me when I ran away with Ellis. You know, the one my father called a scoundrel. By the time I figured out my father had been right, I was pregnant."

"We all make mistakes," Jenny said, patting Lora's arm.

"I made more than one," Lora continued. "Ellis didn't do anything except visit speakeasies, spend the money I'd made doing odd jobs to feed us. So, I went home. My parents said I was a bad example for my younger siblings, and took me to the home for unwed mothers in Albany. I suppose they were right about that, too, but I didn't have anywhere else to go. Then the home said I had to give my baby up for adoption…" Lora shrugged. "I couldn't do that."

Jenny had long ago set her fork down and reached over, taken Lora's hand. "You can stay here as long as you need. There's no rush or pressure."

Lora nodded, and then frowned. "Will you stay here forever, Jenny?" She blushed slightly. "I mean, don't you think about getting married someday? Having more children?"

Jenny swallowed hard and gathered the empty plates, carried them to the sink. "No. I like it here." Forcing herself not to think about anyone, especially one specific person, she turned to the table, and smiled. "I like helping all of you."

"If it wasn't for you and Gretchen, I would have ended up back at the home," Lora said. "I know I would have. I'd have had to give up my baby."

Jenny went back to the table and gave Lora a quick hug. "Well, you don't have to worry about any of that. Just think about the precious little baby you'll soon have." Tears were threatening to form as Jenny reached over and squeezed Rachel's hand. "You both will have little babies." Releasing both of them, she picked the glasses off the table. "I'll wash these dishes. You two go back to bed. You'll be able to sleep now that you've had your fill of cake."

Yawning, they both agreed, and Jenny filled the sink with soapy water. Dozens of girls had stories like Lora and Rachel. Including herself.

Her first days at the home in Albany were a blur, but she had refused to sign anything because she'd already deduced that she wasn't going to stay there. She hadn't known where she'd go, most certainly not back to Rochester, because of her family and Donald.

She'd felt as if taking her to that home had been a relief for her mother. Life had been tough after her father had died. He'd been a steel worker and died building a bridge. Her memories of him were limited, having been only age five, younger than Emily, when he'd died. She'd been seven when her mother had married Richard Brown, and she hadn't wanted anything to do with him, with having a new father. The years that followed hadn't been pleasant. They'd never truly become a family.

Eventually, they gave up on that happening. Her mother and stepfather had provided for her, clothes, food, a home, spending money, but they'd never cared where she was, or who she was with, or even if she'd been home. There had always been a camera convention that had taken them out of town for days at a time. She'd thought, hoped, her mother might eventually see things from her point of view, right up until her mother had found her in the bathroom one morning, throwing up.

Jenny finished the dishes, and then moved to the stairway. Looking up it as she clicked off the kitchen light, she questioned going up to bed. There was even more now to keep her awake.

Because she still did think about getting married someday. She didn't want to admit it, but she did.

Chapter Four

Connor had sold more than three dozen phone contracts in the past two weeks. Since leaving Jenny's place, since seeing her meet her daughter at the school bus. His back teeth clenched at the wave of pain that filled him.

He'd done the math. Jenny had to have gotten pregnant as soon as she'd left Rochester, or within a few months there afterwards. *Gone to live with family out of state.* Not hardly. She'd run off with someone, that's why her mother had been so mum about it. He'd never met her mother or stepfather until he'd gone to see her after returning home from New York. They had never been home when he'd picked Jenny up for their dates. A housekeeper had been. An older woman, who hadn't seemed to care who was picking up Jenny. Her home life hadn't appeared to be a happy one. She hadn't said much about it, other than her father had died when she'd been little and that her mother had married Richard Brown, the owner of a camera company, a couple of years later, and that he and her mother traveled a lot for his business.

She had never mentioned another boy, either, someone that she'd liked. He'd searched his mind, trying to come up with someone else from school who'd moved away about that same time, but had come up blank, so it had to have been someone he didn't know.

Which was fine. He didn't want to know.

He didn't want to know her, either.

All the years he'd spent wondering about her, years of nursing a broken heart, she'd been married, raising a family.

Anger boiled inside him. They had been young. Some might say too young, but he'd thought what they'd had was special. Obviously not. She must have started dating someone else as soon as he'd left town.

What angered him even more was that now he was going to have to start forgetting her all over again. It would be easier this time. His questions had been answered.

Other than, where was her husband?

Jenny hadn't been wearing a wedding band, and no one in Twin Pines had mentioned a man living at Gretchen's place, but there could be. He hadn't been looking for signs of a male presence. He'd been too focused on Jenny.

He laid his foot on the gas and told himself it didn't matter. She'd made her bed and he had to get to the Village of Newark, New York, before nightfall. Only forty miles from Rochester, the Village of Newark already had phone lines, including his, and he needed to call Seth, his engineer, to get a crew ready to start running lines all the way to Syracuse.

The trip had been successful, very successful, and he should feel good about that. Every pole rooted in the ground, every line strung, every phone installed, was money in his pocket. The foundation of his future.

A heaviness filled his chest.

A future that was as lonely as his past.

He'd been fascinated by phones as a child, but it hadn't been until he'd figured out that as the second son, he would never be groomed to truly be a McCormick. That had been reserved for the oldest. Even though he and Mick were twins, Mick was older by fifteen minutes. He'd pretended that hadn't bothered him, but it had. How there didn't seem to be anyplace for him in their father's life.

So, he'd set out to make one. His father had been humored by his interest in phones, so that's what he'd chosen. Hoping to make his father proud, instead of humored.

He'd been well on his way, when Jenny had left, and then his father died.

He'd almost given up on his idea then, but couldn't. People expected him to continue, and, well, because he'd been so used to not wanting to disappoint anyone, he'd planted a smile on his face, and continued.

That was him. Connor McCormick. The guy voted most likely to succeed by his senior class.

Of course, they all had expected that to happen simply because he was a McCormick.

Jenny had been the first person, the only person, that he hadn't had to pretend with when they'd been together. He had truly been happy with her. Even just walking beside her had made him happy.

She'd shattered that happiness in him when she'd disappeared.

And again, a couple of weeks ago, upon seeing her daughter.

He had to stop giving her that ability. It was his life.

She could do whatever she wanted with hers, but he was in control of his.

At least he would be from now on.

The setting sun, shining through his windshield, was blinding when he arrived in the Village of Newark, a town established during the time men were digging the Erie Canal. Connor was glad to turn into the hotel lot on the edge of town, and rubbed his burning eyes with one hand as he killed the engine. Ten miles of driving straight into the setting sun, along with the rubbing, left him seeing stars.

He sat there for a moment, blinking and letting his thoughts wander.

Right back to Jenny.

She seemed to fill every waking moment, and plenty of sleeping ones.

Frustrated, he threw open his door. There was one way to fix that. He'd find a speakeasy and spend the night dancing with every doll in the place.

Right after calling Seth.

He checked in to the hotel, deposited his bag in the clean and comfortable enough room, then went downstairs to use the public phone. The call didn't take long. Seth was already on top of it. Not only competent and trustworthy, Seth was a forward thinker and had already ordered supplies and had a crew ready at hand.

A few questions to the concierge and Connor was on his way to the most hopping place in the city. Yes, prohibition was in full force. Yes, speakeasies were illegal, and were supposed to be hidden and private joints. And, yes, they were as easy to find as the Erie Canal.

Connor entered the joint through the back door of a grocery store and then followed the stair steps down into the basement, where the music was playing, booze was flowing, and flappers, with their short skirts and even shorter hair, were pulling men onto a raised dancefloor.

A half dozen or more flappers were perched along the edge of that raised floor like a row of sparrows sitting on a telephone wire.

A redhead was giving him the eye as he walked to the long wooden bar with brass hand and foot rails and men lined up shoulder to shoulder.

"What will ya have, mate?" the bartender asked. A bald-headed man with thick gray eyebrows and a scruffy gray beard.

"What do you recommend?" Connor asked over the ragtime music and laughter echoing off the beamed ceiling. This was a hopping place. Exactly what he needed to get his mind off other things. The redhead would help with that.

"Two clams will get you beer all night, and five will get you gin. Specialties are by the glass." The bartender said all that while filling mugs and sliding them down the bar two at a time.

Connor wanted to have a little fun and not feel it in the morning. Pulling out two bills, he slapped them on the bar top. "I'll take a mug."

The bartender scooped up the bills with one hand and slid him a froth-topped mug at the same time.

Connor grabbed the mug and stepped away from the bar, giving room for the next guy to get a refill.

"Butt me, pal?" the guy asked.

"Sorry. Don't smoke," Connor replied as he walked past the guy.

He found an empty spot against the wall, leaned his

back against it and planted the sole of one foot on the wall as he sipped his beer.

The redhead still had her eyes on him, and smiling, she crossed the room. She was certainly cute enough to be a distraction for his mind.

"Haven't seen you here before," she said, fingering the long string of pearls hanging around her neck.

"I've never been here before," he answered.

"I'm Molly."

"Nice to meet you, Molly."

She shook her head slightly, making the red curls near her chin bob. "You looking for a good time, or just the hooch?"

Connor took another swig off his mug as a knot twisted in his stomach. The same one that he'd been ignoring for years. The one that said he could dance all night long, play it up as if he was having the time of his life, but come morning, nothing would have changed.

The knot in his stomach let itself be known with a vengeance. He'd wanted a distraction to get his mind off Jenny. That hadn't happened in years and wouldn't tonight, either. "Sorry," he said, and set his mug on the closest table. "Maybe another time."

"I'll be here," she said as he walked away.

Connor had no doubt that she would be. He wouldn't be. Not because this was a bad joint. It wasn't. Gaiety filled the room. People from all walks of life were having a good time. Flappers and gents were dancing the night away and bellied up to the bar, telling tales and raising the roof with their laughter.

He'd done that plenty of times, trouble was, it was all for show. He wasn't the happy-go-lucky guy he pretended to be. Inside he was hollow. Had been for years.

Because of Jenny. There had to be a way for him to quit allowing her to have that power over him.

He wasn't going to find a way for that to happen here. With the music and gaiety echoing in his ears like mocking laughter, he walked out the door. Went to the hotel, lay in the rented bed, and stared at the ceiling.

When sunlight began to shine in through the window, he crawled out of bed, bathed, dressed and checked out of the hotel. He wasn't going to let Jenny get to him this time.

Was not.

This time, he was going to put an end to it all. The only way he could do that was by finding out the truth. The entire truth.

Then he could go on with his life. Just like she had with hers.

It was a little after ten in the morning he pulled into Jenny's driveway. The old truck Gretchen used to deliver her flowers wasn't parked near the sheds. The doors on the sheds were open, exposing the rows of flower plants inside. Other than a few leaves fluttering on a breeze, there was no sign of movement inside the sheds.

Connor parked the Phaeton near the house, climbed out and scanned the neatly trimmed yard, flowerbeds, and the area around the clothesline on the side of the house as he walked to the front door.

He raked his fingers through his hair, then jaw set, knocked on the door. If she wasn't home, he'd wait. Plant himself on one of those wicker chairs in front of the windows and wait until she was home. There would be no leaving this time. No giving her time to trust him again.

Growing frustrated, he raised his hand to knock

again, but just then heard a scream coming from inside—a woman, shouting Jenny's name.

He grabbed the doorknob and thrust the door open. Concerned, and hearing the thuds of footsteps echoing overhead, he jogged across the neat living room, into the kitchen. Guessing the hallway in the back of the kitchen would host the staircase to the second floor, he made a beeline in that direction. Turning the corner, he grabbed the handrail and took the stairs three at a time. At the top of the steps, he followed the sound of voices down the hallway, past closed doors to one that was open at the far end.

"Don't hold your breath, Rachel," he heard Jenny say. "Breathe through the pain."

Connor increased his speed, and then skidded to a stop at the doorway. Jenny stood at the foot of the bed and another woman stood near one side of the bed, while a third woman lay upon the bed, groaning as if in great pain. "What's happened?" he asked.

Eyes wide, Jenny twisted toward him and shouted, "Connor! Get out of here! Now!"

"Do we need to take her to the hospital? My car—"

"I said get out!"

"She's injured!" he argued. "In pain!"

Jenny propelled herself toward him until they were nearly nose to nose. Being almost a foot taller than her, he still had several inches on her, even as she rose up on her tiptoes. "She's having a baby! Now get the hell out of here!"

Little else would have made him take a step back, but that did. "A baby?"

"Yes!"

He glanced toward the bed, where the woman lay with

a sheet over her and a pain-filled grimace on her face. Shifting his gaze, he caught a better look at the second woman. She was clearly pregnant. "The one in the bed or the one standing up?"

Anger snapped in Jenny's brown eyes. "The one in the bed!" She pushed on his chest, attempting to shove him backward. "Now get out!"

He took another step backward, into the hallway, and she slammed the door shut.

Connor stood there for a moment. He couldn't leave; Jenny might need help. Not that he wanted to have anything to do with delivering a baby. Or two. From the size of that other woman's stomach, she'd be going into labor soon, too. He had no experience whatsoever with delivering babies, but he did have some experience with little kids—well, not really, he mainly just bought things for his friends' kids—but he'd gotten a quick glance of a fourth person in that room. He knocked on the door. "Jenny?"

The door was wrenched open a moment later. "For crying out loud, Connor! I told you—"

"I know!" He held up both hands. "I'm not coming in, but what about the baby—"

"It hasn't arrived yet!"

The door had been open just a crack, but he caught the door before she closed it. "I'm talking about the one in the playpen. Do you want me to take him downstairs or something?"

Her face softened as she glanced over her shoulder, toward the little guy standing in the playpen.

"We'll just sit in the kitchen," Connor said. "Or outside. It can't be any fun for him to be in there." He was certain of that.

She turned, looked at him again. "You wouldn't mind?"

"No. No. I won't mind." Not wanting to enter the room, he continued, "Bring him to me. We'll be downstairs."

Leaving the door open a crack, she walked over and lifted the baby out of the playpen. On her way back to the door, she kissed the baby's cheek. "His name is William."

Connor nodded and held out his hands. "William. Good to know."

Hesitating, there was reluctance in her face.

"He'll be fine. I promise," Connor said.

"Jenny, I think another contraction is coming."

Connor wasn't sure which woman in the room had spoken. He grasped the baby's waist. "Go. William will be fine."

She released the baby. "Thank you, Connor."

The door closed and Connor looked down at the baby, who had a head full of golden curls going in all directions. "Let's get out of here, William."

A big grin formed on the baby's face.

Connor chuckled. "I thought you'd agree with me. You might as well learn early on that the male species has to stick together."

Jenny's mind wandered to Connor and William, many times, but only between Rachel's contractions, which came every few minutes over the next hour or more. Every baby was different in the amount of time they took to enter the world, and she focused on keeping Rachel calm. Lora helped with that, and everything else that was needed.

When the actual birth happened, Jenny shed a tear,

as she always did. It was such a miracle. Other than that, she kept her composure until everything had been completely taken care of for both Rachel and her new baby daughter.

When she finally walked downstairs, it was after one in the afternoon, and though it had been a harried morning, she felt exhilarated. Bringing a baby into the world was so very special.

Rachel's water had broken at eight this morning, shortly after Gretchen and Joyce had left, so in reality, the labor and delivery had been a relatively short one.

The kitchen and living room were empty, but she could see the back of Connor's head through the living room window. Sucking in a deep breath, she paused long enough to hold it until her lungs burned, and then let it out before she grasped the doorknob.

Of all the people who could have knocked on the door today, she'd never have guessed Connor. She had been on her way downstairs, to answer the door, when Lora had shouted for her, convinced the baby had been arriving.

It had simply been another contraction, albeit, stronger than the ones before. She'd barely arrived back in the room when Connor had appeared in the hallway.

She released the doorknob to press a hand to her chest, against the rapid increase of her heart. Huffing out another breath, she smoothed back the hair at her temples and fluffed her bangs. Sweat had rolled off her brows upstairs. Though she'd delivered many babies over the years, each one was unique and challenging in their own right.

And precious. So very, very precious.

Jenny opened the door, and what she viewed as she

pushed open the screen door was also so precious that her breath locked in her lungs.

Connor was sitting in one of the wicker chairs as she'd assumed from seeing the back of his head through the window. Eyes closed, his head was leaning back, against the headrest of the chair, his feet were propped up on the table and William was asleep on his chest.

Why did he have to be so handsome, so prince-like? That's how she'd always thought of him, like a fairytale prince, which was foolish. Fairytales were just that. Tales. Made-up stories. Pretend.

Jenny stepped onto the porch and quietly eased the screen door closed.

Connor opened one eye and the grin he flashed her sent her already pounding heart tumbling.

"He fell asleep right after eating lunch," he whispered.

"You fed him lunch?" she asked, even though he'd just said that he had.

"Yes." Connor rubbed William's back as he whispered. "I wasn't sure what he could eat with so few teeth, so I boiled him some eggs."

"He likes eggs," Jenny answered, stepping closer.

"Yes, he does." Connor nodded toward the house. "Has the baby arrived?"

Bliss warmed Jenny all over again. "Yes. A perfect little girl."

"Congratulations, I hope the mother is doing well."

"Thank you, and yes, both mother and baby are doing well." She reached out. "I'll take him, put him in his crib."

Connor lifted his feet off the table. "I'll carry him, so he doesn't wake up. Just lead the way."

Normally in the living room, the playpen was still

in Rachel's room, where Jenny had placed it after Rachel's water broke. The reality of all that had happened quickly set in. Connor was sure to have questions, and she didn't want to answer them, because she didn't want him to know so many things. "You've already done so much, more than enough. Thank you. I can take him. I'm sure you have other things to do."

Shaking his head, he stood. "No, I don't have anything else to do. Lead the way."

Although standing so close to him made her heart race, she remained where she was, blocking his way. "I'll take him. His crib is upstairs. Thank you again for taking such good care of him. I really appreciate it."

"It was no problem, and carrying him upstairs won't be a problem either."

He took a step forward, which was too close for comfort, forcing her to take a step back. And another. Short of attempting to pull William from Connor's arms, a battle which she doubted she'd win and would only upset William, she opened the screen door.

Connor held the door, while holding William securely with his other arm, and nodded for her to enter first.

She led the way through the living room, kitchen, and up the stairs. There, she opened the door to Joyce and William's room. Connor followed her in and carried William to the crib near the window and carefully laid him inside.

He covered the baby with the thin blanket hanging over the edge and then turned to her.

Jenny fought to keep her thoughts in line, as well as to avoid his gaze. His care and kindness toward William were doing funny things to her heart, to her entire body. She spun around and hurried to the door.

Lora was in the hallway. "Both Rachel and the baby are sleeping. I'm going to make something to eat. Are you hungry?"

Jenny knew the moment Lora saw Connor in the room behind her, because Lora blushed red.

"I—I'll make enough for both of you." Turning about, Lora took off down the hallway.

Between contractions, and to ease their worries, she had told Lora and Rachel that Connor was an old friend and that William would be perfectly safe with him. She had believed that. Completely, or would never have let him take the little boy out of the room. That had truly been a blessing.

Jenny huffed out a sigh, knowing that Connor had smiled at Lora. She knew, because she'd just been transported back in life, to high school, where every girl that Connor had smiled at had reacted exactly as Lora just had. Including her. He had this magnetic charm that leaped forward when he flashed one of his smiles. It was hard to explain, and even harder to describe what that smile did, but it had an effect. She couldn't deny that, and was afraid to look over her shoulder. His smile had already sent her heart tumbling on the porch, and she certainly didn't need that again.

Keeping her gaze straight ahead, she said, "We can leave the door open."

He followed her out of the room, but stepped up beside her once in the hallway. "Are you running a home for unwed mothers?"

Her breath caught for just a moment, because of how close to the truth he'd guessed. Then, she accepted that considering what he'd seen today, that was a conclusion most people would have. "No, we offer a safe haven for girls who are pregnant."

"What's the difference?"

She huffed out a false chuckle that only those who knew the difference would understand. A seriousness overtook her, because the matter was very serious. "I would like to ask a favor, Connor."

He stepped in front of her, forcing her to stop and turn to look at him. "Of course. What do you need?"

She kept her gaze on his chest, not his face. "Silence. I need you to not tell anyone."

"Tell anyone what?"

"What you saw here, who lives here."

"Why?"

She shook her head. "It's important, Connor. Your silence."

"Are these girls runaways or something?"

Again, he was too close for comfort. To her and to the truth. "I can't say more, Connor."

"Yes, you can," he said. "And you can trust me."

She shook her head and sidestepped to walk around him, but his bulk filled the hallway. "It's none of your business, Connor."

"I'm making it my business."

Anger snapped inside her. She met his gaze, which was as stern as the one she was sending his way. "You don't have that right."

"Right?" He folded his arms. "The only right I'm concerned about is the one in right and wrong. If something wrong is happening here, I will not remain silent. Who are these girls? Where are their husbands, the fathers of their babies? Where's your husband?"

Chapter Five

Although they were whispering, Jenny couldn't take the chance of disturbing Rachel, or William. "I need to go help Lora make lunch."

He waved at the steps. "Fine. We'll go downstairs. Just know I'm not leaving this house until I get the answers to those questions. And more."

She swallowed against the thickness in her throat and walked toward the stairs. Those questions were ones she wouldn't answer. Couldn't. She just had to figure out how not to, because he would persist.

They descended the stairs silently. With him at her side every step, as if he expected her to take off running. She wouldn't do that, even though escaping him had crossed her mind.

Lora was at the counter, making sandwiches with the chicken left over from last night's supper.

Jenny walked to her side. "I'll do this. You can sit down and rest."

"No, I'd rather stay busy," Lora said, piling the chicken on slices of bread. "I do hope your friend likes mustard. I already put it on the bread."

Jenny's insides flinched at Connor being called her friend.

"Yes, I do," Connor said, standing close.

Lora twisted, and once again, her cheeks flushed as she caught sight of Connor. "That's good."

Jenny clamped her teeth together, flustered all over again.

"I'm Connor McCormick," he said.

"I—I'm Lora. Lora Bradford."

"It's nice to meet you, Lora," he said.

"You, too."

The nervousness in Lora's voice had Jenny rubbing her forehead. She had to get rid of him fast. Given the chance, he could soon have Lora, or Rachel or Joyce, telling him all they knew, without realizing how that could affect others. She grabbed a plate off the counter and set a sandwich on it. Spinning around, she handed it to him.

"Thank you," he said.

"Would you like a pickle, or some applesauce with your sandwich?" Lora asked him.

"No, thank you, the sandwich is fine. It looks delicious."

"You can sit at the table," Jenny said, not sounding as polite as Lora had, or Connor.

"I'll wait for you," Connor answered. "You and I can eat our sandwiches on the front porch."

Jenny grabbed another sandwich, set it on another plate. "All right."

"Oh, here," Lora said, lifting another sandwich off the counter and carefully holding it out to Connor. "I thought you might like two."

"Thank you." He held his plate out for her to put the sandwich on. "They do look good."

Jenny was already on her way across the room. She held no animosity toward Lora and her thoughtfulness; she just didn't want anyone to be nice to Connor because she didn't want him to feel welcome. He wasn't welcome. Not here or anywhere else in her life.

He caught up with her in the living room, and opened both the house and screen doors for her to exit first. They'd barely sat down in the wicker chairs when Lora arrived. "Sandwiches can be dry," Lora said, setting two glasses of water on the table.

"Thank you, Lora, that was very thoughtful," he said.

"Yes, very thoughtful. Thank you," Jenny said. "You rest for a bit after you eat."

"I will, but I'll listen for Rachel, and her baby and William," Lora said.

Once she'd gone, Connor said, "She doesn't appear to be very old."

"Seventeen," Jenny answered.

"Where's the father of her baby?"

Committed to getting this over as quickly as possible, she picked up her sandwich, and before taking a bite, said, "I have no idea."

Connor's gaze never left her, causing her to need to take a drink of water because her mouth had gone so dry that she was sure to choke on the mouthful she was attempting to chew.

"What about the girl upstairs? The one who just had a baby. Where's the father of her baby?"

Her mouth was still full. Jenny took another drink of water and shrugged while shaking her head.

Connor picked up his sandwich, and ate it, while looking around as if he was scanning the lawn, sheds, and flowerbeds, for clues. Or answers.

Jenny forced herself to eat her entire sandwich, while also refusing to allow her thoughts to tumble into the past, remember how she and Connor used to laugh and talk while eating together. They'd had fun, laughed, no matter what they'd been doing together.

He'd finished both of his sandwiches by the time she was done with hers. She took a deep breath, watching as he leaned back, rested an elbow on the arm of the chair and his chin on the back of his knuckles.

"I was as serious as a headstone upstairs, Jenny. I'm not leaving here until I have answers."

She sat back and squared her shoulders. "I was serious, too, Connor. It's none of your business." Without giving him time to respond, she continued, "I appreciate, very much, how you took care of William today, but that does not mean I owe you any type of explanation."

"What about leaving town, without a word?" he asked. "While I was gone. You just disappeared. I expected you to be there when I got home, and you weren't. Does that justify an explanation? I think it does."

She shook her head. "You weren't out of town."

"Yes, I was. I left the morning after I told you I was going. Took the morning train to New York City, and when I returned, two and a half months later, you were gone."

The back of her throat burned at how easily he lied. That's what had gotten to her so strongly back then. How he'd lied to her. She'd never, ever, have expected that from him. Steadfast to remain strong, she said, "That was seven years ago. It's in the past."

"That doesn't mean you don't owe me an explanation," he said.

"It doesn't mean I do, either." She pinched her lips

together to keep them from trembling for a moment. "Do us both a favor, Connor. Leave. Forget what you saw here today."

He shook his head, and then used one hand to flip the triangle of dark hair off his forehead. "I can't do that, Jenny. I've wondered what happened to you for too many years."

She had wondered, too. He was the very reason she never picked up a newspaper, because if she saw his name, knew where he was, she might have reacted to that knowledge.

"Who was it?" he asked. "Or should I say *is* it?"

"Who is what?" she asked.

He gave her a look that held no charm, but was full of disdain. "The man you fell in love with, ran away with, the father of your daughter."

She closed her eyes at the way her insides flinched. There was no love, never had been, but she loved her daughter and would do anything to protect her. That's what this was about, protecting Emily, and the girls here, their children, and those in the future who would need help. She had to protect each and every one of them.

Connor held his breath, mainly in order to keep his feelings in check. Who shouldn't matter, he just didn't want it to be someone he knew, or had known. That would make it easier to hate whoever she'd fallen in love with. Which was stupid, but also real. Very real.

Jenny opened her eyes and blinked several times, and the shine he saw in her eyes, the dampness on her lashes, was from tears. Unshed ones.

His heart constricted. "Jenny—"

She shook her head. "It doesn't matter who Emily's father is, Connor."

"It does to me. Where is he?"

"I don't know," she said.

Anger filled him at the man. "He deserted you and your daughter?"

The door opened and the black-haired, brown-eyed Lora said, "Jenny, Rachel is asking for you."

Jenny leaped to her feet at the same time Connor did. As she shot toward the door, she told him, "Stay here."

He wasn't about to do that, and followed her into the house, all the way to the staircase off the kitchen.

She spun around as the younger, pregnant woman started up the steps. "I mean it, Connor. Stay here! You come up these steps and I'll never forgive you!"

He ran a hand through his hair. She sounded serious, looked it too, but what if she needed help upstairs? Someone to carry that new mother downstairs, and her baby, drive them to see a doctor.

Jenny had disappeared up the stairs, and he paced the floor for a short time, hearing the soft cries of a baby. A tiny one from the sounds of it. He didn't know much about babies or new mothers, or doctoring, but couldn't just stand here, not doing anything.

He grabbed the handrail, but before taking a step, he listened. There wasn't any shouting, or hurried steps. All he really heard was the pounding of his heart. His nerves were dancing under his skin as if the woman and her baby weren't mere strangers.

Jenny wasn't a mere stranger, and if that woman and her baby needed help, he had to offer it.

He had to help Jenny, too, if her husband had deserted her and her daughter. Any man who did that was not a man. He was a piker, a coward of the worst kind. A snake that needed to be shoved back under the rock that he'd crawled out from beneath.

Connor stared up the steps and wondered if William was still asleep in his crib. He'd had no idea what to do with the little guy when he'd first held him, but had figured it out easily enough. The little guy couldn't walk on his own, but had liked trying when they'd gone outside. Connor had held on to his tiny hands and helped William walk across the thick lawn in his chunky little white shoes.

Willie, as Connor had called him, had also liked playing with the rag ball, and he'd really enjoyed holding on to the steering wheel in his car.

When Willie had kept trying to chew on the steering wheel, Connor had figured he must be hungry and had brought him back inside, and looked for something to feed him. Ultimately, he'd figured boiled eggs would be safe. Easy to chew.

The poor little chap had almost fallen asleep in his high chair, and Connor had almost fallen asleep outside after Willie had sacked out on his chest. Though his hair was blond, and Riley's red, Willie reminded Connor of Riley, the five-year-old boy who lived with his grandparents next door to his mother's house. Connor always brought a candy bar or chewing gum whenever he went to visit his mother, knowing Riley would see his car and come over to say hello.

Jenny appeared at the top of the steps and his heart slammed against his ribcage with the force of a baseball landing in a catcher's mitt. "How are they?" he asked.

"Fine." She walked down the steps toward him.

"What about Willie?"

"What about him?"

"Is he still asleep? He might need his diaper changed."

Stopping on the second step up, so they were eye level, she gave him a quizzical look. "Are you offering to change his diaper?"

He wasn't totally offering. He was just at a loss as to what to do. "If he needed that, yes, I would."

The twinkle that appeared in her eyes reminded him of the old Jenny, the one that had made his heart skip a beat just like it was right now. "Really? Have you changed a diaper before?"

"No, but it can't be that hard."

She grinned and walked past him. "It's not hard, but it doesn't always smell very pleasant."

He followed her to the kitchen doorway. "What did the new mother need?"

"She's hungry. I'm going to make her some tea and toast."

"Shouldn't she be seen by a doctor? And the baby?"

She twisted, looked at him. A long look. "They will be."

"When?"

She walked across the kitchen. "After I send word that the baby has arrived, Dr. Dillon will drive out to see them."

He leaned against the painted white archway and crossed his arms. "How will you get word to him?"

"Her," Jenny said, filling a tea kettle with water.

Confused he asked, "Her who?"

"Dr. Dillon is a woman."

A doctor was a doctor! As long as they knew what they were doing, he didn't care if they were a man or a woman. "How will you get word to her?"

After putting the kettle on the stove, she took a loaf of bread out of the tin box on the counter and sliced off two pieces.

Tired of waiting, he asked, "Do you need me to take a message to this Dr. Dillon?"

"No. Mr. Whipple will do that." She put the bread in the oven.

"How? Where is he? Who is he?"

She turned around and leaned against the stove. "This really is none of your business."

Although she attempted to look stern, all he saw was her uncommon natural beauty. Even wearing a simple pale green dress, with her long hair loosely braided and pinned up, she was beyond pretty. She'd matured into a very beautiful woman. He pushed off the wall and walked into the kitchen. "You've already told me that."

"I have, and yet you're still here."

He stopped within a foot of her, blocking her from moving away from the stove. "And I'm not leaving, other than to get word to this Mr. Whipple fellow, so he can tell Dr. Dillon to get her carcass out here."

"I will tell Mr. Whipple."

"When? How?"

She turned and opened the oven door to check on the bread.

Connor was holding on by his last thread. The want to place a tiny kiss along the slenderness of her neck, was enough to drive him crazy. Throw in her aloof answers, and he would soon be fit to be tied. "Damn it, Jenny, why can't I get a straight answer out of you?"

She closed the oven door, and leveled a solid stare on him. "Mr. Whipple is the school bus driver. When he drops Emily off, I'll ask him to let Dr. Dillon know that we need her to stop out here at her earliest convenience." She picked up the kettle that had started to steam. "Now that I've answered your question, you can leave. I have things to do."

He stepped back so she could pour the water in a teapot on the counter. "One question. You answered one question. I asked several others. You haven't answered any of them."

She dropped a teabag in the pot and replaced the lid. "There is a newborn baby upstairs, along with the woman who just delivered her. I have another woman who could go into labor at any moment. A year-old infant who will be waking up from his nap shortly, two greenhouses full of flowers that need to be watered, and a daughter who will soon be home from school." She lifted a plate out of the cupboard and set it firmly on the counter before she grabbed a pot holder. "In other words, I don't have time to answer any more of your questions."

He couldn't deny any of that, but wouldn't be denied his answers, either. He'd been haunted by what those answers could be for too long. Though it may have looked as if he'd gone on with his life, the way he'd continued to hang out with friends and build his phone company, that had all been on the outside. Inside, he'd been hollow, stuck. Trying to get through it, he'd told himself that he loved his life, and had continued to tell himself that, hoping that someday he'd believe it. A wave of anger washed over him. Jenny hadn't been stuck. She'd gone on with her life as if he'd been nothing but a casual acquaintance she'd once known.

She took the bread out of the oven, and set it on the plate to butter.

"All right," he said.

There was a definite look of surprise in her brown eyes as she twisted her neck to look at him. "All right what?" she asked slowly.

"You have a lot to do. I see that. I've seen that since I arrived." He walked toward the back door that led to a screened-in porch.

"Thank you for understanding, and thank you for all your help with William, earlier."

Her tone was softer than a moment ago, almost meek. He kept walking, right out the door. "You're welcome."

Once outside, he took a deep breath, and walked toward the greenhouses. He didn't know anything more about taking care of flowers than he did about babies, but if they needed to be watered, then that's what he'd do.

The greenhouses were outfitted with everything he needed, including a hand pump and rubber hoses to fill center ditches that ran through the long rows of flowers in their raised beds. Ingenuity had always amazed him, and right now, that included the flower business that took place here. He didn't know all the different varieties, but there were numerous plants, from seedlings to those that were already blooming.

He checked each row, looking for those that were dry, then positioned the hose and pumped water into the long, shallow ditch for those plants. The ones that were moist, he skipped over. That much he'd learned from his mother and the flower beds she had along the side of the house he'd grown up in and had to weed often enough while growing up.

"What are you doing?"

He was in the second greenhouse, having just finished filling the ditches in the beds with water. Barely glancing at Jenny standing in the doorway, he continued rolling the rubber hose around his hand and elbow in order to replace it near the hand pump. "What does it look like?"

"It looks like you are still here," she said. "I thought you'd left."

"Did you hear my car leave?"

"No, but I hadn't heard it arrive, either, so I assumed—"

"That's because it's a Phaeton," he interrupted. "Runs as quiet as a kitten purring, and as smoothly." He hung the hose on the metal hook nailed to the wall by the pump. "And to answer your question, I just watered the plants for you. Only those that appeared to need it. Too much water can make their petals turn brown."

"How?" She shook her head. "I didn't—"

"I know you weren't asking for my help," he interrupted again. "And I know about the petals turning brown from my mother. How are the baby and new mother doing? Did she eat her toast?"

"Yes, and they are fine."

"And the other pregnant girl?"

"She's fine."

She still stood in the doorway, even as he began walking toward her. "And William?"

"He's fine, too."

He rolled down his shirt sleeves and buttoned his cuffs as he walked. "It must be about time to get your daughter off the bus."

"It is." She huffed out a breath and shook her head. "Thank you for watering the plants, Connor, but I need you to leave. Now, before Emily arrives."

"Why?"

"Because she isn't used to men being here. I don't want to frighten her."

He stopped in front of her, and once again, the desire to touch her flared inside him. Watering the plants had given him plenty of time to think, and to remember that he wasn't here to fall in love with her again. He was here to find out the truth so he could finally forget her and get on with his life. "Why? Because her father deserted you?"

Jenny averted his gaze. "He didn't desert us."

"Is he dead?" That was the only other explanation that he could think of for them being alone.

"Not that I'm aware of—now please, Connor, you need to leave."

"Not that you're aware of? What the hell kind of answer is that?"

Chapter Six

"The truth!" Jenny pinched her lips together in order to quell the frustration filling every part of her being. She truly had thought he'd left and purposefully hadn't gone to a window to see if his car was gone because a part of her had hoped he hadn't left—which was so utterly ridiculous! Her best defense was to stay focused on why he couldn't be here. "Something you are incapable of doing!"

"Incapable of doing?" He shook his head as if flummoxed. "What am I incapable of doing?"

She had to stop this. Now. "We've already been through all this! You need to leave before I have the police remove you!"

Laughter echoed on the ceiling overhead. "How are you going to contact them? You don't have a phone, furthermore, Twin Pines doesn't have a police department. The state police would have to come in from Syracuse or Rochester. If it's Rochester, it could be my brother Mick who shows up."

A shiver of fear coiled around her spine. "Your brother is a police officer?"

"Yep. He's with the city, but helps out the state department all the time because he's the best detective around."

A detective? Could this get worse?

"You can't pack up and run away this time, Jenny."

Anger made her sputter. "Pack up and run away? I didn't pack up and run away from anything! I didn't lie and hide in the shadows, either, like some people!"

"Well, you sure as hell weren't there when I got home!" He threw his arms in the air. "And what the hell are you doing now if not lying and hiding in the shadows?"

Totally furious, she stomped forward and shoved a finger against his chest. "I'm taking care of those I love! Those who need to be taken care of, which is a hell of a lot more than you can say you ever did!" Her percolating fury flooded through her. "But how could you? You don't even know what love is!"

"Really, and you do?"

"Yes, I do! I know how it can crush a person! Make them do things they would never have otherwise done! Now get in your fancy Phaeton car and get out of here! Don't ever come back! Ever!"

He shouldered past her, and she stood there trembling and sucking in air. The sound of his car door slamming and the engine roaring into life made her insides jolt, but she refused to turn around. Not even when she heard the tires of his car kicking up gravel as it drove away.

It took several deep breaths before she was stable enough to walk into the greenhouse, to the pump, where she pumped water into her hands and splashed it on her face, washing way the tears. Lifting a towel off the stack kept near the hose, she pressed it against her face and held it there, telling herself Connor was not worth crying over.

She'd told herself that so many times, it shouldn't have to be repeated.

By the time she removed the towel, her insides were calmer and she was able to straighten her shoulders, but her insides were still a jumbled mess. There wasn't anything she could do about that, so she set the towel down and left the greenhouse.

The tire impressions in the dirt provided no help in her attempts to collect herself completely before meeting the school bus. It took the sight of Emily jumping out of the back of the bus for that to happen. Holding her hand out, for Emily to run forward and grasp it, Jenny stepped closer to the driver's window.

"Hello!" Mr. Whipple greeted, his eyes squinting due to his broad smile. "How are you today?"

"I'm well, thank you," Jenny answered. "Could you please let Alice Dillon know we need her to drive out when she has time?"

"Of course. As soon as I get back to town. Is there anything else?"

"No, that's everything." She and Emily stepped away from the bus.

"Say, did you hear they finally fixed the road at the railroad crossing up the road?" he asked.

"No, I hadn't," she answered. "But I'm glad they fixed it. It's needed gravel for months."

"It sure had!" With a smiling nod at her and a wave to Emily, he shifted the bus into gear.

She and Emily waved as he drove off. "How was your day?" she asked as they began walking up the driveway.

"Is there a new baby?" Emily asked rather than answering.

Jenny smiled. "Yes. Rachel had her baby this morning."

"Oh, goodie! A boy baby or a girl baby?"

"A girl."

"Yay! Can I see her?"

"After you change your clothes and eat the biscuits and apple butter on the table for you."

"Yum! It's my lucky day! Two snacks! Mr. Whipple gave us a cookie today for the ride home."

Jenny laughed. "It must be your lucky day." It hadn't been hers; that was for sure.

Emily was still eating her snack when the sound of a vehicle coming up the driveway made Jenny's heart drop to her ankles. He couldn't be back. Please, no. She couldn't take much more of him.

The short amount of time it took to walk to the front door wasn't enough to fully put her in the state of mind to face Connor again, but thankfully, it wasn't needed. The car wasn't his.

Jenny opened the door and stepped onto the porch as the black, older-model Ford pulled up in front of the house. "How on earth did you get my message so quickly?" she asked as the car door opened.

"He said I needed to get out here right away," Alice Dillon said, lifting her bag out of the backseat.

Jenny sucked in a gulp of air so quickly, it hurt. "Who?" She knew. Oh, yes, she knew. Mr. Whipple hadn't had time to make it to town yet, but someone else had.

"Connor McCormick." Alice hurried forward. "What's

wrong? Were there difficulties with the delivery? The baby? The mother?"

"No, the delivery went well and they are both fine," Jenny answered. "They just need to be checked, at your earliest convenience. Not immediately."

Alice let out a tiny laugh. "Well, I'm here, so let's go check on them, then."

Jenny had to once again quell the frustration filling her over Connor's interference. An interference that was not necessary. She was fully capable of taking care of everything that needed to be taken care of. The girls, the house, her daughter, the greenhouses. She'd been doing it for years and the idea that he was attempting to undermine her efforts and capabilities went beyond irritation.

Alice was in the midst of her examinations when the sounds of another vehicle pulled into the yard, this one easily recognized by the rattles and clangs unique to Gretchen's delivery truck. Gretchen and Joyce bounded in the back door moments later.

"Rachel?" Gretchen asked, walking to the sink. "I saw how low she was carrying that baby last night."

"Yes, Rachel," Jenny answered. "A baby girl around noon today."

"It went well?" Gretchen asked while washing her hands.

"Yes, both are fine. Alice should be down to confirm that soon."

"Rachel named her baby Annie," Emily provided. "Isn't that a nice name for a baby?"

Gretchen dried her hands and then used the corner of the towel to tickle the tip of Emily's nose. "Yes, it is. Almost as nice as Emily."

Emily giggled, and then turned back to focus on tying William's shoes as he sat in the high chair.

"Lora?" Gretchen asked.

"She's resting," Jenny replied. "She was a great help this morning."

"It's always a little scary, watching someone else go through labor, when you are so close yourself," Gretchen said.

"Yes, it is." Jenny would never forget helping with her first delivery, only days before she'd gone through it all herself.

"I'll take these two outside," Joyce said, lifting William out of the chair. "They can help me unload the truck."

"How did the deliveries go?" Jenny asked as the children and Joyce walked out the back door.

"The deliveries went fine." Gretchen sighed and shook her head.

Jenny's heart sank. The Albany Moral Hospitality Institute, the home as they all referred to it, had a new director, making it more difficult for girls who wanted a different option than the two offered—sign the adoption papers before the baby was born, or afterward. If they signed before, their families were provided a reduction in the cost of their stay at the home. Along with that option came visitation rights. At a cost of five dollars more per week, for those who didn't sign, also came "housekeeping" chores.

Most girls were residents of the institute for a few months, but her mother and stepfather had paid for her nine-month stay in advance, on the night they'd dropped her off. Cloaked in the darkness of night, her stepfather had driven down the long narrow driveway, lined with trees and canopied by heavy branches that had darkened the road even more. He'd stayed in the car while her mother had escorted her into the large brick building, where they'd been met by Dr. Amos Mayor, who'd taken them into a room and examined her to confirm her pregnancy.

Her stomach clenched at the memory and her gag reflex kicked in, making her move to the sink as she cupped a hand over her mouth.

The swooshing noise in her ears faded enough for her to hear someone say her name. She held up a hand, saying she'd be fine in a moment. The memory just had to fade away.

The disruption in her stomach eased, and she closed her eyes, drew in a breath and blew it out.

A glass of water was handed to her. She took a sip and stared out the window above the sink, where she could see Emily holding on to William's hands, helping him take awkward steps through the grass.

The image did the job of sending memories back into the far recesses of her mind. She drank more water, then dumped out the glass, rinsed it and set it on the side of the sink.

When she turned, Gretchen and Alice were in the kitchen. Although there was concern in their eyes, neither said a word. There wasn't a woman who passed through this house who didn't have flashbacks.

Jenny pulled up a smile. "How are Rachel and Annie?"

"Perfect," Alice said, setting the red-and-white kitchen scale on the counter. "Six pounds, ten ounces, and nineteen inches long."

"That's about as perfect as they come," Gretchen said, pouring coffee into a cup.

Trim, with brown hair and eyes, and bright red lips, Alice took the cup and saucer from Gretchen. While holding the saucer in one hand, she lifted the cup with the other and took a small sip. A frown formed between her dark brows as she said, "I truly thought there was an issue by the way Mr. McCormick acted."

Jenny refused to glance at Gretchen as she said, "He was here when the delivery happened and I don't believe he's ever experienced something along those lines."

"Births can tend to agitate some men," Alice said. "I thought he was there to tell me it was time to install a telephone line. I can't even say how excited I am about that. It will make all the difference in the world for my patients to get hold of me. You are having one installed, aren't you?"

"No," Jenny answered. "We aren't."

"Why not? I'm glad it's his company covering this area. I've heard good things about it and his prices are far better than what other people have paid. A telephone truly could be a lifesaver. Well worth the cost." Alice took another sip of coffee. "I was impressed by him. A man so young owning such a thriving company, and out selling lines himself."

Jenny's ears began ringing. She shook her head against it and against Alice's comment. "Connor doesn't own the Rural Rochester Telephone Company." He'd said he worked for it, not...

"Yes, he does," Alice said. "I read an article about him in the Rochester Chronicle last year. It had suggested he would be running telephone lines from Rochester to

Syracuse this spring. I'd started to be concerned that it wouldn't happen."

Jenny's back teeth clenched. He'd lied to her again. For no reason, he'd flat out lied to her.

"He's also the reason the railroad crossing finally got new gravel hauled in," Alice said. "He called the county and two days later, it was fixed. Impressive if you ask me." Alice set her cup and saucer on the counter. "Thanks for the coffee. I'll stop by next week to check on Rachel and Annie, and I highly suggest you reconsider having a phone installed."

A nod was the most Jenny could muster as Gretchen followed Alice out of the kitchen. Hell could freeze over before she'd have one of Connor's telephones in her home.

Connor raised a brow at the man sitting next to him on the chrome stools in the only diner in Twin Pines. "You don't say?"

"I do," Howard Fletcher said, rubbing at the whiskers covering his double chin. "And it's the gospel. Gretchen filled his hide with enough buckshot that old Doc Dillon was still plucking it out a week later."

"Dr. Dillon?" Connor asked.

Howard nodded as he took a large bite of the gravy-covered beef. He owned the gas station next door and seemed to know everything about everyone—the very reason Connor had asked Howard to join him for dinner.

"Alice Dillon," Connor said, just for clarification. He'd sold a phone to the doctor's office in town a couple of weeks ago, but hadn't put two and two together until after leaving Jenny's house. Then he'd driven straight to the big white house on the edge of town to send the doctor out to Jenny's place. His mind had been too plugged up with other things when Jenny had said the doctor's name.

"Oh, no, no." Howard took a drink of milk and wiped his mouth with his sleeve before continuing. "Not Alice. Her pappy. Roland. He died, oh, gosh, must be going on five years ago now. That's when Alice moved home, took over his practice. She'd been down in New York City, working in one of those big hospitals. That's why she never got married, you know. Never had time. They had her working day and night. Way I hear it, she lived right there at that hospital. That can't be good for a young gal like she was back then. She's a good doctor, though. Everyone trusts her. Mainly 'cause we trusted her pappy. He was home-grown. She was, too, as far as that goes. We got some good home-grown folks here."

Connor had watched the doctor leave town, and had watched for her return. She'd assured him that all was well with the new baby and her mother. That eased his mind about that situation, but there were still others filling his head.

He pushed his plate to the opposite edge of the counter. The roast beef had been the only choice written on the small chalkboard on the wall. That wasn't completely true; he'd had a choice of having either green beans or fried cabbage on the side. The board had also said there was a choice of a ginger bar or an oatmeal cookie for dessert, but he'd been informed that the cookies were all gone on account of Mr. Whipple buying a dozen to give to the children on the school bus for the ride home.

He'd forgone the dessert. What he ate wasn't as important as the conversation. Jenny had been wrong when she'd said that he didn't know what love was. He knew. He also knew how it could crush a person. If she wouldn't give him the answers he wanted, he'd get them elsewhere, and his companion could very well be that person. In a town this size, everyone knew everyone else's business, and Howard had been more than willing to talk while pumping gas into his Phaeton a short time ago.

"This Andrew Jewel, that was his name, right?" Connor asked.

"Sure was." Howard nodded toward the small plate beside Connor's larger empty one. "You gonna eat that bread?"

"No." Connor slid the small plate closer to Howard. "Go ahead. This Andrew was caught sneaking around Gretchen's after dark a few years ago?"

Howard took the bread and while swiping it in the gravy on his plate, said, "He claimed he'd blown a tire on the road and walked up the driveway to get help. Don't know what kind of help he expected." He popped the gravy-soaked bread in his mouth. "But I bet it wasn't buckshot."

Connor slid an extra napkin toward Howard. "Why did Gretchen shoot him?"

Howard used the napkin to wipe the gravy off the front of his grease-stained overalls, but used his sleeve to wipe the gravy off his whiskers. "Showing up uninvited." Leaning closer, he glanced left and right before whispering, "She's got those young girls and their babies out there."

"Yes, she does," Connor said.

"There you have it." Howard emptied his glass of milk and set it down with a thud. "Hillary sure puts on a good spread, don't she?"

"Yes, she does." Connor made sure the waitress and owner, as well as the cook, were well out of earshot. "So this Andrew has been the only man anyone's heard of being out at Je—Gretchen's place?"

"Sure is." Howard guffawed. "Except a traveling salesman now and again. They're getting one of your telephones, aren't they?"

The waitress was making her way toward them so Connor pulled out his billfold. "Yes," he told Howard. "They'll have a phone installed." Free of charge, he'd see to it himself.

"Need anything else, Howard?" the waitress asked.

Howard patted his round stomach. "Nope."

"How about you?"

"No, thank you." Connor handed her several bills. "It was all very good."

Her red lips puckered as she looked at the money. "You paying for Howard's meal, too?"

"Yes, I am." Offering a believable explanation, he added, "It gets lonely eating alone every night."

"I'll be right back with your change."

"No, the rest is for you." He gave her a wink for good measure.

Touching the side of her blond hair, she grinned. "Well, sugar, you stop in any night."

"Tomorrow night it's fried chicken," Howard said. "Best you've ever eaten. Comes with corn or peas and apple cobbler."

Not wanting to commit to anything, Connor said, "I'll keep that in mind if I get back in town in time."

Howard pulled out a grease-covered rag and blew his nose. "Where you going?"

"Running lines all the way to Syracuse. Still have

plenty of people to sell service to." That was a flat-out lie. He was going back out to Jenny's tomorrow.

"Your phone line is the talk of the town. Folks haven't been this excited about something for years. Not since the president's train rolled through."

"Oh? When was that?"

"Let's see here..." He rubbed his beard. "Best I can recall, that must have been right around 1892."

"Then it's time for excitement." He patted Howard's shoulder as he rose off the metal stool. "Thanks for joining me for dinner."

"Thanks for the invite." Howard climbed off his stool. "Glad you stopped in to fuel up the gas tank in that fancy car of yours." He let out a low whistle. "She sure is a beauty."

"Thanks." Connor pushed open the door. He and Howard parted ways on the sidewalk. He crossed the road to the small inn where he'd booked the same room he'd stayed in before, and Howard walked to his fueling station next door to the diner. He had an apartment above the station that he'd lived in since he'd opened the fueling station after his wife had died and he'd sold his farm to none other than Gretchen Olsen. That had been fifteen years ago, according to Howard.

Entering the Bird's Inn, a wooden building in need of another coat of white paint, Connor waved through the arched doorway, at the owners sitting side by side in rocking chairs and listening to the radio in the living room. "Just me."

"Grand Ole Opry's on the radio if you care to join us," the husband, Eric Robertson, invited.

"That's a good show, but I'm going to call it a day. Thank you, though. Another time."

"Good night," Ava Robertson said.

"Thank you, same to you." Connor climbed the narrow staircase, admitting that he hadn't been to a town this friendly in a very long time. Rochester was his town. Full of hustle and bustle, nightlife and family and friends. Twin Pines didn't have a nightlife other than fireflies, there was no hustle and bustle and the only person he really knew was Jenny, but he was more than willing to stay here as long as necessary. Afterward, he'd return to Rochester, the life he'd always known. He'd know why Jenny had left by the time he headed home, and he'd be able to completely put her behind him.

Chapter Seven

The night air blowing in through the window was pleasant and cool, and carried in the hooting of an owl. The bird must be close by, perched in one of the many trees behind the inn. Connor grinned. It had been a while since he heard an owl hooting.

A frown tugged down on his brows as he listened more closely. Either that owl had a sore throat, or it wasn't an owl. He tossed back the covers and picked up his watch to check the time as he climbed off the bed. It was after ten o'clock. He walked to the window and pulled back the curtain.

Startled by what he saw, who he saw, he pushed the window all the way open and leaned out. Even with a scarf over her hair, he recognized her. "Jenny?"

She pressed a finger to her lips and waved for him to come down.

Still dressed, other than his shirt and shoes, he grabbed them and rushed out the door. The inn was quiet and it wasn't until he was at the bottom of the steps that he paused long enough to question if he'd truly seen her, or had been having some kind of dream. One where he was awake and seeing things. A mirage.

There was only one way to find out.

He opened the door, pulled it closed quietly and ran down the porch steps. The rocks dug into his stockinged feet, but he ignored them. He'd put his shoes on after he discovered if it was Jenny, or if he'd been dreaming. While being awake. He knew he hadn't fallen asleep yet.

Rounding the corner of the building, his heart sank at the empty space. There were trees, grass, an old wooden swing, but no Jenny. A wave of disappointment hit him like a tidal wave. He had imagined her.

Huffing out a breath, he turned, even more convinced that he had to get her out of his system.

"Connor."

He closed his eyes, ignoring the way his mind was even conjuring up the sound of her voice.

"Connor. Over here. Past the swing."

Certain the whispered words hadn't come from within, he turned and scanned the trees behind the swing, and his heart somersaulted at the partially hidden shape beneath the long, low hanging branches of a willow tree. A woman's shape. Wearing a dark dress and scarf, just like he'd seen out the window. Cautiously, because he wasn't one hundred percent certain that he wasn't imagining this, either, he took a couple of slow steps.

She waved for him to hurry.

He looked around, seeing nothing, and continued walking forward. "Jenny?"

"Yes. Be quiet."

"What are you doing here? Is something wrong?"

"Just come on. Hurry before someone hears us."

He crossed the lawn to where she stood, glancing around, checking to see if this was some sort of trick.

"It's just me," she said.

"What are you doing here?"

"I have to talk to you."

It was too dark to see her face fully because of the tree branches and leaves. "How did you get here?"

"Gretchen. She parked on the edge of town so no one would hear the truck."

"Why? What's so important you're sneaking around at night? Is it one of the girls? Another baby?"

"I wouldn't—"

A dog barked in the distance.

She grabbed his arm and tugged him to walk farther into the grove of trees. "I wouldn't be here if it was just another baby."

"Why are you here?" His socks were collecting the nighttime dew. "Hold up a minute. Let me put my shoes on."

She stopped and released his arm, then wrung her hands together while looking around as he slipped on his shoes.

"What's going on?" he asked while tying the first shoe.

"I need a ride to Albany."

"Oh. All right." He tied the second shoe. "When?"

"Right now."

"Right now?" He wasn't opposed to giving her a ride, but felt he needed to point out, "That's over a three-hour drive. It'll be the middle of the night when we arrive."

She planted both hands on her hips. "I know that, but girls don't run away in the middle of the day, they run away in the middle of the night!"

"What are you talking about? Girls running away?"

Full understanding struck. "Those pregnant women at your place, they are runways!"

"Yes, but not from their homes, from *the* home." She grasped his arm. "I wouldn't ask if I wasn't desperate. Will you take me or not?"

He'd take her. That was a given. He could see the desperation on her face now that she was no longer shadowed by the trees. "I'll take you, Jenny, but I need to know what I'm getting into."

"I'll explain everything you need to know on the way," she said hurriedly. "Please, we must leave, now. Something is wrong. I know it."

Her urgency triggered one inside him. "My car is out front. Go get in it. I have to go to my room and get the keys."

Jenny pressed a hand to the churning in her stomach as Connor climbed in the car and started the engine. She'd thought about it, tried to come up with someone else she could ask, but there wasn't anyone else. Connor was her only hope.

Gretchen agreed.

"Can you turn your lights on and off three times?" she asked.

"Why?"

"For Gretchen," Jenny explained. Twin Pines was small enough that the entire length of town could be seen from both ends, and Gretchen would see the lights from where she sat in the truck on the west end. "She's watching and will know that you agreed to take me once you flash your lights. She'll go back home then. Lora could go into labor at any time. One of us has to be there around the clock for when that happens."

He flashed his lights, and then pulled onto the road. "What is *the* home?"

She hated asking for help. It was not something she did, and asking him was the worst. He might figure out the truth behind Emily's birth, but she had to take that chance in order to help others. "A home for unwed mothers. It's actually called the Albany Moral Hospitality Institute. Not that there is anything moral or hospitable about it."

"The women at your house? That's where they ran away from?"

"Yes." She swallowed against the burning in her throat. "It's a terrible place, Connor. Terrible. The girls are told they are immoral, disgraceful and that the sin in their blood will carry over to their babies. That their babies will be outcast as bastards if they don't give them up for adoption, and that the only way they'll be forgiven for having a baby out of wedlock is if they give up their child, just like God did. It's terrible—the girls don't feel as if they have any other option."

"And you give them one, let them live with you," he said.

"Yes, many of them want to keep their babies. Gretchen started helping girls who had run away from the home several years ago, and we usually see two, sometimes three a month, but it's been over three months and I'm convinced that any who attempt to run away are getting caught."

"Why do you think that?"

Jenny was questioning her sanity by involving him in this. Gretchen had said he'd want to know everything, and if she truly trusted him, she would have to tell him. "I have to know you won't tell anyone about this. Not anything about it. You have to promise, and you have to be honest, keep that promise."

"I've always been honest with you."

"You didn't tell me you owned the Rural Rochester Telephone Company."

"You didn't ask."

"You told me Seth O'Brien works with you at the phone company." She'd searched her mind for every time he'd mentioned the phone company, after Dr. Dillon had left and before she and Gretchen had sat down to discuss all that Naomi at the flower shop had said today and formulate a plan to find out what was happening with girls not going to the shop, not seeking out help. Lora had been the last one, and that had been almost three months ago.

"He does."

"Why didn't you say he works for you?"

"I don't know. Because I don't think of it that way. He oversees the installations and is excellent at it. I think of him as a partner more than an employee. He's been with me since the beginning."

"Then why didn't you say that?"

"Because we weren't talking about the phone company, we were talking about your friends, and that he's married to Franny. I'm sorry if you think I was being dishonest. That wasn't my intent."

She could feel him looking at her, and kept her gaze out the passenger window.

"What else do you believe I've been dishonest with you about?"

The muscles in her neck stung from how hard her teeth were clamped together.

"What is it?" he asked. "I can tell it's something."

She turned, but only to look straight ahead, not at him. "That you never went to New York City."

"Yes, I did. Took the morning train, just like I told you the other day."

Frustration filled her. Maybe she'd been wrong in asking him for help, but there had been no one else. If anyone in town learned the entire truth, they might not be as supportive as they had been for years. "No, you didn't."

"Yes, I did."

Even with everything else on her mind, pain still filled her. "Then why did I see you two weeks later?"

He didn't say a word, but she heard his intake of breath, and she hated that he wouldn't just tell her the truth. Admit that he hadn't wanted to see her any longer back then.

"I'm sorry, Jenny."

A shiver whispered over her entire being like an icy wind. She'd always believed he hadn't gone, but deep in her soul hadn't wanted it to be true.

"I did come home, but only for a few hours. I'd promised my mother I'd be there for my father's surprise birthday party. I took the afternoon train home, stayed for the party and took the night train back to New York. Not contacting you was hard, but I knew we'd barely have time to say hello."

Her stomach clenched at how he turned one lie into another.

"That's the truth, and the rest of the truth is that I was afraid that if I saw you, I wouldn't go back to New York," he continued. "It had been hard enough to leave the first time."

"Stop it, Connor," she snapped. "No more lies! You

didn't look like you were having a hard time when I saw you that night."

"I'm not—You were at Pinion's that night? Why didn't you—"

"I wasn't at Pinion's," she interrupted. The nightclub was for members only, of which she wasn't. "I was in the parking lot, and saw you running for a car, laughing, with a—"

"Beth, my cousin," he interrupted sharply. "I only had a few minutes to catch my train and she gave me a ride. Mick was supposed to, but he was busy talking to my father. Like always. That was the reason I had to go to New York, and stay there the entire summer. It was my only chance to prove to my father that I could amount to something too, that I wasn't second best at everything."

Second best? She'd never heard him say anything like that. Had never heard the frustration in his voice, either.

"I told you all that in my letters," he said.

"What letters?" Just when she was questioning if he was telling the truth, he lied again. "You never wrote me any letters."

"Yes, I did. Every chance I got. I just never got around to mailing them."

"Why?" If she'd gotten a letter those first few weeks, everything would have been so different.

"Because I didn't want you to know. Didn't want anyone to know."

"To know what?"

"How focused I was on proving to my father that I wasn't second best. That I was a son he could be proud of, too."

Surprised, and concerned, because the Connor she'd always known had never been anything except completely confident. Always happy. "I'm sure he's proud now that you own the phone company."

"I like to think so, but I'll never know for sure." He glanced her way, briefly. "He died that winter."

Her heart dropped and she had to stop herself from touching his arm. "I'm sorry—I wasn't aware of that." She'd tried hard to not know anything about any of the McCormicks the past several years.

"It was a few months after you disappeared. A car accident in a snowstorm."

Silence filled the car, and she considered offering her condolences again, but it felt like too little too late. If only she'd have known the truth, things would have been so different. Then and now.

The silence remained as they drove through the quiet, deserted streets of Syracuse. Her mind spun in circles the entire time. She'd bought into the belief that he hadn't gone to New York so easily. Bought into the belief that he was dating someone else and had only been after one thing from her.

She'd given that one thing to someone else, that very night. Connor may have been trying to prove he wasn't second best, but she'd just wanted to be loved. She would have settled for second best.

Actually, she'd settled for far less than that. Donald had been the one wanting one thing from her, and had laughed afterward, saying how he'd finally gotten one over on Connor McCormick. That they both had.

It had made her sick to her stomach, and the memory did so again now.

"What were you doing at Pinion's that night?" he asked.

She blinked at the tears burning her eyes. "Just driving by."

"With your parents?"

Holding in a bitter laugh, she said, "No." Her mother and stepfather hadn't even been in town that night.

"Well, I'm truly sorry if you misunderstood what you saw. It really had been my cousin Beth, and she gave me a ride to the train station. I took the train back to New York and came home again two days before school started that fall."

By then, she'd already left the home and was living with Gretchen. "I'm sorry, too, Connor."

He cleared his throat. "Well, uh, so, why do you think these girls are getting caught?"

That was a better idea, to focus on the future because the past could never be changed. "Because Naomi knows girls have been told to go to the flower shop, but then they've never shown up."

"Who is Naomi? And what does the flower shop have to do with it?"

"Naomi owns a flower shop in Albany. Her sister used to work at the home, but quit because of the way the girls were treated, and ever since then, keeps a lookout for girls who run away and directs them to go to the flower shop if they don't have anywhere else to go."

"All right, let me get all this straight. There's a home for unwed mothers in Albany that girls run away from. They go to this flower shop, owned by Naomi, where I'm assuming Gretchen picks them up when she delivers flowers to the shop, and brings them back to your house, her house."

"Yes."

"What happens to them next? After they have their

babies. This Rachel who had her baby today, what will happen to her now?"

"She can stay as long as she wants. Most of them leave by the time the baby is a few months old. Sometimes they go back home, or go to live with other family members. Several have obtained jobs through people that Gretchen knows, and some have married the fathers of their babies."

He remained quiet for several minutes, and she feared what he was thinking. It was about her, she was sure of that, and why she hadn't married Emily's father. She wouldn't tell him. That was not information he needed to know.

"How do they end up at the home in Albany in the first place?"

"Their families take them there. Families who are ashamed that their daughters became pregnant out of wedlock, or refuse to allow them to marry the baby's father."

"Why doesn't the home let the ones who don't want to be there leave?"

"Money. They charge the families a weekly fee for the girls to be there. The people adopting the babies pay, too. The girls do all the cleaning and cooking, some stay there afterward, taking care of the babies in the adoption ward, or delivery ward." There were so many more aspects of the home that people just didn't know about. She hadn't either, not until working with Gretchen to help others. "Before their babies are born, the girls have to sew clothes for the babies, diapers and blankets, and clothes for all the girls to wear."

He was staring ahead, as if focused on driving, and

his tone was cold as he said, "That sounds cruel. More than cruel."

"It is. So are other things that happen there. When the girls arrive, they are given a new name. Not allowed to use their real name so they won't be able to tell anyone about others they'd met there. They are given two sets of identical clothing and a pair of shoes, and have to wear their hair pinned up, covered with scarves so everyone looks the same. They aren't allowed to talk about their families, their pasts, nor are they allowed any visitors. As soon as a baby is born, it's taken to the adoption ward. The girls are knocked out with ether when they go into labor and wake up not knowing if they gave birth to a son or a daughter. They remain in bed for a few days and then if the family still owes for their stay there, they have to stay and work off their bill, if not, they can leave. For some, their families take them home and pretend they'd been at a boarding school or living with family, out of state. For others…"

She closed her eyes, knowing that was what her mother had told people. Including him. There was more she could tell them. Like how some of the girls ended up institutionalized from the trauma, or how some families adopted the baby and took their daughters home, to live as siblings rather than mother and child. There were just too many different situations to start attempting to explain them all.

He cursed under his breath. "This place needs to be reported, Jenny. They—"

"They aren't breaking any laws, Connor."

"Then tell me why we're going here tonight?" he asked. "What's the plan?"

"Gretchen and Naomi had agreed today that another

flower delivery should happen tomorrow so that Naomi and her sister can survey the streets of Albany tonight, and if they find any girls, they'll bring them directly to the flower shop for Gretchen to pick up tomorrow morning."

His long sigh echoed in the car, and made her spine shiver slightly.

"So are we picking them up tonight, rather than Gretchen tomorrow?"

He sounded frustrated, angry. "Yes, if we find any while surveying the street near the home."

He ran a hand through his hair. "Does this place look for their runaways?"

She bit down on her bottom lip until it stung, before replying, "Not if their bills were paid in advance." Afraid he might change his mind, she grasped his arm. "It's not like we are doing anything against the law."

"It's not? Creeping around at night, helping runaways escape. I don't think that's completely legal. We should be calling the cops. Putting a stop to it all."

"We can't." Her fingers felt as if they were on fire when she pulled them off his arm. "What they are doing to these girls should be illegal, but it's not. The cops won't help us. Cheryl, Naomi's sister, tried to tell people about the conditions there, about how the girls were being shamed, coerced and humiliated into giving away their babies, but no one would listen."

"Why?"

"Because they agreed that the girls are immoral and promiscuous, and should be glad they have a place to go, being as sinful as they are." Anger filled her. "It's not right. These girls didn't set out to get pregnant. And they are young. Just young girls who…" She shook her head, unable to go on. To her, no baby was a mistake. God didn't make mistakes. Others didn't see it that way. He probably didn't, either. Wouldn't understand that no matter how she'd been conceived, Emily was the light of her life. The best thing that ever happened to her.

"I agree with you, Jenny," he said. "No one should be treated the way you described, nor should they hold all the blame or face the consequences alone. I've heard of homes for unwed mothers—there is one in New York City, but I never thought that much about them. About the girls who go to them. I never imagined the conditions are what you described."

"There are many homes for unwed mothers, all across the nation, the world, and they all aren't the same. Some are havens for girls—they truly help them. The one in Albany isn't like that. They have no compassion. They are focused on money, not helping people."

"Well, we'll help them tonight. Do whatever we can. We are almost to Albany. You'll need to tell me where to turn."

"I will. It's on the south end of town. Past the big park on the Hudson."

Silent for a moment, he then asked, "Are you talking about that big old monastery building?"

"Yes."

"With the tall brick wall?"

"Yes." She hadn't seen the building in years and wasn't looking forward to seeing it again. "That's the place."

Chapter Eight

Connor knew the building; situated along the Hudson River, it looked like some sort of eerie old castle that would only be found in some medieval land and host a torture chamber in its bowels deep below the ground.

The old building wasn't making his mind circulate over and over again; the information Jenny had shared was doing that. He now knew where she'd gone when she'd left Rochester and why. He'd thought knowing the truth would be satisfying. It wasn't. It was disturbing. The things she described were from memories—hers. He hated the idea of her going through so much, and it made him want to know who Emily's father was. Not for satisfaction. Well, maybe, because if he knew the guy, he was going to knock him into next week. And if he didn't know the guy, he'd find him, and then knock him into next week.

He was mad about the other girls, too. What they were going through, all on their own. It should be illegal.

"You'll need to turn at the next crossroad," she said.

He turned at the next corner, and followed the highway through town, toward the river. The streets were

deserted, the businesses and homes dark. The only movement was the moths fluttering their wings as they collected near the streetlights.

For Jenny's sake, he hoped they found a girl who
was attempting to run away from this unwed mothers'
home, because it meant so very much to her. She felt it
was the only way to help. He wasn't so sure about that.
About any of this.

The girls did need help. That was a given, and there
were a dozen questions he wanted to ask, but now wasn't
the time. He'd have to bide that. A few other questions,
he could ask. "What are we going to do once we arrive
at the home?"

"Wait." She let out a long sigh. "I have no idea where
Naomi and Cheryl are stationed."

"Maybe we should go to the flower shop."

"No. They won't be there until morning. What time
is it?"

He glanced at his wristwatch as they drove past a
streetlight. "Ten after one."

"Lights-out is at nine, but those working in the kitchen
are never done before midnight."

"How do they sneak out?"

"Different ways, those who want out find a way."

"How did you?" The question escaped before he realized it.

"The coal chute in—" She clamped her lips shut.

"I'm sorry. I—I shouldn't have asked that."

"I knew you'd figured it out." She was looking out
the passenger window, exactly as she had been for most
of the trip.

"Yet, you still asked me to help," he said.

"I had to. There was no one else."

He nodded, feeling slighted at being her last choice.

"I didn't mean it to sound like that. It's just that there was no one in town that I could ask to take me and Gretchen's truck is too recognizable to be driving around in the middle of the night."

"Why couldn't you ask anyone in town? They certainly take the secrecy of the girls at your place seriously."

"For the most part, they do, but some don't like it. Every once in a while, they'll get worked up and start a ruckus, say that Gretchen needs to take those girls to a home so that the children of Twin Pines are not influenced by the immorality they are being exposed to. It tends to die down quickly."

Connor was thinking of Howard when he said, "Because Gretchen is home-grown?"

He happened to drive past a streetlight right then, and the smile she flashed at him nearly robbed his ability to breathe.

"Yes."

"The town puts a lot of emphasis on that."

"They do, and there is hardly an empty seat in the church when one of the babies is baptized."

"I'm glad that you have some support, some help with what you are doing." He meant that. In all the years he'd wondered where she'd gone, he'd never thought along these lines. Regret sat heavy inside him. He should have told her more about his plans when he'd left for New York, that he'd be back home for his father's birthday, but at the time, he couldn't. His focus had been on impressing his father.

"Thank you for helping tonight. If word spread

through town that the girls are runaways, things might change."

"Where do the people in town think the girls come from?"

"A friend of Dr. Dillon. Not Alice, her father. He'd helped Gretchen in the beginning, and asked Alice to come home when he became ill. She's been wonderful and has tried hard to make changes, but…" She heaved out a sigh. "Dr. Dillon, Alice's father, schooled Gretchen in midwifery."

"And she taught you."

"Yes." She pointed at a driveway ahead. "Don't turn in there. That's the main entrance. We need to go to the next block and drive to the back side."

While driving past the road that led into the entrance, he let out a low whistle at the number of lights on the side of the building and on poles in the parking area. "That place has more lights than a Christmas tree."

"It never used to be like that," she said quietly, as if afraid someone would hear.

All these years, he'd been focused on how her leaving had affected him, but she'd gone through hell. He couldn't help but wonder where her family had been through it all. He wanted to ask, but sensed she wasn't ready to answer those questions.

"There is a new administrator," she said. "One that is more strict than the previous one."

He reached over and took hold of her hand, giving it a gentle squeeze. The warmth that spread up his arm went straight to his heart. He still cared about her. Would always care about her. A first love was special, and she had been his. He'd assumed it had been the same for her, and that was his problem. For assuming too much.

He wasn't assuming now. She needed his help, and he'd do whatever it took to help her. He released her hand and turned off his headlights before turning onto the street that ended up near the back of the building.

"Why did you turn off your lights?" she asked.

"So we aren't seen." Though the car had a powerful, straight-eight engine with over a hundred and thirty horsepower, the motor was quieted by the exhaust system. Unless they were listening for a vehicle, the car wouldn't be noticed over the crickets and rustling of the large maple and oak trees surrounding the monstrous building.

The street, like the others they traversed along, was empty, and Connor asked a niggling question he'd had since leaving Twin Pines. "How do you know girls will try to escape tonight?"

"Because Naomi and Cheryl were going to be on the lookout," she said, while scanning the roadway and trees.

"And?" he asked, elongating the word.

"Cheryl has a friend who still works here and drops hints about where a girl might look for help if they choose to leave."

Once again, he had to believe there was a better way to help those who didn't want to be here. He wasn't sure what, but would think of something. Mick might be able to help him, but he wasn't overly sure that he wanted to ask his brother. The only person who knew how Jenny's disappearance had truly affected him had been his brother. He hadn't even needed to say anything; there were just times where they knew how the other was feeling, and that had been one of them.

It went both ways, when Mick had dated an actress for a while, an inner, unexplainable feeling inside Connor had told him that she hadn't been right for his brother. That she'd make him unhappy. That's exactly what had happened.

Growing up, Mick had been too busy working to date or even participate in school activities, but after his short relationship with the actress, it was as if Mick had completely written off women. Connor had wondered if he should consider that, too.

In a way, he already had. Though he dated, went out with girls on a very regular basis, it was all for show. A way for him to keep up the happy-go-lucky, got a girl on my arm, and life is good, persona that people had come to expect since he'd been in high school. It was a farce. He'd created it to pretend it didn't hurt to be second best, and after Jenny's disappearance he'd needed to continue it in order to pretend that nothing affected him. He'd hoped it would help him believe that, too.

"Connor, there's someone by the far end wall." She pointed toward where the wall was partially hidden by the trees. "Do you see them?"

There was a shadowy figure near the corner of the large stone wall that was made out of the same square-cut stones as the building and ran along the entire length of the property. "Yes, I see them," he said, more focused on what he'd noticed ahead of them. "But we can't stop."

"Why?" She gasped. "There's more than one! I saw two. One could be Cheryl or Naomi. We have to stop!"

"We can't. There's a uniformed man, my guess is a police officer, near the other end of the wall at the entrance to the driveway."

"Oh, no! Do you think he's looking for them? What if—"

"He sees us," Connor said.

She clasped ahold of his arm. "What are we going to do?"

"It's going to be fine. Just act natural." He increased his speed and drove forward, to where the police office had stepped into the street. "Maybe we can distract him long enough for them to get away."

Stopping next to the cop, Connor shifted the car into Neutral and released the clutch. "Hello, officer, perhaps you can help us. We are traveling, and looking for a motel. Had pulled in here because of all the lights, but it doesn't look like it's a motel."

"Why are you driving with your headlights off?" the officer asked.

Acting surprised, Connor reached down and clicked on the headlights. "No wonder it was so dark. I must have bumped the switch with my knee. As I was saying, my wife and I are on our way to Niagara Falls, but we need to get some sleep. Too tired to keep driving."

Rubbing his neck, Connor kept talking because the officer leaned closer, to get a better look at him and Jenny. "Been driving all day and really need to find a place to rest for a few hours."

The officer pulled out a flashlight and shone it into the backseat.

"Is there something wrong, officer?" Connor asked.

"Just looking for some suspected runaways," he answered, clicking off his flashlight. "You see anyone out on the road?"

"No, but we were looking for a hotel," Connor answered.

The officer looked at Jenny. "Did you see anyone, ma'am?"

"No," she replied.

Connor wasn't sure if the yawn she covered as she turned and glanced out the window was for show or real. He guessed show, but either way, it was convincing.

The officer nodded and gestured with one hand. "There's a motel up on the highway, about a quarter of a mile or so, on the left."

"Thanks, does this road go back out to the highway, or I should turn around?" Connor asked, just biding more time for whoever had been in the shadows to make their escape.

"It goes back out to the highway," the officer said, taking a step back.

"Are the runaways dangerous?" Connor asked. "Convicts or something?"

"No, just young girls who don't know how good they have it," the officer replied gruffly.

"That's too bad," Connor said.

"It happens often enough around here."

Connor shifted the car into gear. "I hope you find them."

"They'll get caught," the cop replied. "Hotel should have a vacancy sign outside."

"We'll look for it," Connor said. "Thank you very much."

The cop took another step back and waved them to drive forward.

Sensing Jenny was about to twist and look behind them, he said, "Don't turn around—I can see him in the mirror and he's watching us."

"What's he doing?"

"Just watching us."

"Why did you say that to him?" she asked, in somewhat of a hiss.

"Say what?"

"That I was your wife and we were on our way to Niagara Falls!"

He turned the corner and drove toward the highway. "Should I have said that we are looking for runaway pregnant girls to haul back to Twin Pines?"

"No, of course not."

"Then that's why I said it."

"Sure, because you don't know that Niagara Falls is the honeymoon capital of the world."

"I didn't say I didn't know that. Everyone knows Niagara Falls is the honeymoon capital of the world, but that doesn't have anything to do with us or what is happening tonight."

Jenny's cheeks were on fire over the direction her mind had gone. He was right; what he'd said to the police officer had nothing to do with what they were doing. She was just near her wit's end. Gretchen had offered to be the one to go to Albany tonight, but Jenny hadn't been sure that Connor would agree to take Gretchen. She hadn't been sure that he'd agree to take her, either, but thought he would. And he had.

The other thing was that since he'd told her about his father's birthday party, she'd been thinking about how different things could have been if she'd only have known.

"You want me to say that I lied to the officer? Fine, I lied to him. You knew that from the moment I opened my mouth." He huffed out a breath while turning onto the highway. "But I didn't lie to you about going to New York, or about anything else."

Old habits were hard to break, yet at this moment, she

needed to apologize to him. She hadn't been accusing him of lying; she'd been reacting to how his claiming that she was his wife had made her heart stop. There had been a time when that had been her greatest dream. One she hadn't quite gotten over. "I'm sorry, I—"

"No, I'm sorry. I know you're upset, tired and worried." Glancing at her, he continued, "We're going to drive up the road to that motel and park the car in case that officer drives by to check. You are going to wait there while I walk back here and find those girls."

"You can't. They'll run from you, and what if the officer sees me waiting in the car? We'll both walk back."

"Do you argue with everyone, or just me?"

Her spine stiffened. "I only argue when someone is too stubborn to listen."

He laughed, and the sound evoked other memories, those of having fun with him, laughing with him. It was enough to make her want to smile. She tried to hide it, but it won out.

She didn't let him see it by looking out the passenger window as he pulled into the motel and parked near the back of the lot. They had only dated for a short time, but it had been the happiest time of her life. It had also heartbroken her like nothing else ever had, and she would never do something foolish enough to let that happen again.

As soon as he shut off the car, she opened her door.

"Slow down," Connor said. "We aren't just going to go running down the streets. There are two blocks of houses between here and the *home*."

"I know," she answered while climbing out.

He stepped out of the car on his side and collected his jacket from the backseat. While putting on the suit coat, he walked to the front of the car. "Don't want my white shirt sticking out like a sore thumb." Nodding in the general direction of the *home*, he continued, "I think our best bet would be to go to the river and follow it to the property—hopefully the runaways are coming this way."

Jenny hoped so, too. "With the policeman stationed near the front, I would think this is the direction they'd go."

"Where did you go when you ran away?"

"Toward town, but there wasn't a policeman at the entrance when I left," she answered as they started walking. There was no use keeping certain things secret. Other things, she'd never tell. "I met Cheryl in the park the next morning, and she told me to go to the flower shop."

"Where is it?"

"Downtown, about twenty blocks from here."

"That's over two miles. You had to have been scared."

It felt strange talking about it to him, yet wasn't difficult. "Yes, and no. Anything would have been better than staying there."

"How long had you been there?"

"Almost a month."

They were walking along the edge of a lawn belonging to a large brick home, and when he took her hand, she wasn't sure if it was for comfort, or because the lawn had started to slope down a hill that led to the river.

After a long moment of silence, he asked, "Your mother wouldn't let you return home?"

"I never contacted her. Haven't seen her since the night she dropped me off. She'd made it clear that I'd been disowned and that paying for my stay at the home was the last thing they'd ever do for me."

His hold on her hand tightened. That simple gesture warmed her soul in a way that nothing else had in a long time.

"Jenny—"

"I was fine with that," she said, stopping him from saying more. Sympathy was not something she needed. "And still am. I would never have been allowed to keep Emily had I contacted them, and I wanted my daughter." Quiet, peaceful night sounds surrounded them. The chirp of crickets, rustling of leaves, the soft splash of the river rolling along the banks. Oddly, there was a peacefulness inside her. An acceptance that she'd acquired long ago. "Things were so different after my father died and my mother married Richard. We were never a family after that., I felt like I was a burden, baggage. Richard traveled a lot, selling his cameras, and my mother joined him, leaving me home with a housekeeper, like that was all I needed, someone to cook me meals and make sure I went to school every day."

He stopped and stepped in front of her, looking at her. "Why didn't I know any of that?"

"Because I didn't want you to know." It had taken her a long time to figure it all out, but now she knew, and accepted her childhood. "I didn't want anyone to know just how unwanted I was. Or how lonely." The only time she hadn't felt unwanted or lonely had been when she'd been with him. He'd filled her with such joy, such happiness, there hadn't been room for anything else.

He nodded. "Just like I didn't want you to know about me and my father."

The softness of his touch, of one knuckle touching her cheek, made her eyes sting. They'd both been so young. So naïve. "I guess so."

"I'm sorry, Jenny." His palm cupped the side of her face. "I wish I could say more than that. I wish I would have found you. Helped you so you didn't have to go through so much by yourself."

"No, you don't, Connor. Trust me." She didn't ever want him to know who had fathered Emily. And he might have, back then.

He grasped her shoulders, pulled her against him and engulfed her in a hug. It was a haven she'd never known and could easily get lost in it, especially when his lips brushed the top of her head. Therefore, she pressed her hands against his chest to separate them. "But I do appreciate your help right now. Tonight."

The sigh he released echoed inside her, and left her feeling shaky as he took her hand and started walking again.

A short time later, while they were walking along the edge of the riverbank, staying hidden just inside the line of trees and brush between the lawns of the homes and the water, she heard something. A thud and a muffled yelp.

He pulled her deeper into the trees, where they crouched down behind a cluster of thick brush. Side by side, they remained still.

After a long, silent time, without a single unrecognizable sound, she whispered, "Do you hear anything?"

He shook his head. As he rose to his feet, he kept hold of her hand to help her stand. Her heel caught on a twig as she took a step, making her stumble.

Connor caught her around the waist. Her upper torso ended up pressed against his. The contact stole her breath and sent her heart racing.

He pressed a finger to her lips and then pulled her down behind the bush again. "Someone's coming."

Past the thudding of her heart echoing in her ears, she heard a rustling that sounded like footsteps.

Connor tapped on her shoulder, then pointed deeper in the woods, closer to the river.

Three figures were slowly making their way around the trees. Women. All three of them. She nodded to Connor, knowing his silent question asking if it was the runaways or not. She recognized Cheryl's larger shape, which confirmed it was them. After scanning the area and not seeing anyone following the women, she held up a hand, telling him to stay put, and slowly rose to her feet.

He caught her hand and gave it a gentle squeeze, before giving her a nod and releasing her hand.

Being so close to Connor, holding his hand, having his arms around her, was affecting her far deeper than it should. Far deeper than she could allow. Needing to keep everything in perspective, she kept her eyes on the women while slowly making her way toward them.

Chapter Nine

Connor couldn't hear what was being said as Jenny approached the other women, but he was sure they'd found the runaways. He was glad, and couldn't wait to get them all out of here, but his mind was still honed in on Jenny.

On her mother for disowning her.

That angered him.

Deeply.

Yet, recalling how her mother had been cold, distant and indifferent to his concerns when he'd tried find out where Jenny had gone after he'd returned home, he believed all Jenny had told him.

He'd sought his father's approval, but he'd never doubted that he was loved. Would never have been disowned. It was unfathomable to him that a parent would do that.

Anger tightened deep in his stomach, and it was directed at himself. For not knowing how bad Jenny's home life had been. She'd never invited him to meet her parents, and he should have questioned that.

As his thoughts continued, he once again scanned the area, looking for anyone following the women. When his gaze landed on Jenny again, he realized that although he understood more, he still had no idea how she'd become pregnant, or by whom.

She started walking toward him, with two others, while the third one walked in the opposite direction. He moved forward to meet Jenny.

"This is Meg and Tina," she whispered, gesturing toward the two girls who kept their eyes downcast. "Tina fell and hurt her leg," Jenny continued, "but we have to hurry. Cheryl says the police used dogs to find them the last time they ran away."

"Can you walk?" Connor asked the one she'd pointed to as Tina.

The girl nodded.

"All right. I'm just going to hold your arm, to help you because we have to move fast. The car isn't too far away."

She nodded again.

"Stay right behind us," he told Jenny as he grasped the girl's arm to lead her through the woods.

By the time they arrived at the last house, where it was only a mowed lawn between them and the motel parking lot, the sound of barking dogs filtered the air. "We are going to have to run to the car," he told Jenny, then scooped Tina into his arms. She'd been limping too much to run.

They reached the car, climbed in and as he pulled the car out of the parking lot, the barking noise was closer. "I'm sure they are watching the road. We have to take another way back to the highway."

Jenny nodded. "Cheryl was going to keep walking around in the woods, hoping they'd follow her and not us."

He found a road that would take them east, then another north, and after winding around and through neighborhoods, finally connected to the highway that would take them to Syracuse. He still didn't let out a sigh of relief. Instead, he said to Jenny, "This must be how bootleggers feel."

She shook her head at him, but then grinned and nodded.

He winked at her then glanced toward the backseat. The two girls hadn't so much as mumbled a word since they'd climbed in the car. "Are you two all right back there?"

"Yes, sir," one said and was quickly echoed by the other.

"How is your leg feeling, Tina?" He felt bad for both girls, for what they'd been through, for what they still faced. This was all foreign to him, but deep down, knowing he'd helped these girls, helped Jenny find them, he felt good.

"It's fine," Tina answered softly.

"Maybe you should take a look at it," he told Jenny. "There's a toolbox underneath the seat, with a flashlight in it."

She dug out the toolbox, and the flashlight from inside it, then twisted around and climbed up on her knees to lean over the seat.

A jolt shot through him and he forced himself to stare straight ahead, at the road, and not even glance at her enticing behind. It was right there, though, out of the corner of his eye. Spending the last several hours with her had reignited all those long-ago feelings he'd had toward her, and several more.

Using the flashlight, she leaned farther over the seat and accidently brushed against his shoulder. "Sorry."

"It's all right," he said, looking straight ahead.

She talked to the girls, but he didn't have a clue as to what she was saying; he was too busy telling himself to keep both eyes on the road.

It was after five o'clock in the morning when they drove through Twin Pines. Both of the girls in the backseat were sleeping, and though she'd been yawning for miles, Jenny was still awake. They'd spoken little during the long drive, but his mind hadn't been silent. It was speeding along, wondering if there was more that he could do to help her. Help these girls.

"Thank you so much for your help tonight," Jenny said as he pulled the car up next to her house, where Gretchen was already walking down the steps.

"You're welcome," he said, shutting off the engine. "I'll help you get the girls inside."

"No, Gretchen will help. You need to get some sleep."

Sleep? Tired or not, that wasn't going to happen. The sun had yet to rise, but the sky was already pinkening, signaling that old glory would soon rise up over the horizon. "So do you."

She'd twisted in her seat to waken the girls and gave him a slight nod while turning back around and opening her door. "Thank you, again."

He opened his door, climbed out and opened the back door for Tina to step out. She winced and he helped her out and walked her to the front of the car, where Gretchen stood.

"Thank you for your assistance, Mr. McCormick," Gretchen said, taking Tina's other arm.

"Any time," he said.

Jenny was already helping Meg up the steps and he

waited until the girl entered the house before he laid a hand on Jenny's shoulder.

The light from inside the house shone on her face. She was tired; he could see that in her eyes. He could also see her beauty. Words escaped him. He leaned forward and placed a soft kiss on her cheek. "Thank you for asking me to help you tonight."

Closing her eyes, she nodded.

"I'll see you later." He walked down the steps, to his car, climbed in and drove away. All the while knowing something inside him had changed tonight. He wasn't exactly sure what, but he felt different.

He could smell coffee when he walked in the front door of the hotel and climbed the stairs to his room. There, he lay down, convinced he wouldn't sleep, but did, because the next thing he knew, it was after ten in the morning.

After using the bathroom at the end of the hallway, he put on a clean shirt and left the hotel. The doctor's office was a short walk, and he found Alice Dillon in the outer room as he entered.

Fully prepared to tell her that she needed to go to Jenny's house, he was surprised to learn she'd already been there and had given both Meg and Tina complete exams. The school bus driver, Mr. Whipple, had delivered her a message to visit the house this morning, after picking Emily up for school. She also confirmed that Jenny had told her that he'd been the one to drive her to Albany last night and not to worry, that she wouldn't tell anyone of his involvement.

It wasn't his involvement that he was worried about. He accepted the cup of coffee she offered him, because even though he didn't want to betray Jenny, what they'd experienced last night was too dangerous, and was sure to get worse. "It's only going to get harder for those girls to continue to run away," he said. "Something has to be done."

"I agree and I've reported my concerns about that facility to others. I'd hoped a new director would change things, but it appears it's only changed it in the wrong direction."

"Isn't what they are doing, forcing these girls to give their babies up for adoption, illegal?"

"Unfortunately, no."

He couldn't stop his disgust. "The government made it illegal to sell booze, but not babies?"

"Yes, and I wish others shared your frustration over that," Alice said. "The service that homes for unwed mothers provide is needed. There are girls who believe adoption is the best choice for their babies, and there are people who desperately want to adopt children, especially babies." She was sitting across from him, behind her desk, and took a drink of coffee from her cup. "There are homes for unwed mothers across the nation, and some are truly wonderful. They help the girls get settled in new lives with career training, education in motherhood and many other services. They believe women have the right to raise their fatherless children without being scorned or shunned from society. The one in Albany just isn't like that."

His frustration continued to grow. "Jenny is going to want to go rescue more girls and could end up arrested or something."

The doctor nodded. "I agree with you, but she's very committed to helping these girls. Has been for a long time. I wish I knew of something that could be done, but I don't. I've contacted everyone I can think to contact, but just can't seem to get any traction for changes."

"There has to be a way to help."

"A telephone at their house would be a great help," she said.

That was already a given, but it wouldn't stop Jenny. "They'll have a phone." He set his coffee cup and saucer on the desk and stood. "Thanks for the coffee, and the information."

"You're welcome, and thank you again for all your help last night. It made a difference." She grinned. "Who knows—maybe phone calls will do more help than letter writing."

He acknowledged her statement with a nod, even while knowing a phone wouldn't be enough. With a heavy weight bearing down on his shoulders, he walked to the door. A fleeting thought made him pause. "What do you mean phone calls instead of letter writing?"

"The people I've contacted. State senators and representatives." She shrugged. "Once I have a phone, maybe my calls won't fall on deaf ears like my letters have."

An idea struck hard then. "These other homes you spoke of, is there one near here?"

"It's not close, but there is one run by a group of women in Springfield, Massachusetts, that I've heard very, very good things about."

Springfield was close to three hundred miles away, and he wasn't sure that would give him any answers, but he had to do something. Figure out something.

Nodding, he thanked her for the coffee again and left. Drove to Jenny's place.

She walked out the front door as he turned off the engine and the hitch that happened in the center of his chest was enough to warn him to tread carefully. His mission had been to get her out of his heart, not back into it.

The yellow-and-white dress she wore made her look as bright as the sunshine, but he saw the circles around her eyes. "You haven't had any sleep, have you?" he asked as they met near the front of his car.

"Have you?" she asked.

"Yes."

She grinned. "It couldn't have been much."

"More than you."

She shook her head and sighed.

He touched her chin, lifted it so she had to look at him. "I only argue with stubborn people, too."

Her smile made her eyes shine. "What are you doing here?"

"I have to be gone for a couple of days and I'd like to ask a favor."

"Oh? What's that?"

"That you won't go to Albany to save more girls while I'm gone."

Her face fell. "Why? Where are you going? You can't tell anyone—"

"I'm not going to tell anyone about our escapade last night." He rubbed her upper arm. "I just don't want you going there again by yourself. It's too dangerous. I won't be gone long, and if we need to make another run when I get back, we will."

She let out a sigh and shook her head. "Another trip won't be needed for a while. They'll be guarding everyone even more closely after last night."

He was certain of that. Just like he was certain that he needed to go to Massachusetts. He wanted to ask her to come with him, to see the home there, but was afraid that she'd say it was none of his business. If he'd learned anything about her last night, it was that she wasn't the same Jenny he'd known years ago. She was not only older, more mature, she was committed to helping these girls. He was proud of her for that. How she was using her own experience to help others, and he didn't want to undermine all she'd done. He just knew there had to be a way to help all the girls, not just a few.

He glanced at the house. "How are the girls? All of them?"

"Fine. Everyone is fine."

"Like it or not, within a couple of weeks, a phone line will be installed, so you need to decide which wall you want your telephone mounted on."

"We don't need—"

He touched the end of her nose. "Don't argue. We both know who's being stubborn about that, and it's not me."

She pinched her lips together.

He grinned, and winked at her. "An outside wall would work best." Before she could argue again, he said, "I have to leave, but I'll be back in a couple of days."

Jenny knew the right thing to say would be that he didn't need to be back in a couple of days, he didn't need to come back at all, but for some reason she couldn't bring herself to say that, so instead, she said goodbye, waved and watched him drive away. And for the next four days, she found herself staring down the driveway more than she ever had in her entire life. He'd said a couple of days, and it had already been four. She didn't know if she should be worried, or thankful.

Meg and Tina were settling in, Lora still hadn't gone into labor and there was plenty to do with the flowers, but Jenny still found time to dwell on him. She was no longer focused on believing he'd lied to her about going to New York. She believed he had gone, and that she'd convicted him without ever trying to find out the truth. The whole truth. It was clear what had happened, and how everything could have been different.

But it wasn't. Knowing the truth couldn't change the past. Nothing could.

She had to think about Emily. No, she didn't have to, she was thinking about Emily. All the time. She would never do to her daughter what her mother had done to her. No man would ever be more important than her daughter.

Hearing someone say something, Jenny turned from where she stood at the sink. "Excuse me?"

"Would you like me to walk down and meet the bus?" Lora asked. "It should be here any minute."

Jenny realized then that she'd come in from planting gladioli bulbs to wash her hands in order to go meet the bus. Her thoughts just kept stealing her attention. "Thank you, but no. I'm on my way right now."

She hurried out the door and down the driveway. As she walked around the curve, and the road came into view, her heart leaped so fast and hard that she nearly tripped over her own feet.

A red-and-black car—a Packard Phaeton—was pulling in the driveway.

Horsefeathers! He was back.

He was back!

She closed her eyes at the excitement filling her, and then in the next instant, tried to tell herself that she wasn't happy that he was back.

But failed.

How could she not be when he pulled up next to her and flashed her a smile that sent her heart leaping all over again? She'd missed him. Although she hadn't wanted to miss him. Hadn't wanted to ever miss him again.

She had.

"Missed me so much you walked down to meet me, did you?" he teased.

"N-no. I'm walking down to meet the bus."

He laughed. "I know. It's about a mile behind me. Wait here!"

She opened her mouth, but he was already driving the car up the driveway, around the corner. A moment later, she heard the door slam shut and he appeared, jogging down the driveway toward her. He looked so handsome in his short-sleeved white-and-blue shirt. It showed how broad his shoulders were and how—she stopped her mind right there. "What are you doing?"

"Walking to the road with you, to meet the bus."

She shook her head. "No. No. Emily doesn't know you."

"I know, but I bought her a present." He held up a brown paper shopping bag by the twine handles. "Two presents actually."

"Why?" Jenny shook her head at her own statement. "You can't be buying her presents."

"It's just a little something I saw in a store window." He shrugged. "I bought one for William, too, and Rachael's new baby and three more for the other babies when they are born."

"Why?"

"Because I wanted to."

"Connor, you—"

"I don't know much about kids, but Riley, the boy that

lives next door to my mother, likes when I bring him gifts, so I thought the kids here would, too." He grasped her hand and tugged her forward. "Here comes the bus."

The heat that raced up her arm from his touch went straight to her heart.

To her utter dismay, even before he'd stopped the bus completely, Mr. Whipple was shouting out the window.

"Hello, Mr. McCormick! Glad to see you again! How's that telephone line coming?"

"Right on schedule," Connor answered as the bus came to a stop. "Within a couple of weeks, the line will be all through the town and telephones will start being installed."

"Can't wait!" Mr. Whipple leaned farther out the window. "The town council is so excited they said your telephone poles could go right down the center of the road."

Jenny walked toward where Emily was climbing out of the back of the bus as Connor's laughter floated on the air. Her hand was still tingling and her heart still pounding.

"Who is that, Mommy?" Emily asked. "He sounds happy."

"He does sound happy," Jenny agreed, while fighting hard to not feel a touch of happiness herself. Merely because he was here. She shouldn't be happy about that. Not now. Not ever. "That is Mr. McCormick—he works for the telephone company—"

"That's the telephone man? All the kids are talking about him and his telephones! Are we getting one, too? Can we, please?" Emily's braids bobbed as she jumped up and down. "Mr. Whipple says when we are sick, we can call him so he won't have to drive all the way to our houses, and Teddy says he'll be able to talk to his grandma on the telephone. Hear her voice and every-thing!"

Jenny stopped trying to get a word in edgewise and took her daughter's lunch pail from her hand as Emily continued.

"Mrs. Whipple says the school will have a telephone, too, and she showed us pictures of them and showed us where we'll talk into them and how we'll listen, and that they'll ring, Mommy. Ring like a bell. Ding-a-ling, ding-a-ling."

"Do I hear a telephone ringing?" Connor asked.

Emily giggled. "No, it's just me, pretending to be a telephone. I'm Emily."

Something soft and warm curled around Jenny's heart as Connor knelt down in front of Emily.

"Well, Emily, you sure fooled me. I thought you were a telephone. You sounded just like one." He held out his hand. "I'm Connor."

"M—" Jenny had to clear her throat. "Mr. McCor-mick, and we need to move off the road so Mr. Whipple can drive away."

Emily grabbed hold of Connor's hand, but rather than shaking it, she pulled him toward the driveway. "Come on, Mr. McCormick, we gotta move or we'll get dusty. Even in our mouths."

"Oh, we don't want that," he said and jogged beside her as she ran to the driveway.

"Bye!" Mr. Whipple shouted out his window. "Oh, and thanks for getting that railroad track fixed, Mr. Mc-Cormick! We'd been working on that for months!"

Jenny, walking behind Connor and Emily, turned to watch Mr. Whipple drive away, wondering why he'd thank Connor for the railroad crossing. Until it dawned on her. He must have used his influence to get the county to haul gravel out and fill in the crossing.

"Hurry, Mommy! You'll get dusty!" Emily shouted over her shoulder, still holding on to Connor's hand.

Her daughter's friendliness wasn't surprising. Having so many pregnant girls live with them over the years, Emily wasn't shy, and immediately made everyone feel welcomed. Jenny had taught her to be that way, and couldn't be upset that she was just as welcoming to Connor.

Jenny arrived at the edge of the driveway, out of the way of the plume of dust churned up by the bus tires in time to hear Emily questioning Connor about a telephone.

"Do you have a telephone with you? One I could touch? And listen to it ring? And talk in it?"

He once again knelt down so Emily could look at him without craning her neck. "No, I'm sorry—I don't, but I do have something for you."

"You do?" Emily clasped her hands together and held them under her chin as if praying. "What?"

Connor looked at her, and Jenny felt a tug on her heart. He was asking for her permission. He should have done that before telling Emily because now, if she said no, she was the one Emily would be upset with. So would Connor, the pleading was as strong in his eyes as in Emily's. Huffing out a sigh, Jenny nodded.

With a grin, he set the bag on the ground and dug in it. "I hope you like storybooks."

"I do!" Emily said, bouncing again. "I do."

He pulled a book out of the bag.

Emily squealed, covering up whatever he'd said.

"Mommy! It's the teddy bear book!"

Recognizing the popular book, Jenny nodded. "I see that."

Connor handed Emily the book and she hugged it close. "Mrs. Whipple read this book to us! It's so good!"

"Well." Connor stuck his hand in the bag again. "Does Mrs. Whipple have the teddy bear that is in the book?"

Emily shook her head.

He pulled out a mohair stuffed bear. "You do!"

Emily squealed louder than before. "It's Pooh!"

Jenny had no idea how Connor had done it, but he could never have picked out a more perfect gift for Emily.

"Mommy, look!"

"I see, honey." Jenny had to swallow against the welling in her throat. "What do you say to Mr. McCormick?"

"Thank you, Mr. McCormick," Emily said.

"You are very welcome, Emily," he replied. "I'm glad that you like them."

"I do. I really do."

He held the bag open by the twine handles. "Would you like to put them in the bag so they are easier to carry?"

Emily hugged the bear and the book, then nodded and carefully lowered them into the bag. Then, much to Jenny's surprise, rather than pick up the bag, Emily leaped forward and wrapped her arms around Connor's neck.

"I'll love them forever, Mr. McCormick," she said reverently.

The sight of him, so big and strong, hugging Emily so tenderly, was enough to make Jenny's eyes sting.

"I know that bear will love you forever, too, Emily," he said softly. When they separated, he handed Emily the bag. "I'm wondering if you could do me a favor?"

Emily nodded.

"I have a stuffed toy for William, too, and Annie, and the other babies that will be born soon," he said. "Would you be able to pass them out for me?"

"Yes, I can do that. I pass out papers at school all the time."

He stood and took Emily's hand. "I thought you might, and that you would be the perfect person to do this for me. They are in my car. It's parked around the corner."

Carrying her bag of treasures, Emily looked up at him as they walked, "Mr. McCormick, the babies aren't born yet, so I can't give them anything."

He nodded. "That's right. I was hoping you could keep the stuffed toys and pass them out when the babies are born."

"Oh, I can do that! Can't I, Mommy?"

Walking on Emily's other side, Jenny nodded when her daughter looked up at her. "Yes, you can."

At his car, Connor collected another paper bag out of the car and told Emily she could decide which stuffed toy to give to whom.

"Can I go give William his now, Mommy?" Emily asked.

"Yes, you may."

With a bag in each hand, Emily took off for the house at a full run.

Jenny took a step to follow, but Connor laid a hand on her arm. "May I speak with you for a moment, in private? It's important."

The seriousness on his face made a chill ripple over her skin, leaving goose bumps on her arms.

Chapter Ten

Jenny was wearing a red-and-white-plaid dress, with a red scarf tied at the nape of her neck, leaving her long hair to hang down her back, and a dirt smudge on her left cheek, and Connor swore there had never been another woman who looked more beautiful than she did at this moment. He'd missed her. Despite how hard he'd told himself not to, he had.

He'd finally given in and justified that it was impossible not to miss her because everything he'd been doing had been because of her. It wasn't over yet, either. Neither was the desire to kiss her. That had made itself more adamant since pulling in the driveway. It had grown even more when she'd looked at him with her eyes all soft and glistening after he'd given Emily the gifts.

He hadn't bought the book or teddy bear to gain Jenny's affection, or Emily's. They'd simply caught his eye in a store window in Massachusetts after he'd left the home for unwed mothers and had made him think of all the children here. All the young mothers Jenny had helped.

She was extraordinarily remarkable, and dedicated, and beautiful.

He'd parked his car near the curve, and guided her to the car, where he'd left the envelope he had for her. He truly wanted to help her, wanted to ease her burdens, because despite the years, he still cared for her.

Deeply.

Brushing a clump of hair off her forehead, he said, "I've missed you, Jenny."

She diverted her gaze. "Is that what you wanted to discuss? Because—"

That hadn't been the reason. He was simply being honest. "No, but I do want you to know that, because I have." He cupped her cheek. "I've missed you for years, but the last few days I missed you even more."

She closed her eyes and pinched her lips together, as if she was stopping herself from speaking.

The desire was too great to ignore any longer. "I want to kiss you, Jenny."

Her eyes snapped open and he saw desire blazing in them.

He gave her a moment to stop him, and when she didn't, he leaned forward and pressed his lips to hers. Briefly at first, savoring the warmth of her lips, the pressure of them against his. He understood this wasn't the Jenny he'd kissed so easily in the past. That Jenny no longer existed. Life had turned her wary and he didn't want to do anything to cause her to distrust him again.

Slowly, he pulled back to end the kiss.

She gasped slightly, and then her arms came up, around his neck and she stretched on her toes, keeping their lips touching.

Keeping her vulnerabilities in mind, and his own,

he wrapped his arms around her and gently caressed her lips with his, over and over again. A powerful need filled him, making his blood pound in his veins, echo in his ears. Yet, he held back. Not expecting, or forcing her to respond with more than she was ready, and willing, to freely give.

Their lips parted slowly, with a few, small tender pecks before they both sighed, and he pulled her in closer for a hug.

He'd forgotten just how thrilling kissing her had been, and how right holding her had always felt. Rubbing her back, he quietly said, "I believe I've found a way to help all the girls at the Albany Moral Hospitality Institute."

She stiffened in his arms. "What?"

"A way for you to help all the girls," he said. "Not just those who run away."

Her arms slipped off his shoulders as she stepped back, out of his hold. "What are you talking about?"

He leaned back against his car, and for a moment, wondered what the hell he was doing. Kissing her had not been a good idea. It simply made him want more. This was about her, and the help she needed, not him and what he wanted.

Rubbing his chin to make that thought settle, he said, "It's going to take some work, some serious work. Nothing is ever easy when it involves the state government." He knew that well from years of working on regulations and permits to lay telephone lines, and wanted her to be warned.

"State government?"

He rubbed the tension making his neck muscles tighten. This wasn't like getting permits; it was changing the way people think, and changing laws. He was an excellent salesman. People have said he could sell anything to anyone. But it was going to take more than that for all of this to work.

In spite of knowing all that, there was an excitement inside him that he hadn't felt in a long time. Maybe ever. He'd been driven, years ago, to show his father that he wasn't second best, but the drive inside him now was different. It wasn't self-focused. It came from knowing that he could help these girls, help Jenny.

"Connor, what are you talking about?" She eyed him skeptically. "What did you do? Where have you been?"

"Massachusetts, and then New York City." He crossed his arms to keep from reaching out, from touching her again. "I visited a home for unwed mothers in Massachusetts, one that cares about each and every girl that enters their doors. The people there care deeply about what they are doing. They know that pregnant women need adequate medical care, support and a safe haven, and the right to keep and raise their babies, when that is what they choose." He had been impressed by the home, and the administrator who answered every one of his questions, gave him tours of different wings and also gave him suggestions on the only way changes would ever be made to certain establishments in New York State.

"You what?" She threw her arms in the air. "Why would you do that?"

"Because I don't want you to end up in the hoosegow some night." He glanced at the house. "And I don't want other young girls to be chased down by dogs like they were criminals. That's not right and it doesn't have to be that way."

"It's not right, but we can't make the Albany Moral Hospitality Institute change. It's impossible."

"It's not impossible. After leaving Massachusetts, I went to New York and met with a state senator I know personally, and he's willing to introduce a bill that would mandate all homes for unwed mothers be subject to certain regulations." He reached inside his car, for the envelope. "I have this list from the administrator of the home in Massachusetts. I gave a copy of it to the senator. He served on the New York City Board of Health before becoming a senator and is very interested in helping you, but he needs more information."

She took the envelope, but didn't open it. "Information?"

This was the part he'd been worried about. She'd been through so much, all of the girls had been, he wasn't sure any of them would be willing to talk to the senator. "True stories, from people who have experienced things at the home."

She shook her head.

"I know it'll be hard, very hard, for any one of the girls, but it's the only way that lasting changes will be made." Watching her continue to shake her head, he said, "It doesn't have to be you, Jenny. I told him all I could, but from me, it's hearsay. He needs specifics from actual patients. Nothing the institute is doing is against the law, therefore, we have to change the law."

Still shaking her head, she closed her eyes. There was moisture on her lashes when she opened them again, looked at him.

"He's a good man, Jenny, who wants to help. I've worked with him before on telephone regulations." He held his breath for a moment. "There's one more thing. The session will soon be over, he needs to hear from people soon, within a week or so, in order to get a bill written, otherwise it won't happen until next year." Aware that she may be feeling rushed into making a decision, he gently held her upper arms. "I know it's all happening fast, but think about the girls, scared, just trying to get away, being hunted down by dogs for the entire next year." He didn't like that idea at all, nor did he like the idea of Jenny trying to help those girls and getting hurt, caught. "Think about your daughter. What would happen to her if you ended up being arrested?"

"Stop, Connor. Just stop." Taking a step back, she twisted her arms out of his hold. "Why are you doing this?"

The past four days had been a whirlwind of people, places and conversations that he'd never thought he'd be a part of, and driving. Many hours had passed with him behind the wheel. Just him and his thoughts. At times, he'd been able to convince himself he was doing this because there were young, unwed mothers who deserved better treatment than what they were receiving. Other times, he'd told himself it was because of Jenny, of all she went through and because she was so stubborn, she damn well could end up in jail.

Then there were those times when the ache in his chest was so overpowering, he couldn't stop the anger from rising up. At himself, for not telling Jenny the truth years ago, and at others. For making Jenny going through all that she had alone. He wanted to make this all right for her. Had to make it all right for her.

Therein lay the reason he was doing this. She'd asked for his help, and he was going to give it to her, until there was nothing left that could be done.

"I'm doing this because you asked for my help," he said.

"I asked you to give me a ride to Albany." She planted

her hands on her hips. "A ride, Connor! Not for you to start poking your nose in places it doesn't belong or to throw the McCormick name around like it can save the world! It can't! It never could and it never will!" She stepped closer and shoved a finger against his chest. "This isn't some railroad crossing that needs gravel! It's people's lives! My life! And I don't need you to tell me to think about my daughter!"

She used the same finger to point at her own chest. "She's my daughter! Mine! And is the only thing I've been thinking about for seven years. I've made a good life for her and don't need you or anyone else to be thinking about her, and I sure as hell don't need you to be buying her presents! Now get in your fancy car, drive out of here and don't ever come back. Ever!"

Connor held in a few choice words about her stubbornness as she spun around to walk away. "I can't do that, Jenny."

Arms swinging at her sides, she marched toward the house. "Yes, you can. I don't need your help. We don't need your help."

"You're wrong. Senator—"

"No, you're wrong." She spun around. "Do you think we haven't thought of that? That we haven't contacted lawmakers? That we haven't written letters and filed complaints? We have! Dozens of them and nobody cares because it doesn't involve them. Just like it doesn't involve you. It never has and it never will." She shook her head and looked at him with loathing. "So stop pretending. Just stop."

Connor's stomach clenched and for a moment, he couldn't decipher who he was more angry with, her or himself. Because she was right. He had been pretending.

Pretending that if he helped her, they could go back to where they'd once been.

There was no going back, and he was done pretending that could happen.

Without a word, he climbed in his car, started it, turned around and drove out of the driveway. Her driveway. One he'd never see again and that was perfectly fine with him. It had been foolish to have anything to do with her again.

He was done being foolish. Done being hurt. Done caring about her.

Jenny stared at Gretchen, filled with disbelief. "What?"

"You heard me." Gretchen lifted an empty crate out of the truck. "We need Connor's help."

It had been a week since he'd driven away and Jenny was just getting to the point where tears didn't form every time she thought of him. Almost. Her eyes were stinging again now. She grabbed an empty crate and followed Gretchen into the greenhouse. "No, we don't."

Gretchen set down her crate and then grabbed the one out of Jenny's hands before she flipped her long braid over one shoulder and took both of Jenny's shoulders. "I love you like the daughter I never had, would do anything to protect you, but I also have to think of the other girls, and they need his help."

Jenny's heart was crumbling inside her chest, because despite what she'd told herself over and over, she knew what Gretchen said was true. She just couldn't face him again. It hurt too much. She was tired of the never-ending parade of pain that lived inside her. She'd made so many mistakes and refused to make another one where he was concerned.

"We've already tried what he suggested."

"I know we have, but we didn't have his backing then," Gretchen said. "It's an ugly world we live in at times. Women may have been given the right to vote, but our voices still aren't being heard. We can scream, shout and rally together, but the very ones we need to hear us aren't listening, and they won't until one of their own steps forward. Connor is one of their kind. A man of influence. I hate to admit that, I want to believe that women, that everyone, will be treated as equals, but it's not going to happen today. We need Connor in order to make the changes happen."

Jenny's eyes and throat burned and her heart was twisting inside her chest. "No, we don't."

"He got the railroad tracks fixed."

Jenny rolled her eyes. "That just took a load of gravel."

"I know, but it was something we'd been asking for, and never received."

Her back teeth chomped together as she sucked in air. Damn him. He'd woven himself back into her life whether she liked it or not.

Gretchen pushed on her shoulders, forcing Jenny to sit down on a stack of crates. "Naomi said the home was locked down tighter than Fort Knox, that guards are stationed at every door and the girls aren't even allowed outside during the day. That's our fault. What we did by rescuing Meg and Tina made things worse than ever. Connor can make people listen to the girls, hear their stories and do something about it. We can't."

"We can contact the senator ourselves, without Connor."

"We've tried that. Just like we'd tried to get gravel." Sitting down on another crate, Gretchen sighed heavily. "I know you're still fighting your feelings for him, and—"

"I don't have feelings for Connor." She might be able to believe that, if the memories of how she'd instantly responded to his kiss the other day would go away.

"Denying them won't make them disappear, not until you face them." Gretchen's eyes filled with compassion. "I wish you didn't have feelings for him, then you would be able to see how badly we need his help, and to trust him."

It was as if a fist had hold of her heart and just kept squeezing it harder and harder. She knew the girls needed help, but there had to be someone else besides Connor. That day, seeing him with Emily, when he gave her the stuffed bear—the very bear that hadn't been out of her sight since he'd given it to her—changed something.

Jenny had to swallow in order to breathe because the change that had happened that day had been deep, very deep, inside her. It scared her, too. She did have feelings for Connor, and they had grown that day. Or maybe they'd just fully come to the surface where she could no longer keep them hidden, even from herself.

She'd been young and so honored to have his attention years ago, and that was something that had truly frightened her when she'd seen how quickly Emily had taken to him. That was Connor; his charm was impossible to ignore. She couldn't let Emily be hurt by him.

Not only couldn't.

She wouldn't. Emily was already so attached to the teddy bear that it even went to school with her.

"I saw his car at the Bird's Inn this morning, and if you don't feel you can do it, I'll go talk to him this evening," Gretchen said. "We don't have much time before the session ends this year, and can't afford to wait another year."

"Connor's help won't guarantee new rules and regulations," Jenny said.

"No, but it gives us far more hope that it could than we've ever had before. The McCormick name alone holds weight." Gretchen stood and walked out of the greenhouse.

Jenny rubbed her forehead as she hung her head. After the things she'd said to him, Connor had no reason to help. He'd had no reason to help her when she'd asked before, either. Nor when she would ask again.

The air that left her lungs was so heavy she coughed, and shook her head.

She had to ask for his help for the girls, no matter how damaging it was going to be to her and her heart. Hers. Not Emily's. She'd set down a solid set of rules there. No more presents.

Drawing in a fortifying breath, she left the greenhouse. Gretchen was still unloading the truck, and Jenny barely slowed her steps as she said, "I have to meet the school bus."

Life would have been so much easier if Connor had never reappeared in hers. Then, again, her life didn't have a history of being easy. There was no reason to think it could magically become otherwise.

However, she had learned a lot over the years, and was no longer desperate for attention, like she once had been. Not from Connor or anyone else. As for trust, she trusted in herself, and no one else.

She was in charge, in control of her life, and Emily's, and it was a good life.

Emily leaped off the school bus practically before

the wheels had stopped turning. "Mommy! Mommy! Guess what?"

"It was an exciting day at school," Mr. Whipple shouted out the window.

"It must have been!" Jenny waved at him and held out her hand for Emily. The excitement on her daughter's face thrilled her, and proved that her daughter had everything she needed to be happy.

So excited she was jumping up and down as they walked up the driveway, Emily said, "Mr. McCormick was at school today!"

Jenny's heart stalled in her chest.

"And he brought telephones for all of us to see! Oh, Mommy! They were so pretty! And he made one ring so we could hear it!" Emily spun around to walk backward as she continued, "And he showed us how to dial the numbers! That's what you do when you call someone. Dial the numbers. And we got to pretend to talk in the phones and answer them. Oh, Mommy, it was so fun, and then, and then... Guess what? Mr. McCormick gave us each a candy bar! They were so good! Mrs. Whipple let us eat them after lunch. It was the best candy bar, ever! Oh, and guess what? He left the telephones at school so we can practice using them! When we get our own telephone, I'll know how to answer it and dial and everything!"

A little more than two hours later, Jenny pulled Gretchen's truck in front of the inn in Twin Pines. Connor's car was nowhere in sight. He must be out, selling more telephone lines. Or giving children candy bars. She'd have to wait, which might give her time to calm her insides.

That was doubtful. If he thought he could gain good graces by being nice to her daughter, he...

She slapped the steering wheel. She really had to get over him. Completely. Including the kiss they'd shared. Why would he have done that? Why would she have done that? It made her angry that she hadn't tried to stop it.

Jenny lifted her gaze as a car approached from the opposite direction. It wasn't Connor's, but Alice Dillon.

The doctor pulled up next to the truck. "What are you doing in town?" she asked through the open windows on both vehicles.

Jenny attempted to smile and act normally as she explained, "I'm waiting for Connor. I need to speak with him."

Alice shut off her car so they didn't need to shout over the engine. "Well, you're going to be waiting a long time."

"What do you mean?"

"He went back to Rochester earlier today," Alice said. "Shortly after he visited the school. Margaret Whipple had asked if he could bring a telephone in to show the students. I hear it was a big hit."

Jenny's stomach sank at hearing he'd been invited to the school. She'd thought otherwise. "Did he say how long he'd be gone?"

"I didn't talk to him. While fueling my automobile earlier today, Howard told me about the school visit and that Connor had gone back to Rochester." Alice shrugged. "Maybe he's done with his sales. I really don't know, but I'm going to Rochester and could get a message to him for you."

"When are you going to Rochester?"

"Tomorrow morning. I need to replenish supplies, but

would have time to contact him, tell him that you need to talk to him."

Jenny's heart not only sank deeper, her stomach met it somewhere near the floorboard of the truck. A message wouldn't guarantee that he'd come back to Twin Pines, not after the way she'd told him to leave and never come back.

"Or you could ride with me to Rochester," Alice said. "Talk to him yourself. I'd enjoy the company."

Goose bumps pimpled Jenny's skin. She hadn't been to Rochester since the night her mother and stepfather drove her to Albany and had no desire to ever go back.

"I'll be leaving first thing in the morning and could pick you up, however, I will be meeting a friend while in town, so won't return until late evening," Alice said. "It would be good for you to get away for the day, Jenny. You'd be welcome to join my friend and me for dinner."

No, it wouldn't be good for her to get away. Nor would it be good for her to see Connor again. She wasn't sure if she was falling in love with Connor again or had never fallen out of love with him, but either way wasn't good. At the same time, what Alice offered was her only option. Other than to drive herself, which wasn't really an option. The truck would be needed tomorrow to deliver flowers. Joyce would be able to make the delivery by herself, along with the help of Meg or Tina, and Gretchen could remain home in case Lora went into labor.

Furthermore, after listening to Tina's story of how she'd been treed by the dogs while attempting to run away previously to the night she and Connor had gone to Albany, Jenny knew something had to be done, and soon.

"You truly wouldn't mind?" she asked Alice, hoping for a reason that what Alice offered wouldn't work.

Which was selfish. Her fear of seeing Connor again shouldn't override just how desperately his help was needed.

"I'd love it," Alice said, smiling brightly. "I'll pick you up around seven tomorrow morning, and wear your best dress—we'll be going out for dinner. You'll have a wonderful time! We both will."

Jenny highly doubted that, but agreed, and was waiting at the door when Alice drove into the driveway the next morning. She had chosen her best dress. One she'd sewn and wore to church for the christenings of the babies she'd delivered. Made of satin-backed crepe in a soft orange color, it had a dropped waist, with a long bow attached above her left hip, and a boat neckline highlighted with delicate white lace. Her crocheted white hat sported a bow made from the orange satin material, and she'd also used tiny scraps of the same material for the miniature bows attached to the tops of her white dress shoes.

Two strands of white pearls, one longer and one shorter, along with matching ear fobs and a bracelet completed her outfit. She'd tried hard to quell her wonderings if Connor would like her outfit while dressing this morning, which had included help from Emily. Her daughter had gushed, insisting she looked more beautiful than even Mrs. Whipple. A true compliment considering Emily loved her teacher, even more now that Mrs. Whipple had read the teddy bear book to the entire class and allowed the bear to sit on her desk during the school day.

The entire household shared Emily's proclamations of how pretty she looked, and assured her that all would be fine while she was gone.

Jenny wasn't.

Connor could refuse to see her, and she didn't know what she'd do if that happened.

Call it nerves or the fact that Alice would be interested, Jenny explained her reason for needing to see Connor as they began their two-hour drive to Rochester.

"Bee's knees! He's already spoken to a senator?" Alice asked.

"Evidently," Jenny answered.

"After you brought home Meg and Tina, I'd told him about contacting lawmakers, but how my letters fell on deaf ears, and about the home in Massachusetts. I never dreamed he'd follow up on it so quickly."

Jenny's stomach fell at how she'd accused him of sticking his nose in places where it didn't belong. "You told him about the home in Massachusetts?"

"Yes, and how there need to be lasting changes to the home in Albany. His help could do exactly that, Jenny! This is so exciting!"

Alice was elated, while Jenny was filled with regret at jumping to conclusions again as far as Connor was concerned.

Upon arriving in town, Alice stopped at a fueling station and was told that Connor's house was only a few blocks away. Therefore, long before Jenny was prepared to face him, they were pulling into a brick driveway next to a large home.

It wasn't the brick house that she remembered belonging to his parents. This one was painted white, with black shutters, dormer windows on the second floor and a large porch that had high, solid white side rails.

"I'll wait here, make sure he's home," Alice said.

Jenny nodded and with her palms sweating inside her white gloves, she opened the car door. The sound of her heels clicking against the brick driveway and then the concrete sidewalk echoed in her ears. So did how they clacked against the wooden steps and then over the painted floorboards of the porch.

She felt as if she was about to knock on the door of a haunted house, one full of ghosts of the past that were sure to change her life as much as they had for Ebenezer Scrooge. His had been for the better. Hers wouldn't be.

Forcing herself not to turn around and barrel back down the steps, she raised a hand and knocked on the frame of the screen door.

After what might have only been a minute, but felt like an hour, she lifted her hand and knocked again.

There was no sound or movement from within the house, and not sure what to do now, she turned away from the door.

She'd taken one step when the rattle of a lock, the screech of hinges, had her turning back around.

"Sorry I—Jenny?"

Her heart slammed so hard against her ribs she was sure one had cracked. Bruised for sure.

"Jenny?" he repeated.

She wasn't sure which was more shocking. The look on his face, or the fact that he wasn't wearing a shirt, exposing just how broad his shoulders were, how his chest and stomach were rippled with muscles.

It took all she had to pull her eyes back up to his face and stay upright.

Chapter Eleven

Connor had been stunned a few days ago by the news that Mick was getting married, the very reason he'd returned to Rochester, but Jenny on his porch was even more unexpected than his brother falling in love. Seeing her had his heart flopping like a fish out of water.

"I—I need to speak with you, Connor," she said.

His ears heard her, but his eyes were still taking in the sight of her. Whoa, but she was gorgeous. The pale shade of her orange dress gave her a golden glow, like an encompassing halo around an angel in a storybook.

She lifted a white-gloved hand and nervously touched the back of her head, where her hair was pinned up beneath an adorable, floppy white hat. "It shouldn't take long."

Catching his wits before the last one flew away, he pushed open the screen door. "Sure, yeah, that's fine. Come in."

"Alice Dillon gave me a ride," she said, pointing to the car in his driveway. "She'll be back in an hour to get me, if that's all right."

"Of course." He waved at the doctor who shouted a

hello, and then stepped onto the porch to stand in front of the open screen door. "Come in."

She waved to Dr. Dillon and then walked past him. A subtle scent of flowers drifted in her wake, and he practically sniffed the air like a hound as he followed her inside. He'd gotten a whiff of flowers several times since the last time he'd seen her, and each time he'd been reminded of her.

Then again, everything reminded him of her.

"I'm sorry for disturbing you so early," she said, not turning around to look at him.

He pulled the screen door closed and shut the house door. "I was upstairs, just got out of the bathtub." Realizing he'd only taken time to pull on his pants when he'd heard the knock on the front door, he quickly added, "Let me go get dressed." His manners kicked in as he turned to walk toward the stairway. He spun back around. "There's coffee in the kitchen—can I get you a cup while you wait?"

"No, no, thank you, I'm fine."

She sounded as nervous as he felt, which was odd. They'd argued, they'd laughed, but they'd never been nervous around each other before. Gesturing toward the scrolled-wood-and-tan-upholstered sofa, he said, "Make yourself at home. I'll only be a moment."

He shot up the steps, down the hall and into his bedroom, where he'd already laid out the suit he'd wear to Mick's wedding. There he pulled on socks and an undershirt. It was enough to make himself presentable. If he took the time to put on more than that, she might be gone.

She wasn't, but she was perched on the edge of his sofa like a cat sitting on a fence, ready to leap off and run at any moment.

He didn't want that to happen. "Are you sure I can't get you some coffee? I could make tea."

"No, I'm fine, but thank you." She fiddled with the handle of the white purse sitting upon her knees. "I'm here to apologize." She closed her eyes briefly. "I wasn't aware that Alice had told you about contacting lawmakers, and having them not listen."

"I'm sorry, too. I guess I have a history of not telling you things." He shook his head. There was no excuse for it. "Once again, I was afraid. This time that you'd deny my help."

"Which I did."

"I should have asked you first." He shrugged. "I'm just not used to that." There was more to it than that. She'd made him realize that. "As a kid, I got so used to wanting to please everyone, that when I see something that needs to be done, I just do it."

A faint smile curled her lips for a second. "Yes, you do, and I should have remembered that. How you helped me with the scene boards, without me asking for it." She grimaced slightly. "That's also why I'm here. To ask for your help."

"I see." He didn't, but the given response was the most he could come up with as he walked around one of the matching armchairs and sat down opposite her. "Help with what?" Please don't let her say another trip to the home to rescue more girls. He would take her, though, because it was Jenny. He'd never gotten her out of his system and if the past week was any indication of his future, he never would.

"With the senator you know." Chin up, she continued, "Things have become worse at the home in Albany." An array of emotions flittered across her face as she looked everywhere except at him. "There are guards at all the doors and the girls aren't allowed to go outside even during the day."

Anger, not at her, but at the home in Albany, made his jaw go tight. That place needed to be closed down. He hadn't been able to get that out of his mind the past week, either. "Something has to be done."

"Yes, it does. Sooner than later."

She met his gaze, eye to eye. She looked so fragile, sitting there on his sofa, but in truth, she had more guts than a mobster. It couldn't have been easy for her to come here today. He respected that. He also respected her resiliency, compassion and commitment. She put others before herself in a way he'd never really encountered, and it made him want to help those girls even more. "You've changed, Jenny."

"Becoming a mother will do that to a person," she said.

A soft glow had entered her eyes, and he knew why. "You have a lot to be proud of. I enjoyed meeting Emily, very much. Did you hear that I visited the school yesterday? Showed them telephones." He grinned, recalling the bear sitting on the teacher's desk. "I saw Emily's bear there."

She cleared her throat quietly. "Yes, I heard, and Emily was very excited about seeing the telephones. She doesn't go anywhere without her bear, and has the book memorized." A true smile formed. "I believe William may even have the story memorized with the amount of times she's made him sit and listen to her retell it to him."

He chuckled. "I'm glad she's getting so much use out of it."

"She is."

"She's also beautiful, just like her mother."

Her cheeks pinkened as she bit her lips together. Her lashes fluttered before she lifted her chin again. "Thank you, but about the home. If you're still willing—"

"Yes, I'm still willing," he interjected. "I'll help you with the senator. Do whatever you need, for as long as it takes, to come to a conclusion, but I would like to ask a favor from you in exchange."

Her brows tugged together beneath the brim of her hat. "What sort of favor?"

"My brother is getting married today, in a couple of hours, I'd like you to attend the wedding with me."

Her eyes widened and she pressed a gloved hand against the base of her neck. "Oh, I couldn't. I—I couldn't impose like that. I—Alice will be back to get me in an hour and—"

"We don't have to leave until after that, we'll tell her—"

"No. Uh. Um. She's giving me a ride home."

"I'll give you a ride home." His family would expect him to have a woman on his arm—because Connor McCormick always had a woman on his arm. He had thought about calling one of the dolls he knew who would readily agree to go to the wedding, but his heart hadn't been in it. His heart hadn't been in anything recently. Or for years. He'd gone through all the motions of being a happy-go-lucky bachelor with a different woman on his arm every night for years, but had never truly enjoyed it. Seeing Jenny again had made him understand just how much he'd been faking over the years. Everything from aloofness to happiness.

"Connor, I don't—"

"It will only be a few hours," he said. "The wedding

is at Mick's house—he inherited it when my father died and my mother still lives there with him. That's when I bought this place."

Nibbling on her bottom lip, she nodded. "It's a nice house."

"Thanks," he said, never taking his eyes off her. "Will you go with me?"

"Who—" She swallowed visibly. "Who is Mick marrying?"

"No one you know," he answered. "I barely know her. Mick brought her home from Missouri about six weeks ago to see her father. Her name is Lisa Walters—she's a really nice person. My mother adores her. So does Mick." He didn't know all the particulars because he'd been too busy chasing after Jenny the past few weeks, but had never heard Mick sound so happy as when he'd called home and his brother had told him about the upcoming wedding. More than that, he'd felt Mick's happiness, and knew deep inside that Mick was making the right choice. One that would make him happy for years to come.

He couldn't say the same for himself, but right now, he had to put on a happy face for his brother. Back to acting. It wouldn't be hard. He'd been doing it for years. "I'd really appreciate you going with me, Jenny."

She squeezed the handles of the purse so hard it tipped over on her lap.

Knowing she seldomly left the flower farm, he said, "There won't be many guests. Just family and a few close friends. Afterward we can lay out our plan for the senator."

"We could do it now," she said quickly, "before Alice returns."

Not about to let her off the hook that easy, he shook his head, then realized exactly what he was doing. Was he truly so desperate that he'd coerce her into something she didn't want to do?

That wasn't like him and it wasn't what she needed, now or ever. "Sorry. I still have to finish getting dressed and go buy a wedding gift." He stood. "But, it's fine. You don't have to go. Sorry I asked. You can wait here until Alice returns." Using a thumb, he gestured over his shoulder, toward the stairs. "I'm going to go finish getting dressed and head out." He walked away, saying, "I'll stop at your place tomorrow and we can formulate a plan."

"Connor, wait."

He turned. She'd stood. "It's all right. You can just lock the door when you leave."

A hint of a smile formed as she shook her head.

He felt the shift in her attitude, in the tension between them and it made him grin. More than grin.

"I'll go with you."

"You don't have to."

"I know I don't have to." Her smile grew. "I want to."

His smile grew too, so did the size of his heart. "You want to go to Mick's wedding with me?"

"Yes, and I want to help you buy a wedding present."

He didn't have anything to compare to the bout of happiness that struck right then. "I still have to go finish getting dressed."

Nodding, she gave him a slow appraisal. "Make sure you change your socks."

"I just put these socks on."

"So you planned on wearing one black one and one blue one to the wedding?"

He glanced at his feet. In his rush to get dressed, he'd merely grabbed two socks out of the drawer. Twisting, he gave her a wink. "I guess I needed your help more than I thought."

She laughed and he soaked in the sound of it as he hurried up the stairway. He wasn't going to have to pretend today. The woman who would be on his arm was the one he'd wanted to be there for years.

Once in his bedroom, he told himself to slow down. There was a wall of barriers between him and Jenny. A brick wall. A tall, wide and thick brick wall, but right now, he was willing to take whatever crumbling pieces he could because he was tired of the way he'd been living.

Jenny had changed, and so had he. He was no longer searching for his father's approval. He'd built a flourishing phone company, and it was time he focused on his life, what he wanted. Jenny showing up on his steps this morning had been nothing shy of a miracle.

And the kick in the butt he'd needed to make lasting changes.

Jenny's heart hadn't slowed down since she'd seen Connor standing shirtless and barefoot in his doorway, and she highly doubted it would slow down any time soon. He was fully dressed now, and looked dashingly handsome in his black pinstriped suit—with matching black socks inside his black-and-white wingtip oxford shoes. He'd made a point of showing her that his socks matched before they left his house.

At which point she'd had to laugh, and that had felt good. Very good.

She could have said no, that she wouldn't go to the

wedding with him, but she wanted to go. Not as a favor because he'd agreed to help her—again—but because she simply, truly wanted to go with him.

Alice didn't appear to be surprised by the news that Connor would give her a ride home this evening, and had waved happily as she'd driven away.

They then climbed in Connor's car and stopped at an expensive department store. Her mother had shopped at that very store often when they'd lived in Rochester, but Connor's jubilance didn't give her time to dwell on any memories that popped up.

She didn't let him dawdle, either, as he had near a display of stuffed toys. Along with a bear exactly like the one he'd given Emily, there had been a donkey, tiger, pig and kangaroo. Jenny had shaken her head, silently sticking to her guns about no more gifts for Emily. Even though he'd stuck his lip out in an overly charming pout, she steered him away from the children's section.

Eventually, they purchased a camera, film and a lovely gold filigree photo frame for Mick and his bride-to-be. The store clerk took it all into a back room to wrap, and then met them at the checkout counter. Before she could stop him, Connor snatched up a small wooden black-and-red car and paid for it along with the gifts.

Stuffing the toy in his pocket as they walked out of the store, he said, "It's for a little boy who will be at the wedding."

Jenny met that little boy moments after entering the house. She and Connor had entered through the back door, and had barely said hello to Mick, when a little boy with tight red curls came flying in the house, shouting Mick's name and then leaped into his arms.

It turned out the boy was Riley and he had been staying next door with his grandparents for several months, until last week, when his father had returned from his out-of-town job. Riley and his father, Matt, lived in Albany, but had made the drive to Rochester for the wedding because Riley and Mick, and Lisa, had become very close friends.

Riley was also friends with Connor. As soon as he had the opportunity, Riley asked Connor a plethora of questions about how many telephones he'd sold. Jenny had to wonder if she'd been wrong about being upset over Connor buying toys for Emily and the other children at Gretchen's. It appeared that was just something he did.

He didn't give Riley the toy car until right before the ceremony began and it gave the child something to hold his attention as the adults concentrated their attention on the couple getting married.

The large living room had been set up with several chairs, and the brick fireplace had been decorated with sheer white lace and flowers, which was where the couple met and stood in front of the clergyman to exchange their vows.

The bride was stunningly beautiful in a gown of embroidered gold silk, but it was her face, the way it literally shined as she looked at Mick that made Jenny's heart melt. Jenny had long ago given up the dream of falling in love, marrying a man and having a real family, but watching the ceremony revived that dream, causing her to blink back tears.

Connor touched her hand, and needing something to keep her grounded, she wrapped her fingers around his and held on tight.

The ceremony was short, but the way the groom and

bride pledged their vows with such dedication and love was very poignant.

Once again, Jenny had to close her eyes and tell herself not to dream. She and Emily were a family, the only family they'd ever need.

Jenny kept that thought close, but amongst the gaiety that followed the ceremony, it was difficult to keep it in focus. A meal had been prepared and served, and used to taking care of all that needed to be done, Jenny jumped in to help in any way she could. Connor's mother, Barbara, was a very sweet woman who had greeted her with a warm hug when they'd arrived, and now gushed her appreciation for the extra set of hands.

Guilt formed a knot in Jenny's stomach. She hadn't minded helping, but in truth, had done it more to steer clear and not have to talk to anyone.

Once the meal was over, the bride and groom prepared to leave on their honeymoon, and as they said goodbye, Jenny couldn't help but compare Mick and Connor as they stood side by side.

They were obviously twins, but there was no mistaking the differences. Connor's face was fuller, his features more perfect and his eyes, they were the tell-tale for her. They were a crisp, cornflower blue that twinkled with an undeniable charm.

Just looking at him made her heart feel as if it was too big to fit inside her chest. That's how it had been years ago, and how it was again.

Mick had his arm around his bride, and Connor stood on his other side, holding a suitcase in each hand so he could carry them to their car once the newlyweds had said a final goodbye to Riley and his father. As soon as that happened, Connor turned and winked at her.

Then, he asked Riley to help him carry the suitcases out to the car. The little boy was excited to help, and Connor walked slowly, so the boy could keep his hands on the handle and believe he was carrying the suitcase.

Though she was around children all the time, her life was such that she rarely saw men interact with children. She'd seen that today, from both Connor and Mick, as well as Riley's father, Matt. It made her wonder exactly what Emily was missing by not having a father. Those thoughts were instantly recounted with her own experience of having a stepfather. No father would have been better. From the moment her stepfather had entered her life, she had gone from a happy child, to a very lonely one.

When Connor and Riley entered the house again, Connor was carrying Riley on his shoulders, and had to duck low so the child didn't bump his head on the door frame.

Jenny laughed at the sight as she shut the door behind them. "Goodness, Riley, you certainly became tall all of a sudden. You barely fit through the door."

Laughing, Riley shook his head. "That's 'cause I'm on Connor's shoulders."

"Are you sure?" she teased.

Riley's hands were locked under Connor's chin and while looking down, he tugged Connor's head backward, so he could look at his face. "Yep, it's Connor."

She had to ask, "How do you know for sure?"

In total seriousness, Riley replied, "His head is bigger than Mick's."

Jenny slapped a hand over her mouth, but couldn't stop the giggle that escaped. "Is that so."

"Yep," Riley said. "See, right here." He pulled back

the locks of hair that angled across Connor's forehead. "This part's bigger and—" He poked at one of Connor's eyebrows. "He has more hair here."

"Riley," Matt said with a warning tone.

There was no mistaking the two were father and son. They both had curly red hair, a splattering of freckles and bright green eyes.

"Oh, please," Jenny said in defense of the child. "I asked, and Riley is right. Connor's head is bigger."

The teasing gleam in Connor's eyes sent the blood rushing through her veins in a fun and delightful way. Happiness filled her as she lifted her brows in her own teasing way and shrugged at him.

Matt lifted his son off Connor's shoulders, and after visiting for a few minutes, insisted it was time to leave so they could get back to Albany before dark.

Their departure left just her and Connor, his mother and Lisa's father, Tony, who lived at the house as well and had already excused himself to go lie down, and Dr. George Bolton, a friend of the family's.

Barbara took Jenny's hand as Connor closed the door behind Matt and Riley. "Come," Barbara said. "The only time you've sat down is during the ceremony. I can't thank you enough for all your help, but I can make sure you sit down and enjoy some punch before Connor drags you out of here."

The doctor, a gray-haired man with permanent smile wrinkles filling his face, said, "I'll get punch for both of you." With a twinkle in his eye, he asked, "Would you like me to add a drop of sherry to it?"

Barbara laughed as she nodded. "Or two."

The extra chairs had been put away and Jenny sat down on the sofa that Barbara led her to. Connor handed her a cup and then sat down next to her while Barbara took a cup from the doctor and the two of them each sat in the armchairs on the other side of the coffee table.

"Oh, goodness, that was a lovely service, wasn't it?" Barbara asked.

"Yes, Mother, you truly outdid yourself," Connor replied.

"No, I didn't. Lisa took care of most everything, and Jenny had most of the cleaning up done from the meal before I even entered the kitchen." Her face softened as she said, "Thank you again, dear."

"You're very welcome," Jenny said. "I just hope you'll be able to find everything that I put away."

Barbara waved a hand. "Of course, I will. It's been so long since I've seen you. Tell me, how are you doing? Where are you living now?"

The sip of punch Jenny had just taken got caught in the back of her throat.

Chapter Twelve

"Jenny is a midwife and she lives over by Syracuse," Connor said while laying his hand over the top of Jenny's. Feeling the way she trembled, he continued, "We ran into each other while I was selling telephones."

"A midwife?" Dr. George asked.

George had been their family doctor for years, but ever since Mick had brought Tony Walters here for their mother to nurse, George had become a regular fixture. Connor sensed his mother and the good doctor might be growing into more than friends. That didn't bother him in the least. His mother wasn't yet fifty and deserved to find happiness, love, again. He couldn't think of a better man for her to do that with than George.

"Yes," Jenny answered quietly as she set her cup on the coffee table and glanced at him.

Connor winked at her. He was proud of her for being a midwife and wanted her to receive recognition for all she did for others. And herself.

"Are you happy there?" George asked.

"Yes," Jenny answered, looking perplexed.

"Shoot." George swallowed his cup of punch in one

gulp and set the cup on the coffee table. "I have need for another good midwife in my practice."

"Why?" Jenny asked.

"Because the hospital in town is expensive, many families can't afford to give birth there." He shook his head in disgust. "The amount they charge for ether alone is enough to turn people away."

Jenny sat straighter. "It's not necessary, either," she said. "I believe it's dangerous."

"I agree," George said. "In some instances, it prolongs the labor, causing problems and issues for everyone. Whenever possible, I encourage people to deliver at home, but I only have one midwife in my practice and we can barely keep up."

"I hope you find one," Jenny said. "And I wish more doctors didn't use ether so readily. New mothers wake up feeling sick and not knowing if they have a son or daughter, rather than rejoicing in the miracle of birth."

"Oh, I agree, dear," George said. "Couldn't have said it more perfectly myself."

The pride Connor felt as Jenny and George continued to converse was unlike any other. He wasn't just proud to have her on his arm because she was beautiful. She was that, but also intelligent, compassionate and impressive. He'd been attracted to her, years ago, and now, but he'd never really gotten to know her. There were reasons for that. They'd been young, hadn't known each other long and they'd both had family issues that they'd kept hidden. They'd both had a lot of growing up to do back then. That had happened and he wondered what that meant for them now.

"I've heard of facilities that put women under as soon as labor begins," Jenny said.

"Are you speaking of the Albany Moral Hospitality Institute?" George asked.

Connor wrapped his hand around Jenny's, gave it a reassuring squeeze at George's question and watched her closely as she answered.

"Yes, I am," she replied. "You know of it?"

"Yes, I do," George said with disgust. "I throw their propaganda straight in the trash. That place needs to be shut down, or at least have a board of directors put in place. Right now, they don't have to answer to anybody."

"What is this institute?" his mother asked. "I've never heard of them."

Connor caught the way Jenny glanced at him while George answered.

"A home for unwed mothers." George shook his head. "A very mismanaged one. They pay doctors to send them patients. I advocate against them with other physicians, but to some, money means more than care."

"Do you mean the unwed mothers sent there don't receive good care?" Mother asked with concern.

"From what I've heard, they don't get anything close to even adequate care," George said.

"Well," Mother huffed. "Can't something be done about that?"

As George shook his head, Connor gave Jenny a smile. "Actually, that is what Jenny has been working on. She knows some of the girls that have been at that particular home, and will be setting an appointment for the girls to meet with Senator Hughes."

"Good for you, Jenny," George said. "That's exactly what needs to happen. I filed a complaint against them, but it was from hearsay, and that doesn't hold much weight. The only way real change can happen is for the victims to share their stories."

"Victims?" Mother gasped.

"Yes, victims of mistreatment," George said. "Can you tell us more, Jenny?"

"Yes, dear, please tell us more," Mother said. "Is there anything we can do to help? There must be something."

Jenny glanced at him, and her smile wavered slightly before she lifted her chin. "Connor is helping us, me and the girls, in setting up the appointment."

"I'm hoping Senator Hughes will meet with Jenny and others this week," Connor said. "The session is almost over, so we have to act quickly."

"Do you need me to call him?" Mother asked. "I have his home number. McCormick donations helped him get elected to his first term years ago."

Jenny's back was stiff, and he realized how much his mother and Jenny were alike. Sweet and kind until you ruffled their feathers and then they fought back. His mother's gaze was on Jenny, and that's where his gaze went, too. He was here to help, but she was the one calling the shots. She'd been taking care of herself, her daughter, and many other girls for years and didn't need him to step in and take over. If he'd have realized that in the beginning, things would have gone a lot smoother.

She was looking at him, and he smiled. "It's up to you," he said. "I don't see how it could hurt."

"I don't, either." Looking at his mother, Jenny continued, "But I didn't come here today to solicit your assistance."

"Of course, you didn't," his mother answered. "But as sure as you're sitting there, I'm offering my assistance. And George's. Now, tell us more about these girls, about their experiences, so I have specifics when I'm talking to Brent Hughes."

Jenny, full of gentle, yet compassionate indignation, shared several stories of the conditions and actions at the institute, including the use of dogs to find runaways. Once again, pride for her filled him. These girls truly needed help, and Jenny had been doing that for years.

Clearly outraged by the time Jenny ended, his mother asked, "Why have I not heard of this before?"

Her question was directed to him. "I only heard about it a short time ago," he said. "When I ran into Jenny while selling telephone lines."

His mother turned to George. "You never mentioned it to me, either."

"The institute is in Albany," George replied.

"So?"

"It's not as if it comes up in everyday conversations here in Rochester," George said.

"Well, it should!" Mother insisted. "Young girls are being treed by dogs when they refuse to give up their babies for adoption. I've never heard of such outrageous, insufferable behavior that needs to be stopped." She turned to him. "Does your brother know about this?"

Connor shook his head. "Probably not, Mother. As George said, the institute is in Albany. Mick is a Rochester city detective."

"Well, it's happening in our state, in our nation, therefore everyone should know about it, and you can guarantee I will be telling everyone I know to call Brent Hughes immediately." She pressed a hand to her throat. "Forgive me, Jenny, for sounding so harsh, but this is truly a serious matter and I'm so proud of you to be standing up for these girls. And I want you to know that you are not alone. You have all of our support in any way you need it."

"Thank you," Jenny said, dipping her head in appreciation. "It truly is serious and I do hope the senator is willing to do something about it."

His mother leaned across the coffee table and laid a hand on Jenny's knee. "If he doesn't, we'll take it to the governor."

Jenny glanced at him.

He shrugged. "I'm here to help no matter how far up the ladder you want to go."

Her smile made his heart skip a beat.

"I'm so glad you two ran into each other again." Mother shook her head. "I'm sure it was because he was attempting to sell you a telephone?"

"Yes, it was," Jenny answered.

"He's been obsessed with them since he was a small child, and his father was so proud of him about that." She let out a laugh. "Do you know, that at one time, we had ten telephones in this house? Ten! There were phone lines all over the place. I kept tripping on them and said we only needed one phone in this house. Patrick, his father, loved showing off those phones that Connor had designed so much, that I finally had to compromise to four. With the promise that all the lines would be hidden."

Connor had to nod in agreement when Jenny glanced his way, silently giggling. "It took my father and me an entire weekend to pull the baseboards off the walls and hide the lines behind them."

"Oh, dear, Connor, do you remember all those white feathers the two of you found behind the baseboards?"

"Yes, I do."

"White feathers?" Jenny asked.

"Yes," Mother said. "Years before that, I'd come home from a church meeting—it was known as the woman's guild back then—the name is changed every few years when a new leader steps in with newfangled ideas. Anyway, just as I walked up to the front door, I heard screams and then something hit the inside of the front door so hard it rattled. I couldn't push it open and no one could hear my shouts because they were laughing and squealing so loudly. I ran around the house to the back door and you wouldn't have believed the mess I saw."

Jenny's face was full of rapture as she asked, "What was it?"

"Feathers! White feathers everywhere! You see, it had been in the fall of the year, a real cold, blustery day, so the boys couldn't play outside. Well, Patrick, their father, decided that they should practice sledding down the hill, on the stairway, and because a sled couldn't go down the steps, he got an old feather tick out of the attic and they all three rode down the stairs on that."

Eyes shining, Jenny looked at him.

He nodded and held up one finger. "We didn't crash into the door until the fourth or fifth time down the stairs."

"But when they did crash into the door, the feather tick exploded!" his mother said.

"That really was bad timing," Connor admitted as they all laughed.

The stories continued for a short time, before he said it was time for them to leave. After promises to call the senator and to do anything that might help, his mother walked them to the door.

"Jenny, it was so good seeing you," his mother said. "I'll start calling people right away, but please come again. Don't wait for Connor. We don't need him in order to visit." She kissed his cheek. "Although I do love to see you, too."

Connor kissed his mother's cheek. "Love seeing you, too."

Once in the car, Jenny stared at the house while he backed out of the driveway. "Thank you for attending the wedding, and for helping with the dishes and everything." Every time he'd looked for her, she'd been in the kitchen until nearly everyone had left.

She turned, looked at him with a frown, and then shook her head. "No, thank you for bringing me, and I'm sorry that I almost caused an argument between your mother and George."

He laughed. "You didn't almost cause an argument between them. My mother can get worked up easily—George has seen that before."

"It was very nice of her to offer to help, but I do wonder if I should have accepted it."

"Why?"

She pressed a hand to her mouth for a moment, then with a long sigh, looked at him with anguish in her eyes. "Do they, or you, really want the McCormick name associated with a home for unwed mothers?"

He not only saw, but felt her shame, and that bothered him. More than bothered, he hated the idea of her being ashamed of anything. "The shame would be in not helping those girls."

She shook her head.

They'd only driven a couple of blocks, but he pulled the car over to the side of the road and turned off the engine. Twisting, to look directly at her, he took a moment to study her. "Do you want to know what I see when I look at you, Jenny?"

Her smile was a bit wistful, a bit compliant, as if she wasn't about to believe whatever he would say, or maybe just didn't want to hear it.

Either way, he was going to tell her. "I see the girl I used to know, the one I had missed and dreamed of seeing again for years, but there is only a hint of that girl and it's all on the outside, because she grew up. Grew into a beautiful, strong and amazing woman. You had been put in a difficult situation, but rather than give in, you forged ahead, found a way to change things for yourself and continue to change it for others. That is something to be proud of, Jenny. I'm proud of you, very proud, and feel honored to be helping you continue your mission."

"It's not a mission, Connor."

"Yes, it is. One by one you've changed lives. Not only your own, but others." He wanted to touch her, pull her into a hug, but that, too, had to be her choice. Oddly enough, he'd not only learned a lot about her the past few weeks, he'd learned a lot about himself. "I've never done anything like that."

She twisted, stared at him prudently. "You haven't?" Her laugh was laced with a sigh. "You have the entire town excited by your telephone lines, and you had the railroad tracks fixed. In a heartbeat, I might add. And you are the reason the senator is even willing to listen to us."

That was true, but there was more to it. "I own the phone company—stringing lines and selling service to people is my business. The way I make my living. I'm happy people are excited to get a phone, but it's self-motivated. Expanding my business. As for the railroad tracks. I got high centered on them. Had to push my car off the tracks as a train was coming. Knowing I'd be traveling that road again, I wanted it fixed, so that wouldn't happen again." He shrugged. "And the senator, I contacted him because it would give me a reason to keep seeing you. So, again, self-motivation."

Her gaze grew thoughtful, and then she frowned. "Why did you feel second best with your father? It didn't sound like that to me. He was proud of your interest in telephones from the time you were small."

He let that lull in his mind for a moment. "Insecurity, I guess. Children want to be loved, want to be special to someone. Even though we are twins, and I'm proud of him, love him, Mick was the first born. Named after my father, the first child of the next generation of Mc-Cormicks was destined for greatness. I couldn't compete with that, so I strove for something unique to gain the extra attention I wanted. I used telephones, but also discovered that I could make people pay attention to me by being funny, joking, happy." The truth of all that settled heavily. "Even when I didn't feel happy."

"You always appeared so happy," she said quietly. "Like your life was wonderful."

He took hold of her hand. "Some things about my life were wonderful, and being with you has always made me happy."

She turned, looked out the windshield, and he wasn't sure what to do when a single tear trickled from her eye.

"You made me happy, too, Connor, and you're right, children want to be loved." She wiped away the tear. "I haven't been in Rochester since the day I left."

He held his breath, waiting for her to say more, if she wanted to. At one time, he'd wanted to know everything, would have tried to make her tell him. Now, he just wanted to be there for her.

"I'd thought I was just sick, that I'd eaten something that didn't settle well, but when my mother found me throwing up, she started questioning me." She closed her eyes, shook her head. "Afterward, I could hear her and Richard arguing. Then she came into my room, packed a suitcase and said we were going to see a doctor. It was late night when we arrived in Albany. The doctor examined me, confirmed I was pregnant."

Anger rose inside him, but he focused on her, not himself, and tightened his hold on her hand.

The smile she offered him was strained, and wobbled. "She wrote out a check for my care, and told me I'd made my bed, now I had to lie in it. That was the last time I saw her."

Words failed him. All he had were actions, and he used them, pulled her into a tight hug, held her as she quietly cried against his chest.

He would have held her forever, if that had been what she needed, but it wasn't all that long before she let out a shaky sigh and lifted her head.

"I'm sorry," she whispered. "I, uh..." She sighed again.

He placed a knuckle beneath her chin. "Don't be sorry. Be proud of what you did after all that. You have a beautiful, wonderful daughter, and many other women have their children because of you."

Sitting up straighter, she said, "You're right."

Because humor had been his saving grace many times, he used it again. "Did I just hear you say I was right?"

She grinned and her eyes glistened. "Yes, you did,

but don't let it go to your head. It's already too big. Ask Riley."

He laughed. "He's a character."

"So are you—you're very good with children."

He winked at her. "I'm just a likeable guy."

Giggling, she leaned against the back of her seat and shot him a sideways glance. "I'm not going to say you're right again."

He laughed, and happy that the atmosphere was lighter, brighter, he asked, "It's still early—is there anywhere you want to go, anything you want to see while we're in town?"

Her smile remained, even as she grew thoughtful, almost as if she was releasing ghosts. He hoped so, and he hoped that would help her.

"How about Franny?" he asked. "I didn't say how, where, or why, but I did mention to Seth that I'd run into you, and I'm sure he's told Franny."

"Franny," she said softly.

Not exactly sure what that meant, he said, "Or I could—"

The smile she flashed at him stopped him from saying more.

"All right," she said.

Surprised, he glanced her way. "All right?"

She nodded. "I would like to see Franny. I really would."

With a burst of excitement, he started the car. "All right. Off we go."

"Do you think they'll be home?"

"It's Saturday and they have four kids—they're home."

"You said one is just a baby?"

"Yes, born just a couple of months ago."

In less than ten minutes, he pulled into the gravel driveway of Seth's two-story stucco home. Toys dotted the yard and a shaggy-haired dog ran to meet them, barking his personal greeting. "That's Birdie."

"Birdie?"

He nodded. "Their oldest, Thomas, named the dog when they first got him. Tommy was only two."

As she giggled, the screen door on the house banged, and a squeal split the air.

"Jenny! Jenny Sommers! Dear heavens, it is you!" Franny handed Seth the baby in her arms and ran down the steps.

Climbing out of the car, Connor grinned as Jenny jumped from the vehicle.

"Franny, oh, Franny," she said, hugging the other woman. "It's so good to see you!" As they separated, Jenny wiped at her eyes. "You look exactly the same."

"Banana oil!" Franny said in her boisterous way. "I've got boobs! I never had those before. Only have them now because I had another baby and am nursing her!"

That was something Connor could have lived his entire life without hearing, but he'd live with it because it had made Jenny laugh out loud.

"Look at you!" Franny continued. "You always were such a doll!" As if she just noticed him, Franny asked, "Wasn't she, Connor?"

"Yes," he agreed as he arrived at that side of the car.

"When Seth told me that you'd run into Jenny, I told him if you didn't tell him where she was, I was never going to talk to you again." Franny let out another squeal. "Now, I'll love you forever!" She gave him one of her jubilant hugs and then grabbed Jenny's arm and tugged her toward the house. "Come in, come in—we have so much to talk about. So much to catch up on."

Connor followed in their wake and stopped next to Seth on the porch. "I hope we aren't interrupting anything."

Seth shook his head. "Perfect timing, I'd just called your house. You didn't answer, but I'd been prepared to tell you that I might have to move in with you if you didn't tell me where Franny could find Jenny."

"I'm glad we stopped by."

"Me, too." Seth tickled the baby in his arms beneath her chin. "Looks like you and I will be watching four kids for the next couple of hours."

Connor dug in his pocket. "I have a pack of gum."

"That'll help," Seth said.

When Connor had asked if she'd wanted to see Franny, Jenny had questioned the sanity of that. She'd worked hard to keep herself as separated from her old life as possible, yet talking with Connor had opened something inside her. She had found strength and resilience over the years, but had never found pride. Not for herself, and maybe it was time for that. Time to stop letting the past overshadow all that she had accomplished.

Franny didn't leave time for her to contemplate anything. In no time, they were chatting, laughing and reminiscing; it was as if the years between now and the last time they'd seen each other had completely vanished.

Until long after they'd consumed a pot of tea, discussed a list of people Jenny had been curious about and she'd been introduced to all four of Franny's children, who had then been ushered outside to play under the watchful eyes of Connor and Seth. That's when Franny brought up Jenny's disappearance. She'd known it would come up. It had to, and this was Franny. The years had come back then with a vengeance, and Jenny had to decide how to react to those memories.

Seth had brought the baby inside, for Franny to nurse, and they were sitting in the living room, just the two of them and the baby in Franny's arms. "I'd thought you'd run away to New York, to be with Connor," Franny said. "Until he returned, looking for you."

Jenny smoothed the print on the brocade pillow beside her.

"At first, I thought he was just trying to cover up where you really were, you know, like keeping you hid from your mother or something, but he was so beside himself, that…" Franny's short, dark curls bobbed as she shook her head. "I knew he wasn't lying. That he didn't know where you were, either."

Jenny bit down on her bottom lip. It was hard to imagine how little trust she'd had in Connor back then, and how unfair she'd been to him by instantly believing the worst.

"I'm sorry, I still haven't learned when to keep my mouth—"

"No." Jenny shook her head. "It's fine. Of course you would have been curious as to what happened. If it had been the other way around, I would have been, too." Connor was right about her having a beautiful daughter, and she was proud to be Emily's mother. "I have a daughter. Her name is Emily. She's six."

Franny's mouth dropped open, then she glanced at the door, frowning. "Six? So you and Connor—"

"No," Jenny interrupted again. "Emily isn't Connor's daughter." She shrugged, mainly to herself, because if she hadn't been so insecure back then, things would have been different. Very different. That also meant she wouldn't have Emily, and she'd never wish for that.

A sense of relief, of love, that she did have her daughter filled her. "I became pregnant that summer, while Connor was gone, and when my mother found out, she took me to a home for unwed mothers." After telling Connor, repeating the story to Franny was easy. "I ran away from the home, and ever since then, I've been helping other girls who have escaped."

Franny had a hand over her mouth. "Jenny, I—"

"Please don't say you're sorry," Jenny said. "Emily is an amazing girl, so kind and caring, and lovable, and I love what I'm doing. I've delivered dozens of babies and each one is such a miracle, it's truly incredible."

"I can imagine it is." Franny looked down at the baby in her arms. "I've never even been awake when my babies entered the world, but I've never failed to be amazed the first time I've held them that I created them. Me and Seth. This whole new little person." Her signature laugh echoed off the ceiling. "Then they hit about two years old, and become little monsters. That's when I swear, someone else had a hand in creating them."

Jenny laughed. "Oh, Franny. It's so good to see you. To talk to you."

Growing serious, Franny asked, "Did your mother take you to the home over in Albany? I'm asking because that's where Sarah Foreman went—did you know her? She was a year younger than me."

Jenny shook her head.

"Well, that's the one that Sarah went to, in Albany. They said she had to give her baby up for adoption, so her parents adopted him. They still claim that they adopted him while Sarah was staying with her aunt in Maine, but everyone pretty much knows he's Sarah's son, not her younger brother."

"That's not uncommon," Jenny said. "The home does force the girls to give up their babies, and those who have been disowned don't have a choice, other than running away."

"And you help them. Horsefeathers, that's the real bee's knees, Jenny. Good for you."

"Thank you, but what I've been doing isn't enough. Connor has agreed to help me to see if we can have new laws made, so the girls are treated better and don't have to give up their babies if they don't want to."

"He is?" Franny continued before Jenny could respond. "That sounds like Connor, though, doesn't it? He's still the good guy you used to know."

"Yes, he is," Jenny agreed.

"If there is anything Seth and I can do to help, let us know." Franny lifted the baby and set her over one shoulder while buttoning up her blouse with her other hand. "I have to ask, Jenny. How did you end up pregnant? You never so much as looked at anyone besides Connor."

Jenny sighed. "I acted foolishly one night. Thought I hated Connor and, well, it just happened. I never saw Emily's father again. He doesn't know about her and I need to keep it that way."

"Why?"

"For several reasons," Jenny answered.

Franny nodded, then shrugged. "I was pregnant when Seth and I got married, and when Tommy was born, I was sure everyone was checking the calendar, counting the months between our wedding and his birth, but no one seemed to care. If they did, I didn't hear about it. Then came Bradley, Jill, and now Betsy." With a chuckle, Franny added, "Trust me, nobody cares how many months are between any of them."

"You have a beautiful family, and a beautiful home—I'm so happy for you." Jenny truly was happy. "It was so good seeing you again."

"Wait! Don't you dare say you are leaving."

"I have to soon. It's a long drive home and then Connor has to turn around and come back to Rochester."

"Connor! That man would drive to the moon and back for you." Franny stood. "You aren't leaving because the four of us are going out for dinner. You can't say no because I haven't gone anywhere, except the grocer, since this little one was born."

Chapter Thirteen

"I'm sorry about this; I just couldn't say no to Franny. She hasn't been out of the house since Betsy was born, and was so excited to go for dinner. Practically before I knew what was happening, she was on the phone to her mother-in-law, asking her to come over and sit with the children. Her mother-in-law said yes, and Franny was so excited about what she wanted to wear, I just couldn't say no. Just couldn't."

Connor listened to her apology and her reasonings, the same ones he'd already heard twice, while parking in the lot near Pinion's Supper Club.

"I know it's a long drive for you to take me home and then back again," she continued. "I will give you money for gas, and money to stay at the Bird's Inn, if you want."

He looked at her. "Are you done?"

"Done what?"

"Justifying going out to eat with Franny and Seth."

"I just—well, you're being awfully nice about everything and I don't want to impose any further."

"I wouldn't be here if I didn't want to be here." He leaned closer, looked her in the eyes. "And you wouldn't be, either." Reaching behind him, he opened his door. "So let's just accept it and have fun." He climbed out then, and hurried around to open her door.

She stepped out and looked at the building. "This is Pinion's."

"Yes, it is." This was where she'd seen him with his cousin Beth, as he was leaving his father's birthday. "Is that all right?"

She grinned and nodded. "Yes, it's fine."

He winked at her, shut her car door. "Good, because it's still the best restaurant in town." He laid a hand on her back, to escort her across the parking lot. "And they host the best speakeasy in their back room."

Her heels nearly dug into the concrete as she skidded to a stop. "A speakeasy? Surely Franny wouldn't have—"

He nodded. "This is where she said to meet them."

"She did?"

Putting pressure on her back, he guided her toward the door. "Yes, she did."

As if right on cue, the door opened and Nelson Pinion, the owner, greeted him, "Connor McCormick! I haven't seen you in ages. Come, come, I have your table ready."

"Good evening, Nelson," Connor greeted. "I'm assuming Seth called for reservations."

"That he did," Nelson said as they stepped inside. "But you must tell me how you McCormick men do it?"

"Do what?"

Nelson, the flirt that he was, took Jenny's hand. "Find the most beautiful women in the world. Look at this one. She's the image of the angel in my dreams."

Connor rubbed Jenny's back. "She definitely is beautiful, Nelson. This is Jenny Sommers."

"Jenny, oh, Jenny, you make my heart sing, sweet, Jenny," Nelson sang in a deep baritone.

"Keep trying, Nelson—she's with me," Connor said, winking at Jenny. Her blush was so adorable the desire to kiss her, right here in front of Nelson, struck so hard and fast he had to rock back on his heels to stop himself.

"I see that. You McCormick men always guard your queens." Nelson shook his head. "I hear Mick married his today."

"He did," Connor replied. "It was a small ceremony at the house, but I'll do my best to convince them to have a reception here, just to make you happy."

"Oh, that would. That would. A dual party. For both the McCormick twins. People will come from miles away to attend."

From past experience, Connor knew Nelson would carry on as long as he let him. "Is our table ready?"

"Yes, of course, with champagne on the table for my favorite people. This way."

He led them into the restaurant. The speakeasy was the back room, which was also the banquet hall where members of the supper club could host private parties. Candles, with their little flames flickering, sat upon the snowy-white tablecloths draped over each table, providing a golden glow to the room.

Connor nodded greetings to people he knew as he escorted Jenny to their reserved table, the very one he'd asked Seth to reserve. It was a corner booth, giving them privacy and more comfortable seating than the wooden chairs.

Once she'd slid onto the dual bench seat, he thanked Nelson and then sat beside her.

"Alcohol is illegal," she whispered, looking at the

bottle in the standing metal ice bucket near the edge of the table.

"Selling and transporting it is illegal. Consuming it is not."

"That's hogwash."

Rather than explaining how Nelson always provided his family with champagne during their meals because they were members of the supper club, he said, "No, that's the law." He poured a small amount in each of their glasses. Then held his up. "Cheers."

She touched her stemmed glass, but didn't lift it up. "What are we toasting?"

"Our plan." He knew she couldn't not toast that. "It's a good one and is going to work. Get new regulations and laws in place."

She lifted her glass and clinked it against his. "Cheers."

He watched her take a small sip, then lick the sweetness of the champagne off her lips. The desire to do that for her forced him to look away. He'd tried hard to forget the feeling of kissing her, but that event had done nothing more than remind him of seven years ago, when they'd both been young and kissing each other had been an experiment they'd performed over and over until they'd perfected the merger of their lips into something spectacular.

Her eyes twinkled as she asked, "What are you thinking so hard about?"

"You," he replied.

"Oh?"

"Yes. I'm glad you're here." He clinked his glass against hers again. "I'm glad I'm here, too."

"Me, too," she said. "Me, too."

The arrival of Seth and Franny instantly filled the table with laughter, and for the next hour they ate and laughed as if everything was right in the world. That the four of them being together, as couples, was exactly how the universe wanted things.

"So," Franny said, with a clap of her hands after their plates had been cleared away. "Tell Seth and I how we can help with your plan to help unwed mothers."

Connor leaned back and draped his arm along the back of the booth. He was glad that so many people were stepping up to offer their help.

"I'm not sure." Jenny glanced at him. "We are hoping to take a couple of the girls to share their stores with the senator and some of the other ones are writing letters."

"I could ask Sarah to write a letter," Franny said. "She was at that home."

"Does she know you know?" Jenny asked.

"Yes," Franny said.

"Sarah who?" Seth asked.

"And what does she know that you know?" Connor asked, growing lost.

"Sarah Foreman, the blonde that works at the department store," Franny replied.

Connor knew her, and explained to Jenny, "She helped us with the wedding present today." His mind was then caught up, and he asked Franny, "She had a baby at the home for unwed mothers?"

"Yes, her little brother, but not too many people know, so it's not chin music."

"When?" Seth asked.

Connor didn't remember Sarah from school, but was wondering just how many girls did go to these homes.

"When we were seniors," Franny answered Seth.

Connor looked at Jenny; that would have been around the same time she'd been at the home.

She shook her head in answer to his silent question.

"Sarah has never said who the father of her baby was," Franny said, "but rumors at the time floated Donald Forsythe's name. That could have just been because everyone knew that he was the father of Stephanie Graham's baby. She did go live with her aunt. In California and is now married to an actor."

"You knew Stephanie," Connor said to Jenny. "She was in the play, the girl that Donald tripped and she fell into the scene boards."

She nodded, but didn't look his way. Probably remembering that event. She'd worked so hard on those scenes, and he'd been furious with Forsythe that night.

"Remember how that scumbag flattened all the tires on your car after the play?" Seth asked.

"Yes. The only reason I accepted that part in the play was to irritate him," Connor answered. "He'd always been such a jerk, and had hated me since grade school when I beat him up for picking on the girls. If there's one person I've been glad that I haven't seen since high school, it's him."

"You haven't seen him because Stephanie's older brother was set to kill him when he found out his sister was pregnant," Franny said. "Donald left town and no one's heard from him that I know of."

"She'd be the one to know," Seth said, nudging his wife in the side.

He'd never told anyone about the last time he'd seen Donald. "I saw him the morning I left for New York that summer. He was working at the train station, working as a baggage boy. He tried putting my luggage on the wrong train. On purpose. His boss caught him and the last I saw, he was getting his butt chewed. I just smiled and waved."

Seth slapped the table, laughing. "Serves him right." He scratched his head then, and said to Franny, "I never knew that Stephanie Graham was pregnant, or that she moved to California."

Franny laughed. "Because that was the year you met me, and from then on you only had eyes for me." She kissed her husband's cheek. "And that old jalopy you drove."

"I loved that car," Seth said, waggling his brows at Franny. "Connor helped me rebuild the engine. Remember that?"

"I do," Connor answered. It had been shortly after Jenny had disappeared and he'd used working on the car to get his mind off her. It hadn't worked. He hadn't known about Stephanie being pregnant or moving, either, because his mind had only been on one girl. Jenny.

"That had been right before your dad died," Seth said. "Remember how he let us use his tools, and even helped us that one whole Saturday?"

"I do," Connor replied. "He liked doing things like that."

"He was a good man," Seth said.

Connor's heart warmed. "Yes, he was."

Jenny touched his arm, and he flashed her a smile.

"Well, um, we should be leaving, now," she said softly.

Franny held a finger in the air. "Hold on. I still have an hour before Betsy needs to nurse again, so you two can't give us the bum's rush yet. Let's visit the back room first."

"Connor has a long drive," Jenny said. "Taking me home and then back—"

"It's not that late," he told her. "I'll still get you home well before midnight."

"But then you have to drive all the way back to your house," she said.

"It's not that far, and I've driven all night before."

"Settled," Franny said. "You guys get us a table while us gals visit the powder room."

That's what happened and as soon as the women joined them at a table in the back room, Franny grabbed her husband and led him to the dance floor.

Connor smiled. "Shall we join them?"

Her eyes were on the dancers as she said, "I haven't danced since high school."

"It's like riding a bike," he said.

"I haven't done that since high school, either."

"Me, neither." He stood, and held out his hand. She took it, and he guided her onto the dance floor. There he drew her close and placed his other hand on her waist.

The floor was thick with dancers, from young flappers and drugstore cowboys, to dames and billboards kicking up their heels to the beat of the jazz music filling the air by the full band on the stage.

He two-stepped to an open area, giving them more room, then twirled her under their clutched hands. Seeing the sparkle in her eyes, the smile on her face, he twirled her again. This time he spun, so their backs bumped together midway through her twirl, and rejoiced in her giggle that filled his ears.

This. The burst of happiness within him was exactly what he'd been looking for every time he'd led a doll onto the dance floor, but it had never been there. As much as he'd faked it, his soul had never enjoyed the movements, the connections, until this very moment.

The smile on her face, the shine in her eyes, said she was enjoying it too, and that was exhilarating.

They danced three dances. Each one more exciting than the last. Her face was lit up brighter than the over-head lights, and her laughter more musical than the band.

"Shall we get something to drink?" he asked as the music faded.

"Yes, please." She waved a hand before her face. "It's hot."

"It is!" Stepping off the dance floor, he plucked two glasses off the cigarette girl's tray and handed one to Jenny before steering her to the back door. "We'll go out on the balcony. It's cooler out there."

The breeze blowing off the bay was a welcome relief as soon as they went outside. "That feels good," he said.

"It does." Glancing at her glass, she asked, "What is this?"

"Don't know yet, but it's wet and I'm thirsty." He nodded toward the railing as he took a sip. "It's good—try it."

She waited until they stood near the rail and took a tentative sip. "It's refreshing. Minty." Took a longer drink. "And sweet."

"It is." He held the sprig of mint aside with one knuckle while taking another drink. "It's a Southside Fizz." He winked at her. "Al Capone's favorite drink."

"How do you know that?"

"I have my sources."

Laughing, she shook her head and took another drink. The moonlight shining off the water of the bay below the balcony reflected up onto her face, giving it a golden glow.

"What's in it?"

It took Connor a moment to pull his mind together enough to know she was asking about the drink. "Gin, lemon juice, club soda, sugar syrup." He picked the sprig of mint out of his glass and popped it in his mouth. "And a sprig of mint for fresh breath."

"Fresh breath?" There was no sarcasm in her question. That was in her eyes.

"Yes, fresh breath."

She blinked slowly, then turned to stare out over the water. "I didn't realize this place was right on the Irondequoit Bay."

He set his empty glass on the railing ledge. "It's built in the hill. You can walk out of the basement onto a dock on the bay." He bumped her shoulder with his. "Makes it easy to sneak in booze."

"I can't believe I'm at a speakeasy." Lifting her glass to her lips, she added, "Drinking gin."

"I'm a bad influence, am I?"

She emptied her glass and set it on the ledge beside his glass. "No, I'd give that credit to Franny. I couldn't say no to her."

"But you can to me?"

Her smile never faltered. "That's almost as difficult."

He touched one knuckle to the underside of her chin, and used it to encourage her to twist enough so he could see her full face, not just her profile. "Almost?"

She nodded.

The enormity of his desire to kiss her was too strong to ignore, and the flash of anticipation that slipped into her eyes as he leaned forward sent his heart into a tailspin.

A soft sigh escaped as their lips merged. It could have come from him, but he chose to believe it had been her sigh and pressed his lips more firmly against hers.

She twisted, faced him completely and her arms slipped up around his neck. He folded his arms around her, pulling her as close as possible. The tenderness that filled him was like an old friend coming home. He'd only felt that with her, years ago. He'd searched for it, but had never found it.

Something else opened up inside him. A willingness to sacrifice all he had, all he wanted, for her. For her needs and wants. He would do that this time. Go to whatever lengths it took, face any obstacles, because her happiness was worth it.

He parted her lips with his tongue,, and her eagerness met his as their tongues met, twisted, tasted and explored. It was as if the world was once again a forgotten place. Nothing mattered except the two of them and this moment in time.

Jenny's insides were still humming when Connor closed her car door and walked around the front of the car. She probably shouldn't have kissed him like she had, or even danced with him like she had, but wasn't going to regret it. Not tonight. Not ever. She had enough to regret and he wasn't one. Not any part of him. Today had been amazing. All of it, and she was going to hold on to each and every memory. Forever.

Franny and Seth had been at the table when she and Connor had returned from the balcony, and with remorse, especially from Franny, claimed it was time to go home.

Franny had insisted that they do this again, go out to dinner and dancing, and though Jenny had nodded, and agreed with how good it had been to see Franny, she couldn't promise that she'd be back to Rochester any time soon.

Tonight, today, had proven that she still harbored very strong feelings for Connor. Feelings that she'd never have for another man. She didn't want to have those feelings for another man, but she also couldn't have them for him, either.

It had taken all her will to hide her trembling when the conversation had turned to Donald, and to hide her anger when she'd learned things she hadn't known before. About Sarah, and Stephanie, and how he'd been at the train station when Connor had left for New York.

She'd been so foolish to believe Donald that night, to believe that Connor had lied to her. She'd known Donald had hated Connor, and had fallen into his snare so easily. Yes, she had been young and foolish, and she'd hurt so bad that night, she'd wanted to hate him, but those had only been excuses.

Truth was, she'd been so insecure, had felt so unloved, that she'd just wanted someone, anyone, to hold her, to tell her that she was lovable. Was wanted.

For years, she'd blamed that on her mother. On how that once she'd married Richard, no one else had mattered. She'd forgotten she had a daughter.

Jenny sucked in air, remembering how hard she'd sought for her mother's attention.

"I'm thinking that we should plan on being in New York City for two nights," Connor said.

Letting the memories go, she asked, "Why?"

"We'll drive down Monday, but even leaving early in the morning, it will still be too late to meet with Senator Hughes. We'll do that Tuesday, and then drive back home on Wednesday. Will that work for you?"

"Yes, but I don't understand why we're going to New York City. Albany is the capital of New York. That's where the capitol building is. That's where we've always sent out letters to before."

"Because of Governor Smith. Since he took office, he's been pushing to have the capital changed to New York City. He's turned the Waldorf Astoria into his own private capitol building and rarely goes to Albany. Oklahoma changed their capital several years ago, and he believes it's time New York does."

She hadn't known that, and couldn't help but wonder what else she didn't know by not reading newspapers and staying so secluded over the years. "Why?"

"I can't say for sure, but am assuming it's so he can be the governor that got it done. Others have tried, but been unsuccessful in making it happen." In the next breath, he asked, "Who will take care of Emily and the others while Gretchen is delivering her flowers?"

Having already discussed everything with Gretchen and the other women after she'd returned home last night after securing a ride to Rochester with Alice, she explained, "Gretchen will stay at the house. Joyce and Meg will deliver the flowers. That's what happened today. Lora could have her baby at any time, but Meg is a couple months away from her due date. So is Tina. She'll go with us to New York, and so will Rachel, along with baby Annie. Lora, Meg, and Joyce will write letters for us to deliver to the senator, and Gretchen will contact some of the girls from the past that keep in contact with us to write letters, as well."

"Did you have a chance to review the list of regulations in the envelope I'd given you?"

He probably thought she'd burned it. She hadn't. "Yes. Gretchen reviewed them, too, and we made a few changes…"

They discussed the changes, the trip and the overall plan, for the length of the journey home. It helped keep her focused, but at the same time, it scared her to think of being with him for three full days. Tina and Rachel, as well as Annie, would be with them the entire time, so that would help.

Hopefully.

Because the last thing she needed was to fall completely in love with him again. After today, that could happen.

Easily.

Too easily, and the following morning didn't help ease her fears of that.

Lora's water had broken in the middle of the night, and she still hadn't delivered the baby when Gretchen entered the room.

"I'm sorry, Jenny, but I was so busy getting the truck loaded and the girls out of here, that time got away from me and Emily missed the school bus."

Jenny's heart sank. She'd wanted the time she was gone to be as normal as possible for Emily, but this morning had been overly chaotic. "Where is she?"

"Sitting on the front steps," Gretchen said. "I told her it's just too far to walk, and that I will need her help here today, but it didn't help. She's upset. I'll take over here."

Jenny quickly filled Gretchen in on Lora's progress,

and then went downstairs. She paused in the kitchen to wash her hands and glanced at the clock. Connor was due anytime. It was truly just one of those mornings.

She walked into the living room, where her suitcase, as well as Tina's and Rachel's bags, sat on the floor. Tina was looking out the window.

"Is she still on the steps?" Jenny asked.

"Yes. Mr. McCormick just arrived."

As if her heart didn't know she was already dealing with enough this morning, it fluttered to the point she had to stop and catch her breath. By the time she moved to the door, which was open, leaving only the screen door between her and the steps, Connor had sat down on the steps next to Emily. Her stuffed bear was on her lap and her lunch box beside her.

"Now, why would the prettiest little girl I know be sitting here looking so glum on this fine morning?" Jenny heard him ask Emily.

"Because I'm sad," Emily said.

"Is there anything I could do to make you not be sad?" he asked.

Emily shook her head.

He rested a hand on Emily's back. "How do you know? Maybe if you told me why you are so sad, there might be something I could do."

Emily looked up at him. "I missed the bus, and Gretchen says it's too far to walk and that there's not another way for me to get to school."

Jenny pressed a hand over her mouth, but couldn't bring herself to push open the door yet.

"Missed the bus," he said. "That would make me sad, too."

Emily nodded. "Lora's having her baby and Meg and

Joyce already left in the flower truck. Mrs. Whipple said we could practice using your phones again today. I really wanted to dial that black one again. The one that has the pretty gold numbers on it."

"Well," Connor said. "I have my car—if your mommy says it's all right, I could give you a ride to school."

Emily leaped to her feet. "You could?"

Connor nodded. "Yes, I could."

"Oh, thank you!" Emily threw her arms around Connor's neck.

Connor hugged her back, while saying, "We have to ask your mom first."

Jenny pushed open the door and stepped onto the porch. "Her mom says, yes."

Emily squealed. "She said yes, Mr. McCormick!"

"I hear that." He stood. "Busy morning?"

"Yes, it has been." For the briefest of moments, she wanted to lean against him.

He rubbed her upper arm. "What time does school start?"

"In about twenty minutes," she answered.

"Then we have plenty of time." He winked at Emily. "We could even stop at the diner and get a cookie to stick in your lunch box."

Emily looked at her. "Could we, Mommy?"

"Yes." She knelt down. "How about one more goodbye hug first?"

Jenny hugged Emily as tightly as she had this morning, when they'd said goodbye before she sent Emily outside to wait for Gretchen to walk her out to the road.

"I'll be extra good while you're gone, Mommy, just like I promised."

"I know you will, honey." Jenny released her. "Now

get your bear and your lunch box." She stood and looked at Connor. "Thank you."

"You're welcome." He glanced at the house and gave her arm a gentle squeeze. "We have all day to get to the city, so can leave after you have everything settled here."

Her throat felt too thick to speak, but she managed a nod.

He then scooped Emily up in his arms. "Come on, Jenny Jr., let's get you a cookie and off to school."

Emily giggled. "My name isn't Jenny Jr.! It's Emily!"

"That's right, it's Emily," he said while carrying her down the steps. "So the black phone is your favorite, is it?"

"Yes! The one with the pretty gold numbers."

Jenny stood on the porch, waved and watched, until Connor's car disappeared around the curve of the driveway, and for a short time afterward. This time, rather than try to ignore the warmth filling her chest, she let it spread. Fill her completely.

Chapter Fourteen

As it had been doing all day, Jenny's heart fluttered as she walked into the hotel room. She'd never seen anything so posh and luxurious. From the red-and-pink floral carpets, to the velvet-flocked wallpaper, carved woodwork on the upholstered furnishings and the gold stitching in the brocade draperies, the entire space was breathtaking.

"The girls are next door," Connor said. "And my room is across the hall."

Jenny clutched the handles of her purse. "We didn't need anything this grand or big."

"There's no sense staying somewhere else. This is where we'll meet Senator Hughes. Senate meetings have been held at the Waldorf Astoria for years and years," he said. "This is where they held hearings after the sinking of the *Titanic*. People don't question why state business takes place here, partially because many in the city agree New York City should be the capital of the state. Actually, this building will be torn down in a couple of years, they've already broken ground on a new site for the hotel, leaving this location open for the capitol building to be built."

She nodded while staring at her suitcase that sat on the foot of the bed, ready to be opened. Two bellhops, dressed in a gold-and-red uniform, had met them in the parking lot and carried up all of their luggage. Tina and Rachel, carrying Annie, had followed the bellhops while she'd waited for Connor as he'd handed his car keys to another uniformed man and then spoke with another man at the front door who had known him by name.

"I didn't bring enough money, Connor, not for all of this. I'd assumed we'd stay somewhere else."

He shook his head. "We already discussed that topic this morning. I'm paying for the trip, including the rooms and meals." He crossed the room to the ornate door. "I'll collect you in half an hour. We'll have something to eat, and then you can get some sleep."

"But you've already done so much, including taking Emily to school this morning."

"Another subject we already discussed." He stepped into the hallway. "I'll check on Rachel and Tina and be back in half an hour."

The door shut before she could say more. Not surprising. Her mind was as hopeless as her heart. Neither had been working correctly all day. He'd been kind and generous to Tina and Rachel while driving today, stopping so they could get out and stretch their legs, use powder rooms and take care of anything else that came about, especially with Annie.

He'd never once appeared irritated or short-tempered when Annie had a fussy time, and had stopped the car and gotten out when Rachel had needed to nurse the baby so she had more privacy, and they had talked about

Emily. Including how he'd asked Mrs. Whipple to send the telephone that Emily was so enamored with home with her so it would keep her mind off them being gone.

Jenny plopped down on the bed and began removing her white gloves one finger at a time. That wasn't all. When he'd returned to pick them up this morning, he'd also opened his trunk and given Gretchen several stuffed animals for Emily. The others in her bear book. He'd charmingly asked Gretchen to give them to Emily one at a time, so she'd continue to have new things to keep her busy the next couple of days.

All in all, everything Connor did made her fall deeper and deeper in love with him. That's what was happening. She recognized the same feelings she'd had years ago for him. They'd never truly gone away, and his own way, he'd cultivated them until they were now blossoming like flowers in spring.

She wasn't prepared for that to happen.

It would have too many consequences.

She stood and walked into the private powder room, removed her hat, combed her hair and left it hanging loose while using one of the soft washcloths to wash her face and then reapply her lipstick.

A knock sounded on the door as she was about to pin her hair up again. Thirty minutes couldn't have gone past yet. After leaving the bathroom, she crossed the room and pulled open the door.

"Can you believe this place?" Rachel asked. "I've never seen anything so gorgeous." She hooked her blond hair behind one ear while looking down at the cherub face of her daughter sleeping in her arms. "I'm just sorry that Annie isn't old enough to remember this."

"It is a beautiful hotel," Jenny agreed, holding the

door wide as Rachel, carrying Annie and closely followed by Tina, entered the room.

"Our room has two beds and a crib," Tina said. "And the pillows are so soft. Have you tried one yet?"

The excitement on both of their faces was enchanting. "No, I haven't," Jenny replied. "Are you ready to go down to the dining room?"

The two looked at each other.

"What is it?" Jenny asked, growing concerned.

"We wanted to ask if it would be all right if we tried the room service. Calling downstairs and having food sent to the room sounds so air tight," Tina said. "I'll probably never, ever, get the chance to try it again."

"And Annie could wake up downstairs and start to fuss, and—"

Jenny laughed. "Yes. Yes, you can try the room service. It does sound absolutely wonderful." She'd find a way to repay Connor the cost, for he truly had done enough already.

Tina clapped her hands. She had blossomed the past week, no longer looked thin and pale. Even her long brown hair had gained a shine. "Thank you so much. You can join us if you want to."

"No, I wouldn't want Connor to eat alone, but you two order whatever you want, and enjoy it."

"Thank you, Jenny." Rachel placed a kiss on Annie's forehead. "For bringing us here, I truly hope we can change things for other girls."

"We will," Jenny said. "I'm sure of it."

They spent a few moments discussing the meeting with the senator that would happen tomorrow, including the number of letters that Gretchen had spent most of Sunday driving around collecting that had been obtained by other women. She not only had hope; she had a solid belief that this time, something would be done. Connor was the reason.

The girls returned to their room, and she'd just replaced the navy-blue pill hat that matched her white-and-blue dress when a knock sounded on her door again. Pressing a hand to her chest, where her heart was once again beating faster than normal, she walked to the door. As much as she shouldn't be, she was looking forward to being alone with Connor.

Even though she'd sat next to him for hours in the car, her stomach fluttered at the sight of him when she pulled open the door. He'd added a red tie around the neck of the cloud-white shirt beneath the black-and-white-pin-striped suit he'd worn all day. The front buttons of the jacket were undone, revealing the black silk vest that she'd admired.

He was so downright handsome in every way, all the time.

"Ready?" he asked.

"Yes." She stepped into the hallway, and trying not to focus on how much she enjoyed the feeling of his hand on her back whenever he walked beside her, she said, "The girls wanted to try room service."

"They seemed very intrigued with it," he said.

"When did they mention it to you?"

"When I checked to see if they were happy with their room. I wanted to make sure the crib I'd requested had been put in there."

"You requested the crib?"

"Yes, Annie needed a place to sleep. I requested it when I reserved the rooms yesterday."

There truly was no end to his thoughtfulness.

"Would you rather try room service instead of eating in the dining room? We can if you prefer."

She coughed against the way her heart leaped into her throat. "No." The word burned as it came out. She wasn't made of stone and eating alone with him in a hotel room could very well prove that. Her lips had been tingling all day, remembering kissing him and wanting to do it again, and every time he'd looked at her, even just a casual glance, her insides melted. Having his arms wrapped around her was the most wonderful feeling in the world.

The elevator ride, being confined with him in the small, caged space, had her heart in her throat again, and she had to lock her knees to keep from leaning against him. There was a three-way debate going on inside her. Every ounce of her body wanted to touch his, be touched by him, proclaiming he was what made her feel alive. Her heart thudded wildly, proclaiming a love it had only ever felt toward him, and her mind was busy trying to convince her heart and body that what they wanted could never be.

But it was losing.

His hand remained on the center of her back, sending swirls of warmth throughout her system as they exited the elevator and traversed to the dining room. The absence of his touch when she sat down made her sigh at the loss. It was as if his touch represented what she wanted for the rest of her life.

She knew that was impossible. If Connor ever discovered who Emily's father was, he'd hate both of them. But even that didn't stop the yearning. It simply made her body and heart fight harder against her mind.

He talked about the meeting tomorrow as they ate.

She answered his questions and asked her own, despite the emotions playing havoc inside her to the point it was difficult to breathe. He'd only been back in her life a few weeks, and had turned everything topsy-turvy. She wanted things to change for the girls, for the home to be held accountable for their actions and behaviors. It was the things inside her that were disconcerting.

"Shall we take a walk?" he asked as their empty plates were removed from the table. "After driving all day, it'll feel good."

Jenny agreed, hoping the fresh air would clear her mind, perhaps even allow some common sense to return.

They exited the massive hotel through the ornate front doors beneath the decorative canvas awning stretched along the front of the building that reached high into the sky. Though night had fallen, there were so many streetlights, building lights and headlights on the vehicles driving along the wide road, that it was nearly as bright as day.

"We'll walk this way for a few blocks," Connor said, his hand again on her back.

The hotel was built on the corner of the block, its massive front doors facing the crossroads of two roads that allowed for four lanes of traffic, beside parking along the curbs that separated the streets from the wide sidewalk. There were other people on the sidewalks, couples, groups of people and those walking alone. Connor's hand slid across her back and hooked her side, keeping her closer to him as they strolled along.

It had been years since she'd been in a city at night— other than Albany the night he'd taken her—and she'd forgotten that there were other night sounds than the ones she'd grown used to. Here the chirping of crickets and leaves rustling in the wind had been replaced with people conversing, horns honking, tires crunching, motors rumbling and even a far-off siren of a police car.

"Don't worry, you're safe," Connor said.

"I'm not worried. I was just listening. It's been a long time since I heard the sound of a city at night."

"Do you miss it?"

"I'm not sure," she admitted. There was a theatre across the street, with a line of women wearing fancy hats and evening gowns and men hosting top hats and tails on their suit coats. Since Emily had started school, the idea of her daughter attending a larger school, where she would have more friends, more opportunities within the school and the community, had been in the back of Jenny's mind, but there would be consequences for that to happen. "I like Twin Pines."

Connor graced her with one of his signature teasing grins. "There are good, home-grown people there."

"Yes, there are," she agreed.

"Emily certainly enjoys her school." He gestured to a bench affixed to the sidewalk for people to wait for one of the many city buses. "Shall we sit down?"

She agreed and once seated, said, "Emily does enjoy her school there, but I do worry about when she gets older. I'll have to transport her back and forth to Syracuse every day."

"Is your plan to continue to live with Gretchen?"

A tiny shiver rippled over her. "Of course, why wouldn't it be?"

He shrugged. "You are such a phenomenal midwife, I assumed you'd want to continue."

"I will. Why wouldn't I?"

"There's no reason not to, it's just that once the laws

are changed, young women won't need to run away from the home."

The truth of that rattled her insides. She hadn't thought that far ahead. Gretchen would still need help with the flowers, but she loved delivering babies, and there weren't so many delivered around Twin Pines that Alice would need her help.

"Can I ask you a personal question?" Connor asked.

"Yes," she answered, knowing her answer would depend on the question.

"Has Emily ever met her father?"

"No." That was the easiest question she'd ever had to answer, until another thought collided inside her jumbling head. "Did she say something this morning?"

He shifted, faced her and laid an arm along the back of the bench. "She asked me where my house was, and if any children lived there."

That didn't surprise her, but it should have been something she'd considered when allowing him to give Emily a ride to school this morning.

"And that she wished she had a father like the other children at her school," he added.

Jenny fretted, wondering exactly how she should respond. He wouldn't accept vague answers as easily as Emily. He'd told her the truth about going to New York, and it was time she told him the truth. Even the parts she'd just discovered herself. "What happened between Emily's father and I was a foolish, one-time, act of revenge. I've never seen him since that night." Lifting her gaze to meet his, she knew it was time to admit things she'd never wanted to acknowledge. "The other day, when you said that children want attention. That was me. When my father died, it became just me and my mother.

I had her full attention. That changed when she married Richard, and I hated that. Hated him. I was very rude to him, and when my mother would talk to me about it, I was rude to her. I was invited to travel with them, and refused, challenged my mother to choose between him and me every time they went out of town."

The truth of just how obstinate she'd been to her mother and Richard was hitting hard inside her. Because it was the truth. One she'd never dared face.

"Losing their father and gaining another one would have been hard on any child," he said. "Your mother should have understood that."

Jenny opened her mouth to respond, but closed it again because her mother had tried to talk to her about it, but she'd refused to listen. Many times. Even the night she'd dropped her off at the home in Albany. Her mother had said she was sorry that night, about how far apart they'd grown. How there wasn't anything more that she could do, and that Jenny had finally gotten her wish.

Jenny's insides quivered at the memory, because she had told her mother that she couldn't wait to leave Richard's house for good.

There were other things she had to face, too. "I was very insecure, very immature, when we knew each other. If you had told me about going to New York before you had, I would have begged you not to go. Challenged you just like I had my mother, because with you, I'd had what I'd wanted again. Full attention, and I was in my glory. Every girl wanted to be me." She closed her eyes at the pain encircling her heart. "I was too immature to understand how wrong, how selfish, I'd behaved."

"We were both young and immature, and have learned a lot since then." Connor touched the side of her face.

"My feelings for you were…" He shook his head. "Still are more than anything I've ever felt for anyone. I wasn't ready for that back then, Jenny, and I'm not expecting you to feel the same way, but I would like a chance for us to explore our feelings for one another."

His fingertip caressed the nape of her neck, quickening her pulse, and making her toes curl inside her shoes, yet she shook her head. "It's not that simple, Connor."

Connor had wrestled with several things since finding Jenny again, and he'd come to several conclusions. The most specific one while giving Emily a kiss on her forehead when leaving her at the school this morning. "It is for me," he said. "I'm done looking back. I want to look forward, and I'm hoping the future could include you and Emily."

In the weeks since he'd pulled into her driveway to sell a phone line, he'd been jealous, angry and curious about who Emily's father was, but now, he didn't care. He just wanted to be her father going forward, and Jenny's husband. If she wasn't ready for that, he'd wait. Because someday she would be. "I won't push you, won't force anything on you, or Emily—I'll just be here, waiting to see if your old feelings for me can come back."

She pressed three fingers to her lips and closed her eyes. "Those old feelings have never gone away, Connor. Even when I tried to make them."

He didn't know what a heart attack felt like, but something struck his right then, filled it so full it was about to explode. Running a finger along the side of her face, he asked, "Do you have any idea how badly I want to kiss you right now?"

With the tiniest of giggles, she leaned closer, lining

up their lips as she whispered, "Is it as badly as I want you to kiss me?"

His hand slipped around the back of her neck, holding her face right where it was as his lips touched hers, softly at first, then more firmly.

She returned his kiss, until the honking of a horn made her pull back. "We are sitting on a street corner."

"I know," he answered. What he wanted to do was haul her up to his hotel room and shut the door, close out the rest of the world for a good long time. That couldn't happen tonight, but hope filled him that it could happen someday soon. "I also know it's time for you to get some sleep, so you'll be ready for the meeting tomorrow." She'd been up half the night delivering a baby, and though she'd closed her eyes during the drive to the city, she hadn't slept.

Chapter Fifteen

This was the reason they were in New York, for the girls to share their stories with Senator Hughes, and Connor was proud of how proficiently Rachel and Tina talked about the plights they'd faced. It was emotional for both of them, but their strength shone through.

So did Jenny's. He was particularly proud of her. In so many ways he'd lost count. He'd also lost count of all the things he loved about her while lying in his bed last night, imagining the time when he wouldn't be alone in his bed. He'd love her and Emily until the end of time. Nothing would ever change that.

"I want to thank you for coming to see me," Brent Hughes said, nodding at Rachel and Tina.

They were all sitting around a small, round table in one of the many conference rooms at the hotel, and the senator, a man in his early fifties or so with salt-and-pepper hair and black horned glasses, had been taking copious notes while each of the girls, and Jenny, had spoken. She'd shared that she'd been at the home years ago, but had emphasized what was happening now, girls being hunted down by dogs and locked up like prisoners.

"This is a very serious matter, one that does need attention, immediate attention. I assure you that I have put this on the top of my list of things that need to be addressed before the end of the congressional session." The senator piled the stack of letters he'd been given atop his notepad. "I will read each and every one of these letters and I will encourage my colleagues to do the same. If I discover I need anything in writing from the three of you, I will contact Mr. McCormick."

Connor nodded and stood, understanding the meeting was over. He held Jenny's chair as she stood, and then followed suit for Tina, and Rachel, who was holding Annie. The baby had slept peacefully through the entire hearing.

They each thanked the senator, and shook his hand, before Connor guided the women toward the door.

"Mr. McCormick, I'd like a word with you, please," Brent Hughes said, standing at the table.

Connor gave a nod, and then asked Tina and Rachel, "Can you find your way back to your room?"

"Yes," Tina answered.

Keeping his hand on Jenny's back, he said, "Jenny and I will meet you there shortly."

She looked at him.

He smiled. This was her fight, he was merely an avenue for her, whatever the senator had to say, she could hear.

He opened the door for Tina and Rachel to exit, then closed it and escorted Jenny back to the table.

Senator Hughes didn't say anything, but his eyes held a question.

Connor granted the man a smile and waited for him to speak.

With a nod, the senator said, "I'm sure you are aware that my phone has rung nonstop, both at the office and at home, the past few days."

"Is that a problem?" Connor asked. His mother and George had both followed through on their promises. So had his uncles and other family members. On Sunday, he'd paid a visit to one of his uncles. Mick's wedding had made him realize just how rarely he saw his extended family. He'd spent a lot of time on the road, selling phone lines the past few years, and had shown up when needed, usually with a girl on his arm so everyone would think he was doing fine, going on with life, but he hadn't been. He hadn't been fine and he hadn't been getting on with life. Finding Jenny made him want to change all that. He'd not only told his uncle about Jenny's crusade, and had asked him to contact Senator Hughes, he'd asked what he could do to become part of the family business again.

Turned out, there was a seat waiting for him on the board. After his father had died, Mick had worked with his uncles to implement a restructuring of the business, including seats for both of them on the board. Connor hadn't been interested then. Now, he was ready to put all the pieces of his life back in place and really live again. This time there would be no lying to himself that he loved his life, either. He was going to truly love it.

"No, that's not a problem," the senator said. "I always enjoy hearing from constituents. I was happy to engage in each and every phone call and will continue to." He glanced briefly at Jenny.

Connor held his gaze on the senator and his hand on Jenny's back. "Then what is the problem?"

"I'm not saying there is a problem, per se. The issue

you've brought me has been brought up before and it definitely needs to be addressed. This time, because of your due diligence, I'm convinced I have enough support from colleagues on both sides for a bill to pass the senate and the house." Hughes paused, briefly, before asking, "I'm curious to know if you and your family know that Governor Smith is about to throw his hat into the ring to become the democratic choice for president in next year's race?"

Not a fan of the governor, Connor asked, "What makes him believe he'll win this time?"

"He's wet," the senator replied. "He's never hidden the fact that he's against prohibition, and he believes it's time for it to end."

"I know a lot of wet people," Connor replied. "They've been against prohibition since its conception." He knew a lot of politicians, too, and hated the way they talked in circles and flipped sides to suit their own agendas.

"That's true, but the Midwest is dry. They still believe in prohibition. The only thing Governor Smith has in common with the Bible Belt is his devotion to the church."

Connor began to see the light of where the senator was going. "And a large number of homes for unwed mothers are run by religious organizations."

Senator Hughes sighed as he nodded. "The governor may not sign off on legislation that opposes the actions of any religious group."

Understanding the full impact of that, Connor shook his head. "That would mean two years would go by before anything could be done."

"I will push it through as far and fast as I can, so will my colleagues." With a shrug, the senator continued,

"There is a party tonight, here at the hotel, in the governor's honor. He's going to announce his bid to seek the nomination, and request support."

"Invitation only?"

Hughes pulled an envelope out of his pocket and held it out. "Yes."

Connor took the envelope. "We'll be there."

Jenny didn't say a word until they were in the hallway, then bleakly, she asked, "This has all been for naught, hasn't it? The governor will never sign the bill into law."

He held up the envelope. "It's not over yet."

"What will an invitation to a party do for us?" she asked as they walked toward the elevator.

"A chance to talk to the governor."

"At his own party?"

"Yes, that's how politics works, and might be our only chance." They stopped to wait for the elevator to open. "It's up to you."

She let out a sigh, and then shrugged as she stepped into the elevator. "We didn't come this far to give up now, did we?"

"No, we didn't." He followed her in. "We will go check on Rachel and Tina and then go shopping."

"Shopping? What for?"

"An evening gown, unless you brought one with you?"

"No, I don't even own an evening gown."

Hours later, in her hotel room, Jenny stared at herself in the mirror in complete disbelief. She'd chosen the cream-colored gown because the others had been so colorful, so bright and bold, there would be no way to blend in with the crowd wearing one of them.

Swallowing the lump in her throat, she closed her

eyes, blocking her reflection. There would be no way of blending in wearing this one, either. The flowing, chiffon underdress was simple, with a boat neck and full skirt; it was the overdress, and how it fit that made her insides quiver. Sequined with mock, glittering diamonds in flower burst shapes, the overdress fit her as tight as the matching elbow-length gloves fit over her hands and arms.

The overdress stopped just above her knees and hugged her breasts, her waist, her hips. Opening her eyes, she twisted and peered into the mirror. Dear Lord, yes. It hugged her hind end, too.

"You look like a movie star," Tina said.

"Doesn't she?" Rachel asked, while adding a headband to Jenny's outfit and positioning the single white feather to stand up perfectly.

"I think this dress is too tight," Jenny said. "It hadn't seemed so tight at the store." Probably because she'd just slipped it on and then back off, knowing Connor was waiting on her. He would have waited longer, and not complained, she was sure of that, she just... Oh, for heaven's sake. She hadn't wanted to be away from him any longer than necessary. Because of the kiss they'd shared in the car before going into the store.

It had left her wanting more, just as much as the one they'd shared in the hallway outside her room last night.

They had agreed on their walk back to the hotel to take it slow, really get to know each other this time, with no pressure or expectations.

Then, she'd dreamed about him, and her, and Emily, becoming a family. It had been so real, so right, that she'd awakened this morning with optimism. Genuine optimism that Connor was right. It was time to put the past behind them and focus on the future. They'd talked about that again today. She'd even had a fleeting idea about taking a midwife job with George—if the bill passed and she was no longer needed at Gretchen's.

There were a lot of ifs, but there was a lot of hope inside her, too.

"Applesauce! It's not too tight," Tina said, handing her a glove. "That's how it's supposed to fit. Show off your lovely figure."

"I don't want to show off my figure." Jenny twisted, looked at how it emphasized her shape again. It was… risqué!

"Mr. McCormick is going to like it," Rachel said.

"And how!" Tina expressed her agreement.

Jenny pressed a hand to her chest at the skipping of her heart. She'd tried her hardest to not let anyone notice her growing feelings for Connor, and thought she had done an excellent job of not letting the girls think there was anything between him and her.

"It doesn't matter if he likes it or not," she said, pretending to make sure the pins in her hair were secure.

"Banana oil!" Tina said. "The two of you are crushing. It's written all over your faces."

"No, it's not," Jenny argued, pulling on one long glove.

"And I'm not pregnant," Tina said.

Jenny felt her shoulders droop and looked at Rachel. "Is it that evident?"

Rachel grinned and nodded. "It has been since the day Annie was born."

The second glove fell from her fingers. "No."

"Yes," Rachel said.

"We are all rooting for you," Tina said while hook-ing a short strand of tiny mock diamonds around Jenny's neck.

A bellhop had delivered the necklace to the room a few moments ago. Said Connor had asked to have it delivered to her.

Jenny leaned closer to the mirror, looking at how the stones sparkled and reflected miniature rainbows when she turned her neck this way and that. Especially the three larger stones in the center of the necklace. Those on her gown didn't have the same brilliance. The same warmth. "Rooting for what?" she asked, leaning back.

From behind her shoulder, Tina smiled in the mirror. "You and Mr. McCormick. Being married to him will be like a fairytale come true."

That it would be, but she wasn't going to put the cart before the horse. She was going to take things slow. Just like they'd said.

A knock sounded on the door.

"He's here!" Tina announced, giggling with glee.

Jenny felt gleeful, too, and suddenly hoped that Connor did like the dress as she quickly pulled on the second glove.

While Rachel collected the sleeping Annie off the bed, Tina opened the door, and then both girls, still giggling, bid good-night and left the room.

Without saying a word, Connor walked in, and using one foot, closed the door behind him. He looked magnificent in his black tuxedo, but it was his face, his eyes, that held her attention as he continued to cross the room, never looking anywhere but at her.

Jenny had to remind herself to breathe.

He stopped within inches from her, and she pressed

her heels hard against the floor to keep from toppling forward, into him.

"They sounded happy," he said, eyes still locked with hers.

It was a moment before his words filtered through the pounding of her pulse echoing in her ears. "They are."

"The question is, are you?"

As if she had no choice in the matter, a smile instantly pulled her lips wide. "Yes."

He slid one hand behind her neck and brought his face closer. "That's my girl."

His girl. He'd used to call her that, and she'd loved it. They were both different people now, had learned from their mistakes, but he was still the man of her dreams.

When his lips met hers, she wound her arms around his waist and kissed him, letting him know that she was no longer immature, insecure. She was a grown woman now, and was committed to making things work this time.

So much for taking it slow.

By the time the kiss ended, she wondered if she had sprouted wings, because she certainly had her head in the clouds. Her entire body was floating somewhere so spectacular she might never touch ground again.

"Let me get a good look at you," he said, taking her hand. "I see you got the necklace I bought for you."

She touched the mock diamonds around her neck. "I did, thank you."

"And the dress..." He let out a low whistle.

She stepped back, and then still feeling weightless, and overly happy, she performed a perfect pirouette, giving him a glimpse of how the dress hugged her form.

His eyes were twinkling as brightly as the necklace had in the mirror when she faced him again.

"Do that again," he said. "But slower."

Laughing, she twirled around again, slowly, twisting her neck one way and then the other to be able to watch him the entire time.

"I have never seen anything more beautiful in my life," he said.

A hint of insecurity formed. "You don't think it's too tight?"

"Tight?"

She ran her hands down her sides. "Yes. The over-dress, does it look too tight?"

"Can you breathe?"

"Of course I can breathe."

"Then it's not too tight." He stepped closer. "In fact, I've never seen a dress fit more perfectly."

He kissed her again, and Jenny wished they didn't have to leave the room. But they did, because she really had to get things settled for the girls before she could move on with her own life.

They left the room a short time later, with Connor explaining that there would be food at the party, but he'd made them reservations in the restaurant instead. Jenny was fine with that, and fine with sitting next to him in the corner booth table rather than across from him.

He asked her to tell him all about Emily, from her middle name to her favorite activities, and so many things in between that Jenny didn't know some of the answers. Like if Emily liked cats or dogs better, or if she could live anywhere, where that would be, or what made her laugh the most.

"I truly don't know," she said, laughing at how he

pressed for an answer. "She laughs a lot, about a lot of things."

"Because you are a wonderful mother, and make life fun for her," he said, kissing her cheek.

The touch of his lips made her sigh, wishing she could turn her head so their lips could meet. She could do that, but couldn't because they were in the restaurant, with others nearby. Someday, that wouldn't matter, and that was a day she was hoping would come soon. Very soon. "I just want her to be happy," she said.

"If you're happy, she'll be happy," he said.

Melancholy struck like a bell ringing. "It wasn't that way for my mother," she said. "I was a real brat. It's embarrassing to admit that." For years she'd blamed it all on her mother and Richard, until Connor had said that children want attention and he'd sought it with his phones and by being funny and happy-go-lucky. Then she'd questioned herself, and how she'd behaved. It hadn't been flattering to remember.

"You couldn't have been that bad."

"Yes, I was." She'd acted the same way toward him when she'd thought he'd lied to her.

He kissed her cheek. "That had to have been before I met you."

"No, it wasn't." She would have to tell him the truth. The entire truth. It was the only way they could go forward and forget the past.

He touched the side of her face. "Whether you believe you were a brat or not, your parents shouldn't have abandoned you. I know you'd never do that to Emily."

She wouldn't. Emily could never do anything that would make her abandon her daughter. There was shared fault in her past. She had misbehaved, but as a parent, so had her mother.

Looking at Connor, she nodded. "Once again, you're right."

He chuckled and laid his napkin on the table. They'd finished their meal, as well as a cup of coffee. "It's time for us to attend that party."

Jenny drew in a deep breath for fortification—both for the next hour, and to make a silent vow that she'd tell him about Donald being Emily's father when they got home.

That done, she asked, "Do you think the governor will even talk to us? About the changes we're trying to make?"

He touched the tip of her nose and then stood. "There's only one way to find out."

She took a hold of his proffered hand, and then wrapped her arm around his as they walked out of the restaurant.

The party was in the biggest, most grand banquet room she'd ever seen. Sparkling with light, crystal chandeliers hung from a dark-red-painted ceiling. The walls were painted dark red, too, with gold-and-white ornately carved moldings. Thick red-and-gold carpet covered the floor, and there had to have been at least two hundred people, walking, standing or sitting on the chairs surrounding the many tables filling the room.

Jenny wrapped her arm tighter around Connor's elbow. She wondered if this was how Cinderella had felt walking into the ball.

Connor looked at her and winked.

Jenny grinned. She may not be Cinderella, but he most certainly was Prince Charming.

"Connor McCormick! What on earth are you doing here?"

Something about the woman's voice spiked Jenny's attention, gave her heart an odd hitch. Connor looked at her with a grin that took up his entire face, before he turned to the blonde woman in an elegant blue gown walking toward them. "Hello. Is Wilbur here?"

"Of course." The woman rolled her eyes. "It's the governor's party. Heaven forbid we'd ever miss one of those."

"You remember..." Connor paused and looked down at her again.

Confused for a flash of a moment, Jenny looked harder at the woman.

Recognition hit both of them at the same time. Marjorie didn't squeal like Franny had, but her hug was just as tight.

So was Jenny's.

Marjorie broke the hug first, and took a moment to slap Connor's arm. "I always knew you'd squirreled her away somewhere, just to get her away from her mother and evil stepfather."

Jenny shook her head, but Connor laughed.

"If only, Marjorie, if only." He nodded toward an empty table near the arched doorway they'd just walked through. "Why don't you two sit down? I'll get us something to drink."

Jenny grabbed his arm. "Did you know—"

"No, I didn't know she'd be here." He gave her a wink. "I'll be right back."

Visiting with Marjorie was like it had been with Franny; the years instantly disappeared. However, they didn't talk about other people they knew, instead, Marjorie told her about living in New York, and how she and

Wilbur had adopted two children, because try as they might, she just couldn't get pregnant.

"Your turn," Marjorie said. "Where did Connor whisk you off to?"

"He didn't," Jenny said. "My mother did." She was thinking about Marjorie's saying they'd adopted two children. A boy who was now five, and a girl who was three, but they'd been babies when they'd been adopted—from a home for unwed mothers.

Marjorie stared for a moment and then sighed. "She really did?"

Jenny nodded, not wanting to go into the entire story. Marjorie might not understand, having adopted two children from a place similar to one that Jenny was attempting to change.

"I'm sorry about that comment I made earlier. About your mother and stepfather." Marjorie glanced to where Connor stood, talking to Wilbur Cook, Marjorie's husband.

He had returned with drinks, and with Wilbur, and after making the introductions, had walked Wilbur a distance away, giving her and Marjorie privacy to visit. Just one more reason she'd fallen in love with him all over again.

With her voice lowered, Marjorie continued, "It's just that she was so, well, indifferent about you being gone and when I questioned more, she was downright rude. So was her husband. They said they'd call the police if I came back, asking about you one more time. But that didn't stop me from continuing to look for you."

Jenny opened her mouth to apologize, but Marjorie gasped, with her eyes on Jenny's neck.

"That necklace!" Marjorie said.

Jenny's heart softened and she touched the necklace. "Connor bought it for me."

"Ducky! I saw it in the window at Tiffany's two days ago and knew Wilbur would never lay out that many clams for something that only glitters." Laughing, she added, "It has to be tuned and play music for him to break open the safe."

"Tiffany's?" Jenny asked, her hand starting to tremble. They weren't mock diamonds; they were real. Even she knew Tiffany & Co. was the most expensive jeweler in New York, if not all of America. They didn't sell mock anything.

"Yes, Tiffany's." Marjorie's gaze then went over Jenny's shoulders. "Oh, jeepers-creepers, here comes the flat tire himself. Our big egg, the governor." She exaggerated a moan. "At least he doesn't have his little male gold-digger with him. That's one man I wish would fall off the face of the earth." Whispering lower, she added, "He hasn't changed since high school."

"Who?" Jenny asked, seeing Connor stepping away from the wall.

"Donald Forsythe," Marjorie whispered. "He's as obnoxious as ever. And get this. He's married to the governor's niece. Poor woman."

Jenny's entire body had turned to ice.

Chapter Sixteen

While listening to Wilbur talk about how musical his five-year-old son was, Connor slowly made his way toward the table where Jenny and Marjorie sat. The governor was making a beeline toward him, most likely due to the senator walking beside the governor. Hughes must have pointed him out, and was on his way to make introductions.

That would be fine. The sooner they presented their case to the governor and their hope that he would support the senator's bill, the quicker he and Jenny could leave. Although, that might be difficult. He hadn't known that Marjorie and Wilbur would be here tonight, but was happy that Jenny had been reunited with yet another friend.

She'd gone through some very hard times, and he was anxious to show her that she no longer needed to live in hiding. That's what she'd been doing.

He knew because that's what he'd been doing too, just a different kind of hiding. He'd hidden in plain sight; she'd hidden at Gretchen's, delivering babies for other girls in hiding.

All because neither of them had wanted to put the past behind them and move on.

"Mr. McCormick," Governor Smith said, not caring that Wilbur was still talking. "I've been wanting to personally meet members of your family. I know they've followed my years in office and I'd like the opportunity to make you all aware of the changes I foresee in the future."

The man was between him and the table that Jenny sat at, and short of shouldering past him, Connor had no choice but to stop and shake his hand. "Hello," he said. "I can't speak for my entire family. I can only speak for myself, and relay information as a sitting member of the board on the business." He had yet to attend his first board meeting, but didn't mind dropping that new position.

"Of course, of course." The governor laid a hand on his shoulder. "I'd met your father years ago. He was a good man. A very good man."

Tall, with wide shoulders and mouth that looked too small for his face, until he opened it, Governor Smith was blocking Connor's view of the table, of Jenny. "If you met my father, you'll know how important children were to him. To quote him, 'All men, rich or poor, married or not, are responsible for the children of their community,' and I feel the same way." His father had said that many times, but until this moment, he hadn't recalled it.

"Of course, we all do, we all do. Let's get a drink and sit down to discuss things." Governor Smith glanced around, and shouted, "Don? Don?" Shaking his head, he mumbled, "Where is that imbecile?"

Taking the opportunity to step aside and look over the governor while the man was looking around, Connor noted the empty table. Instantly troubled, he glanced around, searching the crowd.

"I'll find him," Senator Hughes said.

Connor didn't give a nickel about having a drink or talking with the governor right now. He had to find Jenny.

A hand touched his arm; he spun in that direction.

"Jenny went to the powder room," Marjorie whispered. "I told her I'd let you know. Wilbur and I are vamoosing. We'll meet up again when you're done talking to the big cheese."

"Thanks," he replied. "I'm glad you were here."

"I have questions, Connor," Marjorie said. "I need to know where she's been and why, but I'll hold them for another time. I'm just happy to know she's with you. The two of you have always belonged together."

"Aw, there he is!" the governor said. "Don, we need some drinks, right here at this table!" In a more affable tone, the governor continued, "Connor, let's sit down at this table right here. Just me and you."

Because that was the table Jenny had been sitting at, Connor agreed. Even if she didn't see him sitting there right away, he'd see her walk through the door. He hoped she didn't have any issues with that dress in the powder room. It fit her like a glove. The moment her hotel room door had opened, his jaw had nearly hit the floor. She looked cute, beautiful, no matter what she wore, but her in that dress had set his blood on fire. Flames were still licking at his veins. He couldn't wait for this to be over so they could have some alone time to pet. Neck. Flat out neck, that was what he wanted to do with Jenny.

"Bring me my usual," the governor said, "and get Mr. McCormick whatever he wants, and be quick about it."

"What will you have, Mr. McCormick?"

A familiarity in the voice made the hair on Connor's neck rise as he turned his head to look at the man standing next to the table. He'd put on weight, gotten pudgy, but as sure as he lived and breathed, it was the same Donald Forsythe as he'd known back in school.

He still parted his hair in the center, flattened it with so much oil his head looked like a wet football helmet and his brown eyes still stuck out like a frog's.

Loathing struck Connor full force, but that was quickly followed by humor at having Donald wait on him. Donald had to hate that as much as he had hauling his luggage at the train station years ago.

"I'll have an el presidente," Connor said. In part because he didn't trust Donald to not attempt to slip him some bathtub gin—rum was a much safer choice—and two, because the name provided him with a hint of humor over the entire situation. He then added, "Don," because he remembered that Donald had hated being called that.

"And don't dawdle," the governor said.

"Good help is hard to find," Connor said, just because he could.

The governor let out a huff. "He married my wife's niece. Still don't see what she sees in him, but they have three kids and he needs a job to feed them."

Putting Donald out of his mind, because he had far more important people to think about, Connor glanced at the doorway. "Speaking of children, a bill that Senator Hughes is working on concerns children. Infants and their mothers."

"Well, if Brent is working on it, it'll make its way to my desk."

"It's if it'll get signed or not that concerns me," Connor replied, with one eye still on the doorway. "And many other people I know."

"Well, Mr. McCormick, I've put in a bid to run for the White House, and from that desk I'll be able to sign bills into law all across this great nation. I'll need support of course..."

Connor's thoughts drowned out the governor's well-rehearsed speech. It shouldn't take this long just to visit the powder room. Maybe she came in through another doorway and was looking for him, lost amongst the crowd. He gave the room a fast scan, but there were too many people to see beyond those closest to the table.

"It's this bill I'm interested in right now, Governor." Connor stood. "Please excuse me, but I need to find someone."

The governor said something, but Connor was already out the door, looking for the ladies' room. There was a sign at the end of the hall, and halfway to it, he ran into Donald, carrying a tray with two drinks.

"Governor already dismissed you?" Donald asked with a sneer.

Connor made his laugh sound carefree. "Not hardly, Don."

Donald bristled.

Connor picked up the el presidente drink off the tray, swallowed it, and set the empty glass back on Donald's tray.

"Same old McCormick, has to steal the show," Donald said.

"You really need to get over that. High school was a long time ago." For whatever reason, Franny's chin music about Sarah and Stephanie came to mind. Forsythe had always thought of himself as a lady's man and bragged about his conquests. Connor had thought the jerk had been lying, but evidently not. "Didn't your father teach you anything? Like respect?"

Lifting his chin, Donald said, "I work for the governor. People have to respect me."

Connor scoffed. "I meant the other way around, Don." He shouldn't have tried. Forsythe would never change. "Did you get the governor's niece pregnant too, but had to marry this one because she's, well, you know, the governor's niece?"

Donald's neck turned red and his eyes narrowed into hate-filled slits.

Done with him, Connor stepped around him. An old nemesis wasn't worth his time. He had to find Jenny.

"Jealous, McCormick?" Don said. "Let me guess— you found out that little prop girl you liked so much wasn't so faithful after all."

Connor had told himself not to listen, but something about Donald's statement struck him like a knife between the shoulder blades. He stopped, turned to meet Donald's glare with one of his own. "What did you say?"

Donald laughed. "Jenny, wasn't that her name?"

A rage like he'd never known took over. His fists flew. One right and then a left was all it took before Forsythe was on the floor with the crème de menthe from the governor's grasshopper drink covering his white shirt and blood trickling from his nose.

Connor considered pulling Donald to his feet, just so he could knock him down again, but it wasn't worth it. Jenny would never have done that with Forsythe. Never.

Ice formed in his bloodstream.

She wouldn't have, unless Donald had forced himself on her.

Furious, torn between wringing Donald's neck and finding Jenny, Connor chose Jenny. He'd always choose her.

He ran to the sign for the ladies' room, pushed open the door and shouted, "Jenny!"

"There's no one in here by that name," a buxom older woman said, shoving the door closed.

He turned, ran to the first entrance of the banquet room. Luck, a piece of it, had him spying Marjorie. He shouldered his way to her. "Have you seen Jenny?"

"No. She still isn't back from the powder room?"

Scanning the crowd, he shook his head. "No, and she's not in there, either." Settling his gaze on Marjorie, he asked, "Did she see anyone before going to the powder room?"

"No. I saw the governor coming, made a comment about him and Donald working for him, and she said she had to go to the powder room. I told her that I'd let you know."

She had to be in her room, hiding, because of what Forsythe had done to her. He'd see that bastard pay for what he'd done. Pay.

Jenny didn't want to answer the door; Connor was sure to ask why she'd left the banquet room, and she'd have to tell him the truth. She didn't want to do that here. She wanted to wait until—Oh, dear Lord, why? Why did *he* have to work for the governor? Why was this happening now?

The knocking came again, more persistent. Knowing Connor, he'd find a key and open the door if she didn't answer it, so she crossed the room, turned the key in the lock.

As soon as the lock clicked, the door was pushed open and she was in Connor's arms. His hold was so tight she could barely breathe.

"I was so worried about you," he said.

"I'm sorry, I—"

"Why are you in the dark?" he asked.

She couldn't tell him it was because she was hiding. Just like she'd been hiding the past seven years.

He flipped on the switch, showering the room with light. The contrast from being in the dark made her eyes sting and she buried her face against his suit coat so they could adjust.

"Honey, it's not your fault," he said, tightening his arms around her again. "You don't have to keep hiding. It's not your fault."

Confused, she took a step back, even though she'd much rather have stayed in the comfort of his arms, forget Donald Forsythe ever existed. "What's not my fault?"

Compassion or empathy, or something crossed his face as he slowly shook his head. "Jenny, I know."

Fear struck, but there was no way he could know *that*. "Know what?"

"That Donald Forsythe is…"

A swooshing sound filled her ears, blocking her hearing and the room spun. She grabbed both sides of her head, but it didn't help. Her worst nightmare had arrived.

Connor's arms were once again around her, holding her upright when she would have otherwise sunk to the floor.

"It's all right, honey. It's all right."

The darkness that had threatened to overcome her slowly disappeared as Connor held her, hugged her, kissed the top of her head.

"It's all right. I'm here," he continued to say.

Her ability to think, to comprehend returned.

"We'll make him pay for forcing himself on you," Connor said. "We'll make him pay."

The anger she heard beneath the compassion in his voice frightened her. She pushed against his chest with both hands until his arms released his hold on her. "Pay for…" Shaking her head to gain clarity, she asked, "Who told you that? That he'd—"

"No one. I figured it out."

"How did you figure it out?"

He tossed his hands in the air. "Forsythe said something that made me know he was talking about you. I punched him and came up here to find you."

"You punched him?"

"Yes, I punched him. His comment was rude." He grasped her upper arms. "We'll hire a lawyer. Talk to Mick. Find a way to make him pay."

She covered her face with both hands. "No, Connor. No." Fear was pouring inside her like water filling a glass. This was bad. So bad. "You—you didn't tell him about Emily, did you?"

"No." He grasped her wrists. "He doesn't know you became pregnant?"

She still couldn't look at him, and kept her hand over her face. "No. Nobody knows, and I want to keep it that way."

He pulled her hands away from her face. "He needs to pay for what he did to you. He needs—"

"No." Tears sprang forth, hot. So hot it felt as if they scalded her face as they ran down her cheeks. This was getting out of hand. Completely. She had to stop it. Now.

There was only one way to do that. "He didn't force himself on me."

He released her wrists and took a step back, hands up like she was pointing a gun at him. "You willingly..."

The look on his face was pure shock. She almost gagged because the lump in her throat was too big to swallow around. "Yes."

"Within weeks of me leaving, you willingly..."

He stopped again, as if he couldn't say it.

She couldn't either. "I'd thought you'd lied. Thought you hadn't left town, that you'd broken up with me because you had another girlfriend. I saw the two of you at Pinion's and—"

"So it's my fault?"

"No." She had to swipe away the tears in order to clear her vision enough to see him. "It was— When Donald told me you were at Pinion's, I didn't believe him at first, but then—"

"You thought I lied, but you believed him." His hands were still in the air and he ran both of them through his hair. "Then slept with him. Got pregnant by him."

His sarcasm tore at her already crushing heart. "I was going to tell you."

"Really? When?"

"When we got home."

Skepticism filled his face.

"I was. I just—" She shook her head, swiped at the tears. "I never wanted you to find out. Never wanted him to find out. Never wanted anyone to know."

"So you hide out upstate, not caring at all about anyone who might have wondered what happened to you?"

"Yes." Why couldn't he understand? "I had to think

about Emily! I'm her mother. She's my daughter. Mine! No one else's!"

He looked at her for a long, still moment. "If by some odd chance, Emily had been my baby, would you have ever told me? Or would you just have run off and hidden? Hidden from life then, too?"

She stared at him, momentarily dumbfounded. If Emily would have been his baby, everything would have been different. Right from the start. None of this would be happening now.

"So that's your answer? Silence?"

"No." She shook her head, trying to find the right words. "I mean—"

"You really weren't the girl I thought I knew." He spun around. "I need to leave."

She wanted to run, catch up with him, beg him to stay, but he was right. She hadn't been the girl he'd thought he'd known.

The door slammed shut so hard her insides rattled.

There was nothing for her to do, except sink to the floor and curl into a ball to combat the pain overtaking her.

Chapter Seventeen

The pain was still there the next morning, and to Jenny, that simply meant it hadn't killed her overnight.

She hadn't wanted that. To die. She had Emily to think about.

That's what she'd done most of the night, thought about her daughter, still was as she'd stood at the window, watching the sun rise up over the city. A city she wished she'd never come to, and one she couldn't wait to leave.

She would leave soon.

Just had to take care of something else, first.

It wouldn't be pleasant, but she had to protect her daughter at all costs. She also wanted her to grow up into a strong, resilient woman. Within a little more than a decade, Emily would be a grown woman, and needed to know that her mother had fought for what she believed in at all costs.

Even though it had meant losing the love of her life.

Already dressed, because Lord knows she didn't sleep last night, Jenny watched the clock. As soon as the hour hand clicked on the seven and the minute hand paused on the twelve, she picked up the phone and dialed the front desk.

Once two buildings, that had been merged into one, the hotel hosted more than thirteen hundred guest rooms, and one entire floor of the more than fifteen-stories-high building had been dedicated to government officials.

Because it was so dry, Jenny's tongue stuck to the roof of her mouth as the elevator took her upward, and each clang of the cage, as it climbed past another floor, made her stomach clench tighter. To think that Donald had been in the same building since she'd arrived in the city made her want to throw up. She could have run into him in one of the restaurants or hallways.

Anger at herself for how gullible, but also how vengeful she'd been back then, grew amongst the storm of other emotions that had swarmed inside her all night. It was like there was a tidal wave inside her, pushing to get out.

When the elevator stopped, and the attendant, a young, hotel-uniformed man, held the door open, she nodded at him and stepped into the hallway. Her feet made no sounds as she walked along the long, carpeted hallway, checking the numbers on the doors as she moved.

Finding the number given to her over the phone by the front desk, she quickly rapped on the door with her knuckles, knowing if she paused long enough to think, she might back out. That couldn't happen.

The door flung open. "Meals need to be—"

The man stopped talking as his eyes gave her a head-to-toe appraisal.

One that made her skin crawl.

When his gaze landed on her face, he frowned slightly. Almost as if he recognized her, but couldn't place her.

"It's Jenny Sommers, Donald," she said with all the disdain filling her. "We need to talk."

His eyes bugged out even farther, if that was possible, and he touched his swollen nose as he stuck his head into the hallway. "Where's McCormick? Waiting to sucker punch me again?"

Because of him, she'd lost Connor not once, but twice. She'd been at fault, too. Wouldn't deny that. Couldn't. But she couldn't go forward without putting an end to the past. "I have no idea where Connor is," she said, kicking the door open so she could enter the room. "This is between you and me."

Running both hands through his overly greased flat hair, Donald walked backward, staring at her as if he was ready to run. "I didn't know you and he—"

"I said this is between you and me." She stepped farther into the room and closed the door. During the late-night hours, everything she'd tried so hard to forget had returned, plus more, and she was utterly disgusted that she'd accepted his lies so easily.

"What do you want?"

"I'm here on behalf of every woman, every girl, you took advantage of."

"Took advantage of? I never took advantage of anyone. Including you."

"I'm not saying you raped me, but you certainly took advantage of me. You knew Connor had left town. You carried his luggage to the baggage car, yet you told me that he hadn't left town. That he had a new girlfriend." Disgust at herself still filled her, but she was willing to use whatever means possible to accomplish the task at hand. "Is that how you coerced Stephanie and Sarah to sleep with you, too? Along with the others. So many others you can't even count them, can you?" She had no proof, but believed there had to have been others.

He puffed out his blubbery chest. "I was popular. All the dolls wanted me."

She wanted to puke. "No one wanted you then and no one wants you now."

"You do. That's why you're here. In my hotel room."

It was either puke or laugh, so she laughed. Laughed in his face until it made him back up, until the chair behind him stopped him.

Glaring at him, she asked, "Did you ever once think of the consequences of your actions?"

"Bastards? That was their problem not mine. I got three." A sneer formed. "Is that why you're here?"

She would never, ever let this man near Emily. "No. I'm here because a bill will soon be landing on the governor's desk. One concerning homes for unwed mothers. You're going to see that it gets signed."

He laughed. "The governor signs what he wants to sign, and doesn't sign what he doesn't want to sign."

His arrogance made her hands ball into fists. A wave of satisfaction in knowing that Connor had punched him struck, and made her smile. "Your nose is already swollen, almost as big as your head." She crossed her arms, gave herself a semblance of indifference. "Do you not understand what I said?"

He frowned and his face twitched as he stared at her.

"If that bill isn't signed, I will personally visit the governor, and bring along with me every Stephanie and every Sarah who ended up in homes for unwed mothers because of you."

His eyes bugged again as he shook his head.

She smiled and nodded, fully convinced she'd hit the nail on the head. "I'm sure your wife will be interested to know she is not the mother of all your children, and I'm just as sure the governor will have plenty to say about it, and you."

Satisfied, she turned and walked to the door. There, just because she could, she said, "You don't want that to happen, but it will—I guarantee it."

Connor had been pretending life was great for years, and had thought he could do it again, but the ride home had almost killed him. Jenny had said she and the girls would take the train home. He'd put a stop to that idea, and questioned his sensibility afterward. Riding for almost ten hours beside her, catching a whiff of her perfume, hearing the soft, kind way she spoke to the passengers in the backseat, and glimpses of how she stared out of the passenger window nearly the entire way, had been torturous.

The wave that had washed over him as he pulled the car into her driveway a few moments ago wasn't what he'd call relief. It would be over now. Completely. He'd never see her again. She'd accused him of lying, while she'd been lying to him the entire time. It gutted him to think she'd willingly slept with Donald Forsythe.

He'd half expected to see the sniveling jerk this morning, when he'd visited the governor. Before seven. Told him that he and his family would be waiting to hear if the bill Brent Hughes presented was signed.

He hadn't seen Forsythe, and hoped he never did, because he still wanted to strangle that scumbag.

After the women all climbed out of the car, he opened

the luggage compartment to carry their suitcases into the house.

The delightful squeal that split the air filtered past the darkness filling his insides.

"Mommy! Mommy! I missed you!" Emily shouted.

"I missed you, too!" Jenny responded.

Connor couldn't see them, because the open compartment door blocked his view, but he could imagine the two of them hugging. He'd imagined doing that. For a few, amazing hours, he'd imagined being Emily's father. He'd imagined buying her a bike and teaching her how to ride it, taking her to the amusement park, reading her storybooks and a dozen other things. Fatherly things.

"Mr. McCormick!"

He set the suitcase in his hand on the ground as Emily rounded the car on a full run and caught her as she threw herself against him.

"I missed you, Mr. McCormick!"

His heart felt as if someone was wrenching it out of him. Ignoring the pain, he stood, with her still in his arms and set her feet inside the luggage compartment, so she could stand there while he lifted out the other suitcases. And the box containing the evening gown he'd purchased for Jenny. "I wasn't gone long enough for you to miss."

"Yes, you were."

He heard Jenny talking to Gretchen, and the others who'd come out to greet them. Glad she wasn't shooing Emily away from him, he asked, "Didn't your stuffed animals keep you company?"

"Yes. Thank you for them, and the telephone!"

"You are most welcome," he said.

She crossed her arms and the little pout she made

reminded him so much of Jenny his breath caught in his lungs.

Pushing the air out of his lungs, he asked, "What's that look for?"

"Toby Turner!"

He lifted out the last suitcase. Just the box was left. "Who is Toby Turner?"

"A big kid."

"A big kid? What did he do to you?" He would talk to the bus driver or teacher if a big kid was being mean to her, whether Jenny would appreciate that or not.

"He said that my stuffed animals could never live in the same forest, like in the book."

"He did?"

"Yes! He said kangaroos and tigers don't live on the same conti—contine—"

"Continent?"

"Yes, that's it." Her little brows knit together over her pert nose. "Do they?"

The compartment was empty so he lifted her out and set her on the ground and knelt down in front of her. "Let me tell you why Toby Turner is wrong."

Her big brown eyes grew wide as she nodded.

"In books, anything is possible," he said. "Tigers and kangaroos, even pigs, donkeys, and bears, can all live together in the same woods. They can talk and they can sing—they can do anything they want inside books, because books are magical."

Grinning, she nodded her head, making her brown hair bounce. "I'm going to tell him that. Tomorrow morning."

She was so cute, so loveable, and in his opinion, needed a father. A real father, not some scumbag like

Donald Forsythe. Keeping his anger hidden, he winked at her. "You do that."

"I will, and if he doesn't believe me, I'll tell him to talk to you."

He patted the top of her head. "I'd gladly talk to him for you."

Jenny had arrived, and as he rose to reach down to pick up a suitcase, she took hold of the handle.

"We can carry everything inside," she said, nodding to others who'd arrived to help.

They picked up the suitcases, but when one of the girls reached for the box with Jenny's gown in it, she said, "Not that." Picking up the box, she set it in the luggage compartment and then closed the door. "Thank you, again."

That was the most she'd said directly to him since he'd put a stop to the train idea. The ride home had been a quiet, solemn one. Even tiny, little Annie had barely made a peep.

He stuck his hands in his pockets so he couldn't reach out, touch Jenny's hand or arm. His insides were a mess, like someone had crawled inside him and tossed things about, in all directions.

"Bye, Mr. McCormick!" Emily shouted as Jenny held her hand.

He opened his mouth, but instead of saying goodbye, he said, "I'll see you tomorrow."

Jenny shot him a look. Not one he'd call friendly, but she did produce a smile for her daughter. "You run inside. I'll be right there."

"All right, Mommy." Emily waved at him again. "See you tomorrow, Mr. McCormick!" She skipped off toward the house, with her hair flipping and flopping.

"There is no reason for any of us to see you tomorrow," Jenny said.

"Yes, there is." He nodded to the house, where Emily was skipping up the steps. "I need to know if I need to talk to Toby Turner tomorrow."

"I can talk to Toby Turner if it's necessary."

He looked at her, standing there, full of dignity and determination. At this moment, he couldn't say what he wanted, but he could say what he didn't want to end. "I know that you can talk to Toby Turner if necessary, and that you will, but I told Emily that I will talk to Toby if he doesn't believe her, and I will."

"Connor—"

He shook his head. "There are a lot of things unsettled between you and me, Jenny. Things that aren't just going to go away. They didn't go away seven years ago, and they aren't going to go away now. I'll see you tomorrow."

She opened her mouth, but he turned, walked around the car, climbed in and drove away.

It wasn't until he reached the end of the driveway, that he realized some of the pressure had left his chest. The pain was still there, it just wasn't as poignant. He didn't know what that meant. He didn't know a lot of things, other than after not sleeping last night, and driving ten hours today, he didn't feel like driving to Rochester.

He drove into Twin Pines instead and rented his regular room at the Bird's Inn. There, he found the ability to pretend that life was grand while checking in and being caught up on all the latest happenings, as if he'd been gone for months. The highlights were that a car, black and red, just like his, had stopped for fuel at Howard's; everyone had thought it was him, but it wasn't. Obviously. On Saturday morning a rooster had arrived in town and had been waking people up at the *crack* of dawn since then, but no one in the area was missing a rooster, so no one knew who it belonged to or where it had come from.

Connor promised to keep an ear open for anyone missing a rooster, declined the offer to listen to the Grand Ole Opry on the radio, and went up to the room that had become a second home to him the last several weeks.

All because of Jenny.

Standing at the window, staring at the weeping willow tree, where he'd seen her that night when she'd sounded like an owl with a sore throat, a smile formed. Other memories came forward then, two, three at a time, of things that had happened over the course of the past few weeks.

Rather than trying to stop them, he stood there, and let them flood his system. They wouldn't give him any answers, but they felt good. For now, tonight, that was enough.

Chapter Eighteen

Jenny walked out onto the porch as he turned off his car at a little past ten the following morning. Connor sat there for a moment, staring at her through the windshield. She had on a blue dress, partially covered with a white apron, and a white scarf that was around her hair and tied at the nape of her neck.

Connor ran his hands over his thighs, before opening his door and climbing out. "Good morning."

"Good morning." Her reply was cool and hesitant.

"How are you, today?" he asked, stopping near the bottom of the porch steps.

"Fine. You?"

"Fine." He kept a smile hidden upon noticing the faces peeking out from behind the living room curtains.

She pointed toward the chairs on the porch. "Would you like to sit? Or we could take a walk."

Understanding that she knew they had an audience, he said, "Whatever you want."

She nearly shot off the porch. "I need to check the glads."

"Glads?"

"Gladioli. Flowers. I might need to stake some so their stems don't break before they are ready to be harvested."

He fell in step beside her. "Are you missing a rooster?"

"No, we don't have any chickens. We buy eggs from Mr. Mason. Why?"

"One showed up in town on Saturday and is waking everyone up at sunrise. I promised Ava I'd ask if anyone is missing a rooster."

She tried to hide it, but he saw the grin that had filtered across her face.

"How are the girls doing?" he asked. "How are Lora and her new baby, Chester, wasn't it?"

"Yes. She and Chester are fine. Joyce and Meg are delivering flowers today. Gretchen stayed home because—" She gave her head a slight shake and sighed. "Because you were coming over."

"How was Emily this morning?"

"Fine, and fully prepared to tell Toby Turner exactly what you said about books."

"That's good." They'd arrived in one of the fields, where green plants of various heights grew. "Which ones do we need to check?"

She let out a sigh. "None. I just—"

"Didn't want an audience?" he finished for her.

She rubbed the back of her neck. "I—I don't know what more we have to say to each other. I thought about it all night, and I don't know, I just don't know."

He'd thought about it all night, too. "If we are still interested in putting the past behind us, we need to put it to rest." He dug a rock out of the ground with the tip of his shoe. "We both made mistakes, Jenny, but how long are we going to let them define our future? Truth is, I have a phone company because of you. I was distraught when I found out you'd left town, but I couldn't let anyone know that. So I did the only thing I knew how to do. I pretended that I was happy and I focused on telephones. Just like when I was a kid. Everyone thought it was because my father had died, and that I was working so hard because he'd been so proud of me and my telephone inventions. It wasn't. It was because I needed a reason to get up in the morning."

She laid a hand on his arm.

Huffing out a breath, because there was more to the story, he looked at the house, looked at the driveway. "That's what I was still doing when I drove up this driveway for the first time." He turned, looked at her. "And saw you again. That's when I started living again, Jenny. It's been complicated and muddled, but it's been real. Because that's what life is. Complicated, muddled and challenging at times. Days where you don't know what to think, if you're coming or going, and others where you've never been happier. I don't want to go back to pretending, to working all day, every day, because that's not really living." Shrugging, he finished, "I don't know what we need to do, how we can figure this out, but I want to try. And I want to keep on trying."

Jenny pressed a hand to her mouth. She didn't want to go on pretending, either, but there wasn't anything that could fix what she'd done. "I'm sorry," she said. That was a terrible beginning, but she couldn't start at the beginning. She had to start at the end, because if he couldn't accept that, there was no use going any further.

Taking a deep breath, and then holding it as if she was diving in the deepest of oceans, she said, "Before we left the city yesterday morning, I went to see Donald. I told him that if the governor didn't sign that bill, I would tell the governor all about Sarah and Stephanie, the other children he'd fathered. He didn't believe me at first, but he did by the time I left."

"You told him about Emily?" he asked tersely.

"No." She met his gaze, eyeball to eyeball. "I didn't tell him about Emily. And I never will. You may think that's wrong, but she's my daughter, and I don't believe she needs to know, and neither does he. It won't benefit anyone. If someday, that changes, I'll tell her." She held up both hands. "I wish I could change my story, Connor. I wish there was a way I could say it wasn't true, but I can't." Her throat burned. "I can't regret it, either. Because to say that would mean I regret being a mother, regret having my daughter, and I don't regret that. I never will."

"I would never expect you to regret having Emily," he said quietly as his shoulders slackened. "She's a wonderful little girl, and you're an amazing mother." He looked at the ground, kicked aside the rock he'd uncovered earlier. "I don't think Forsythe should know about her, either. He'd use that information against her, against you."

"That's why I'm here. That's why I've stayed here, hidden. For Emily." She had to hold her breath for a moment to quell the tears. "For years, I blamed my mother, told myself that I'd never be like her, pit my daughter against a man." She wiped at stinging in her nose. Her mother held blame, too, but that was her mother's problem, not hers. "I should have been telling myself that I never want to be the person I used to be. Emily taught me it's not about receiving love. It's about giving it."

She had no excuses, only the truth, and it hurt, because the one person she'd thought she'd loved back then, she'd hurt the worst. Him. "I knew Donald hated you, and that's why I let things go as far as they did. Because I wanted to hate you, too."

"Because you thought I'd lied to you," he said gruffly.

The pain inside her just kept mounting, like shovels full of dirt dumped on top of one another. "I thought you'd left me, found someone else, just like my mother had. That's all I had to compare it to, and I retaliated just like I did with her." If only she'd been wiser back then. "When Donald called me, told me that you were at Pinion's, I didn't believe him at first, but the idea that you might be there had me agreeing for him to pick me up, give me a ride there. I don't know how he knew, or how he timed it so perfectly, but we'd just pulled into the parking lot when you and a girl ran out of the door, to a car."

"My cousin, Beth," Connor said. "Donald worked at the train station, probably saw me arrive and knew I had a return ticket for the night train."

She nodded, believing it had been his cousin, and that probably was how Donald knew. "I was ready to jump out of the car, chase you, but he stopped me. Said there was a better way. That I could make you jealous. Let you know what you're missing out on." The ache inside her was nearly crippling. "I don't know why I believed him, but I did, and I agreed. We drove down to the park, talked about how mad you'd be if you saw us kiss, and then…" There was no need to say more, other than, "I hated myself, wanted to forget it, and didn't want anyone to know. Especially you. Less than a month later, I was delivered to the home."

Connor touched her arm, and then stepped forward and fully engulfed her in a hug.

Even knowing that he had to hate her, she wrapped

her arms around his waist and held on as all the emotions inside her exploded, releasing the tears she'd fought to hold back.

"Shh," he said, holding her tighter and rubbing her back. "It's all in the past. All in the past." He kissed the top of her head. "I'm sorry I caused you such pain."

"You didn't, Connor. I did. I should have trusted you. Believed in you."

He lessened his hold, took a step back. "Do you trust me now?"

Jenny felt another layer of the past drift up, slip away. Without any doubt, she nodded. "Yes."

His smile was so tender, her heart somersaulted.

"I trust you, too," he whispered, "and I believe in us. Believe we can have a wonderful future together."

She wanted to believe that with all of her heart and soul. "Even after—"

He pressed a finger to her lips. "It's in the past. Today is what matters." He cupped her face with both hands. "Today is the first day of the rest of our lives."

A blessedly wonderful tremor zipped through her at the shine in his eyes, the smile on his face.

"And," he whispered, "I know how I want to start it."

"How?"

Connor started out by kissing her forehead, then the sensitive spots at the corners of her eyes, one at a time, then the tip of her nose. By the time his lips were in front of hers, happiness was busily working its way through her.

"By kissing you."

The breath of his words mingled with the sigh that escaped her lips. A wonderful sigh because that was

258   A Proposal for the Unwed Mother

exactly what she wanted, too. "That sounds like a good start to me."

In the next instant, they were kissing and hugging, sharing something she'd never dreamed she'd be able to share with him. Love so strong and real and complicated, and wonderful. Most infinitely wonderful.

Jenny rejoiced in how free that felt. She was completely free to love him. Love him without having to hold anything back, keep anything hidden.

When their lips parted and she opened her eyes, she declared, "I love you, Connor McCormick, and always, always, will."

"I'm going to hold you to that, because I'll be right there, loving you back the entire time." He threw his head back and laughed. "For the rest of our lives." Lifting her off the ground, he spun around and around.

While kissing her.

She was dizzy when her feet touched the ground again, but that could have been from happiness.

"When are we getting married?"

Jenny wanted to shout *right now*, but couldn't. She traced the side of his face with one fingertip. "I need to talk to Emily before we set the date."

"May I?" With a hint of a smirk, he added, "I'd like her to become a McCormick as soon as possible."

Tears of happiness struck. "Adopt her?"

"Yes. Adopt her. I want to be her father, and I hope she wants that, too."

Her vision was blurred by tears, but her heart could see clearly, and it saw a beautiful future for all of them. "Yes, you can ask her."

Chapter Nineteen

Talking to a six-year-old shouldn't make a twenty-five-year-old man nervous, but Connor was nervous as he watched the bus approach. He was also excited, and happy, and lucky. So lucky.

He loved his life.

Truly did.

"Still waiting on those phones," Mr. Whipple said out his window as the bus rolled to a stop.

"Next week we'll be putting in poles," Connor replied while walking toward the back of the bus where the only door was located.

"Yeehaw!" the driver shouted. "You're the best thing that's ever happened around here!"

Upon opening the door, Connor lifted Emily off the bus so she wouldn't have to jump, but didn't put her down right away because she'd looped her arms around his neck.

"That's Toby Turner," she whispered in his ear while looking into the bus.

Connor caught sight of a good-sized, blond-haired boy slouching in the seat next to the door. "Did he believe you?"

Emily shook her head. "He said books aren't magical, they're stupid."

"Do you want me to talk to him?"

"He said he doesn't want to talk to you."

Connor gave her a wink, and then said into the bus, "Hold up a second, Mr. Whipple, if you don't mind."

"I don't mind," the driver replied.

Connor leaned in through the door. "You Toby?"

The boy slouched a little lower in his seat. "Yeah."

"Toby Turner?"

"Yeah."

Taking a chance on remembering the locals that had signed up for service, Connor asked, "Is Kent Turner your father?"

Sitting up a bit straighter, Toby said, "Yes, why?"

Connor was glad to see the boy's reaction. It said Toby's father wouldn't be impressed by his son's actions. The universe may never figure out why some kids felt the need to pick on others, but Connor had a good idea of how he could nip this in the bud before it went any further. "Just curious," he said. "I'll be installing a phone at your place soon and will have to mention that you and Emily know each other. That you've talked about books. I'll be talking to your father about books, too. The phone book that will be printed for this area. He'll probably like seeing his name in the book. Most people do."

Toby sat up straight. "He will. I'm sure of it."

"Then I will mention that you and Emily talked about books, and that you agreed with her," Connor said, giving the boy a look that said more than his words.

Red-faced, the boy smiled at Emily. "Books are magical, Emily. You were right."

"And they aren't stupid," Connor added.

"No, sir, they are not stupid."

"Nice meeting you, Toby. And I appreciate you look-ing out for the younger kids, making sure no one picks on them." Connor gave him a wink. "That's what a true man does. Respects everyone."

Toby's chest puffed as his face lit up. "Nice meeting you, too, sir."

Still holding Emily in his arms, Connor stepped away from the opening, closed the door and carried Emily to-ward the driveway. "Thanks, Mr. Whipple!"

With a wave, the bus driver shifted gears, and the bus rolled away.

Emily's arms tightened around his neck again. "Mr. McCormick! Toby doesn't think books are stupid any-more!"

"No, he doesn't, and you tell me if you need me to talk to anyone else." In his heart, she was already his daughter and he would protect her and love her with ev-erything he had.

A thoughtful expression crossed her face, then she shook her head. "I can't think of anyone else."

He set her down on the ground and knelt in front of her. "I'd like to talk to you for a minute, if that's all right?" Not wanting to worry her, he pointed up the driveway. "Mommy is right there, by the curve in the driveway. She'll wait there while we talk."

Emily looked at Jenny and waved a hand over her head. "Hi, Mommy!"

"Hi, sweetheart," Jenny shouted back, waving.

"I'm going to talk to Mr. McCormick," Emily shouted.

"I know," Jenny replied.

"I need to talk to you about something real impor-tant," he said.

"What?" Excitement shone in her eyes.

Like her mother, Emily made his heart sing. He already loved his new life, knew it would get better and better every day. "Do you know what being married means?"

"Yes. Mommies and daddies are married."

"That's right." He glanced down the road at Jenny. Two for one, he really was a lucky guy. "I want to marry your mommy, and am wondering if that would be all right with you."

She put her hands over her mouth as it opened in an O, then held her arms out at her sides, palms up. "Mr. McCormick, that would mean you would be my daddy."

The sense of awe in her voice boosted his happiness up another notch. "Yes, it would, and I would like that very, very much."

Giggling, she jumped up and down, "Me, too!"

Her response was one he was looking forward to seeing on a daily basis. His mind was already making up a list of all things they would do together.

"I've never had a daddy before," she said in a whisper.

"You do now," he whispered back. "And you have a grandma who is going to love you as much as your mommy and I do." There was no doubt his mother was going to be over the moon with Emily.

"A grandma?" she said so quietly he read her lips more than heard her.

"Yes, a grandma, and an uncle and an aunt," he whispered.

She threw her arms around him again and held on tight. "Mr. McCormick, this is the best day of my life!"

"Mine, too, sweetheart. Mine, too." He could have dwelled on all that Jenny had told him, but he wasn't.

He was the winner, all the way around, and was going to make the most of it every single day.

Emily's giggle was soft, secretive, before she asked in a whisper, "Can I go tell Mommy? She's going to be happy."

"She is?"

Emily nodded, and then as if it was the biggest secret in the world, she whispered, "She likes you. She told me so when you gave me my teddy bear."

"I like her, too." Laughing at how Emily giggled, he said, "Let's go tell Mommy."

"Can we run?"

Clasping her hand, he said, "Yes."

Less than two weeks later, Jenny stared at herself in the mirror, blinking back tears of happiness. Everything about her life was nothing shy of wonderful. Perfect. Including her cornflower-blue wedding dress. The same shade of blue as her soon-to-be husband's eyes.

A faint ringing entered the room, and that made her giggle softly. She'd forever love the sound of a phone ringing. It was the reason she'd been reunited with the love of her life.

"Mommy, you look like a princess!"

Jenny turned as Emily bounded into the room. Wearing a frilly dress the same cornflower-blue as hers. The heart-shaped diamond necklace around her daughter's neck sparkled in the sunlight as brightly as the one around her neck. A gift from Connor, signaling how special this day was for Emily, too. "So do you," she said, fluffing the curls that Tina had put in Emily's hair for their special day.

School had ended for the summer yesterday, and

Emily was as excited as Jenny to get their new life started. "Is Daddy going to pick us up soon?"

Emily had switched from calling Connor Mr. Mc-Cormick to Daddy almost instantly, and the sound of it never failed to make Jenny's heart overflow with love. "No. He will meet us at the church. Remember, he said Mr. Whipple will give us a ride there?" Because they all wouldn't fit in Gretchen's truck, Connor had arranged for Mr. Whipple to pick most of them up in the school bus.

"I remember! You're going to like riding on the bus," Emily said. "It's bouncy and makes you laugh."

Gretchen entered the room. "Mr. Whipple just called—he's on his way."

Emily clapped her hands, then ran for the door, "I have to get my bear. I promised he could go to our wedding!"

Wearing a lovely turquoise dress—something Jenny had only seen a handful of times—Gretchen watched Emily run out the door. "I'm going to miss her, and you."

"This is the only hard part," Jenny admitted.

Gretchen smiled. "Don't let it be. You'll only be a phone call away, thanks to that man you're marrying."

"I know."

Gretchen's smile grew. "I knew from the first day he knocked on our door that he'd be back, and I'm so glad I was right." She reached out and took ahold of both of Jenny's hands. "If I had one wish for every girl that has entered this house, it would be for them to find the same happiness, the same love, that you have. I am so proud of you. So proud of the way you worked this all out, got rid of the monkeys on your back, and are moving on. As much as I'm going to miss you, I'm happy to see you go."

"I love Connor so much," Jenny said. "But I love you, too. You saved my life, Emily's life, by bringing us here."

"You saved your own life, and your daughter's, and this was just a temporary place until you and Connor found each other again." Gretchen gave Jenny's hands a final squeeze. "I'm heading to the church now, to put out some vases of flowers. I'll take your and Emily's suitcases with me, too."

Most of her and Emily's belongings had already been taken to Connor's house in Rochester, which was where they would go after the wedding today. He'd offered to take her anywhere in the world for a honeymoon, including Niagara Falls, but Jenny had said she just wanted to go to his house. The home she'd always wanted.

Emily would spend the next couple of days with his mother, and it was hard to say who was more excited about that—Barbara or Emily.

A short time later, Jenny paused before stepping out of the back of the school bus. She'd never seen the small church in Twin Pines so overflowing with people.

"Yeehaw! I always knew this day would happen!"

Jenny laughed and stepped out of the bus to accept Franny's hug. "Thank you for coming."

"Like I would miss this!" Franny stepped aside. "Look who else is here."

Marjorie came forward to give Jenny a hug. "I'm so happy for you, Jenny."

"I'm so happy for me, too," she replied. "So happy."

It seemed impossible, but that happiness continued to grow as the day went on. There were many spectacular moments, but a particular one, that Jenny would never forget, was how Connor, after sealing their love with a kiss in front of the church full of people, picked up Emily, kissed her cheek, and then not caring who saw him, when Emily said her bear needed a kiss, too, he kissed the bear.

Only a real father would do that. An amazing, wonderful, father.

After a luncheon in the backyard of the Bird's Inn, she and Connor climbed in his car. The top was down, and before they drove away, she turned her back to the crowd, and tossed her bouquet of flowers over her head.

At the uproar of clapping, she twisted to see who had caught the bouquet. Laughing, along with everyone else, Connor's mother waved the bouquet over her head.

Connor honked the horn, and then drove away, with her snuggled up to his side and waving at the crowd.

"Would you like me to stop and put the top up?" he asked as Twin Pines disappeared behind them.

"No." She held her face into the breeze flowing over the windshield. "It makes me feel like I'm flying."

"You make me feel like I'm flying," he said.

She hugged his arm with both of hers. "We're married, Connor! Married!"

He honked the horn, several times, as they laughed with glee.

The sun was setting, filling the sky with an array of yellows, oranges and pinks that reflected in the windows of his house as they pulled into the driveway. "We're here," Connor said, looking at his new bride. Her beauty never failed to amaze him, and though he'd been looking at her all day, his heartbeat increased when their gazes met.

"Not here, home. We're home." She kissed his cheek. "I love you, Connor McCormick."

He brought his lips close to hers. "I love you, Jenny McCormick."

Their kiss was sensuous and promising, and broken by her giggles. "I used to practice writing that. Jenny McCormick."

He kissed her again and then opened the door. While she was sliding across the seat, to exit the car via the driver's door after he'd stepped out, he grabbed her suitcase out of the backseat. Then, hand in hand, they ran to the house.

They barely made it inside the house before a kissing marathon started. He kicked the door shut with one foot and dropped the suitcase in order to give her his full attention. He had hers, too.

At some point between kisses they managed to make it upstairs, into his bedroom. He couldn't keep his hands off her. Hers were just as frantic. They were everywhere. Touching his hair, rubbing his neck, unbuttoning his shirt. He loved it. He loved her.

With mutual, unspoken consent, they shed their clothes. The only thing she still had on was the necklace around her neck. The diamonds sparkled with brilliance, but her eyes… He sucked in a breath at their brilliance. At the love and passion they exposed.

Her hands settled on his shoulders. "I've waited years for this. Years and years."

"I have, too."

Their kisses renewed, and Connor found himself walking on the edge of control as they settled onto the bed. He'd never been here before, reveling in the unabashed love flowing between them. He wasn't just kissing her, touching her, he was loving her.

Jenny.

The only woman he would ever love in this deep, all-consuming way.

He cherished every part of her, and took his time, moving slow, watching her expression and rejoicing in her responses to his every touch, every caress.

Their coming together as husband and wife was joyous, exhilarating and profoundly exquisite. Leaving them clinging to each other, gasping for air, and gloriously happy.

"Oh, no," she said dropping her arms out to her sides.

The smile on her face said there was no reason for him to be concerned, yet, he asked, "Oh, no, what?"

With stars glittering in her eyes, she said, "That was even more spectacular than I'd imagined."

He kissed the tip of her nose. "What's wrong with that?"

"Nothing, except the fact that I may never leave this room, and never let you leave it."

He ran a finger along the line of her shoulder. "What just happened can be repeated in many places."

"Really? Where?"

"Well, there's the kitchen or the—"

She pressed a finger to his lip. "How about you show me instead?"

He kissed her finger. "Or how about we repeat it right here?"

"Ducky!"

Chapter Twenty

Settling into her new life as Jenny McCormick, Mrs. Connor McCormick, was the easiest thing she'd ever done in her life. Emily was overjoyed having a daddy, and a grandma, and Mick and his wife Lisa were the most loving aunt and uncle possible.

The month of June flew past, full of visits from family and friends, trips to the zoo and amusement park, days of riding with Connor as he oversaw phone installations, quiet days and evenings at home, and telephone calls.

Jenny had never known how one device could keep people so connected. Connor had even taught Emily how to use it, and how to answer it properly.

Connor was at work, and Jenny was spreading meringue over top of the pie she and Emily had made when the telephone rang.

"Can I answer it, Mommy?" Emily asked.

"Yes." Jenny's heart thudded at the thought the caller was most likely her husband. He often called to let them know he was on his way home.

Climbing onto the stool near the counter where the telephone sat—one of the many telephones in their house—Emily picked up the receiver. "McCormick residence. Emily McCormick speaking," she said clearly and with pride.

Jenny's own pride increased. Emily's last name was legally McCormick now.

"Yes. Who is calling please?"

Emily set the receiver on the desk and climbed off the stool.

"She wants to talk to you, Mommy."

Jenny wiped her hands on her apron. "Thank you, honey."

"Her name is Ah... A. Brown, I can't say her other name."

Jenny's heart stopped. So did her feet. Having never heard it before, Audrey would be a difficult name for Emily to repeat. Connor had found her mother's home telephone number—after she'd asked him to—but when Jenny had called last week, her mother hadn't been home. She'd left a message, but after a few days, figured her mother had chosen not to return her call.

"Do you want me to ask her other name, Mommy?"

Forcing herself to breathe, Jenny shook her head. "No, honey, that's fine. You go get your bear." Her hand shook as she picked up the receiver. "Hello."

"Jenny?"

A person never forgot the sound of their mother's voice. Jenny slowly sank onto the stool next to the counter. "Yes."

After a silent pause, where she heard nothing but a faint buzzing noise, either from the telephone line or her ears, Jenny heard, "Richard and I just got home, and received the message that you called last week. I can't tell you how happy that made me. Makes us."

She nodded, then realizing her mother couldn't see that, she said, "I just, um, wanted to know how you are doing?"

"We're fine. We live in Boston now. Richard has another camera factory. A larger one than the one he had in Rochester." After what sounded like a sniffle, her mother continued, "I'm sorry, Jenny. Sorry for so many things. We looked for you, after that night."

Jenny didn't know what to say.

"But you'd disappeared and we couldn't find you, anywhere," her mother said. "I—Oh, Jenny, I've missed you. How are you?"

Her mother was crying. So was Jenny. "I'm sorry to have worried you." It wasn't much, but all she could think to say. Then, she remembered, the choice was hers. She could let the past back in to rule her, or she could decide to rule the future. They both had been to blame, and it would take both of them to make it right. She drew in a breath and let the past go. "I'm wonderful, Mother. Very happy. That was my daughter Emily who answered the phone. She's six."

"She sounded very polite."

The love inside Jenny made her smile. "Her father taught her how to answer the phone."

"He did a fine job."

"He does a fine job of everything," Jenny said.

"She said her last name was McCormick. Do you live in Rochester?"

"Yes, we do. I'm married to Connor McCormick."

The was a hesitation in the line before her mother asked, "If Richard and I were to drive down would—"

"Yes," Jenny said. "We'd love to have you visit."

"Tomorrow?"

Joy burst inside her. "Whenever, Mother. Whenever is fine."

"Tomorrow?" her mother repeated.

Just as she was about to respond to her mother, she heard Emily shout, "Daddy," and Connor's response along with the closing of the front door.

"Jenny?" her mother said.

"Yes," Jenny said. "Tomorrow would be fine."

"We'll leave first thing in the morning, so you can expect us by late afternoon." There were more sniffles. "I can't wait to see you. And Emily."

"I can't wait to see you, either," Jenny said, looking at her husband carrying their daughter into the kitchen. She hung up the phone as he walked closer.

Connor could read her like others could read a book. He set Jenny down and dug in his pocket, pulled out a blue piece of satin ribbon. "I found this ribbon for your hair today." He dug in the other pocket. "And this one to tie around your bear's neck."

"Oh, Daddy! I will go put it on him right now."

As Emily shot out of the room, he walked closer.

Jenny lifted her face for him to deliver a kiss on her lips, which he did, and he swiped aside the tears on her cheeks.

"Who was on the telephone?"

"My mother."

Connor's heart skipped a beat. He'd assumed that by the tears on her face. He wanted her to be happy, to have her past completely settled, but it had been her choice. He'd even waited until she'd asked if he could find a telephone number for her mother to give her the slip of paper with the number on it that he'd already found for her. The shine in her eyes told him all he needed to know, other than, "When are they coming to visit?"

She stood and looped her arms around his neck. "Tomorrow."

He hooked her waist with both hands. "I'll take the day off work."

Stepping closer so their torsos touched, she said, "You don't have to do that. They won't be here until late afternoon."

His hands caressed her sides as he looked into her eyes, searched for a signal of how he should proceed. He took his role as her husband seriously. He loved her beyond all he'd imagined, and would protect her with his life. "I'll still take the day off."

"I love you." She kissed him, not once, but twice, making the second one much longer. When their lips parted, she continued, "Because of you, there's no room inside me for pain or regrets. I'm too happy. Too full of love."

He felt that way, too. The past was the past, and if she wanted her mother in their lives, he'd support her every step of the way. "You are an amazing woman." He kissed her forehead and hugged her tight. "I didn't think it possible, but I love you more every day."

"I love you more every day, too." She gave him a final squeeze. "I made you a lemon meringue pie today. Which I have to put in the oven right now so the meringue can brown."

He released her and leaned against the counter as she walked over to open the oven door. The news he had to share was going to make her happy, too. Very happy. It certainly had him. He'd almost called to tell her, but had decided in person would be better. He knew how much it would mean to her, and many, many other women. "I received a phone call today, too. At the office."

She picked up the pie sitting atop the stove and slid it in the oven. "From who?"

"Senator Hughes."

She closed the oven door and slowly turned, looked at him. "And?"

He let his smile go. "The governor signed it. It's a law."

Slapping a hand over her mouth, she smothered a tiny squeal, then stopped trying to prevent it and let out a shout of joy. Along with a little jump. "Connor! That's wonderful!"

"I know. It goes into effect September first."

Laughing, she zipped around the table to hug him again. Kiss him again.

"That would never have happened if you hadn't—"

He stopped her by pressing a finger to her lips. "It happened because of you. Not me. I wouldn't have been involved if you hadn't come to the Bird's Inn, hooting like a hoarse owl in the middle of the night."

She pushed aside his finger. "A hoarse owl?"

"Yes!" He pretended to cough while hooting like an owl.

"I didn't sound like that!"

"Yes, you did." He mimicked an owl again, and the coughing.

She stopped him with her lips. A good, solid kiss that he took full advantage of by parting her lips and twirling his tongue with hers.

"Hey! Did I hear an owl?"

Emily's question ended the kiss, and Jenny turned

around. He kept his arms around her, and locked his hands over her stomach.

"It was Daddy," Jenny said, rubbing his arms. "He was trying to sound like an owl."

He loved being called Daddy, by both her and Emily. "Mommy can sound like an owl, too."

Jenny elbowed him playfully.

"There's an owl in my teddy bear book," Emily said.

"Yes, there is," Connor said.

He felt more than heard Jenny's giggle. She knew he'd read the bear book so many times he could recite nearly every page.

"I can hoot like one, too!" Head tilted back, Emily proceeded to demonstrate her hooting abilities.

Chuckling, Connor whispered in Jenny's ear, "Like mother like daughter."

She laughed. "You mean like father like daughter." She grasped his hands and pulled them apart so she could exit his embrace. "I have to get my pie out before the meringue burns."

He kissed the side of her neck, let her go and then scooped up Emily. "That's what we are. A family of hooting owls."

While Jenny took the perfectly browned pie out of the oven, he and Emily filled the room with hoots. After she'd set the pie on the counter, he grabbed Jenny's arm and pulled her into the center of the room. "Come on, Mommy, let us hear you hoot!"

Laughing, she let out her famous croaking hoot. Famous to him. That sound had changed his life.

And now, his life couldn't get any better.

Epilogue

Jenny bundled the perfect baby girl in a thin blanket of cotton and then laid the infant in her mother's arms. "She's perfect, Charlotte. Absolutely perfect." Touching the baby's tiny cheek, she added, "She even looks like an Emma."

"Thank you, Jenny," the new mother said, looking at her precious baby. "Emma was my grandmother's name."

Jenny stepped away from the bed. "The two of you need to get some rest now. I've already called Dr. Bolton, and he'll be over tomorrow to check in on you. And Jason has my phone number. Call me if you have any questions."

Charlotte nodded. So did her husband, Jason, who was standing on the other side of the bed. It was the young couple's first baby, and all had gone very well. In the hours since the baby had been born, Jenny had cleaned, washed the birthing bedding and towels, and made a large pot of stew for the couple to eat this evening and tomorrow.

She'd already carried all of her utensils and supplies out to her car. This was just always the hardest part for her, saying goodbye to people she'd come to know well. "I'll be back in a few days to check on you."

"I'll walk you out," Jason said.

Jenny shook her head. "That's not necessary." Running through everything she'd already mentioned, she chose two final reminders. "The stew is on the stove, and there is a bottle of infant formula in the refrigerator—just warm it in hot water if Emma needs something before your milk comes in, but keep nursing, because it will come in faster the more you nurse."

"I will," Charlotte said.

After a couple more reminders, Jenny knew she was merely repeating herself and took her leave. Closing the door on the small, clapboard house, Jenny paused on the stoop. The sight of her husband leaning against the fender of his car made her heart swell.

"What are you doing here?" she asked, stepping off the stoop. She had called him after the baby was born, just so he knew she would be home tonight.

He pushed off the car and walked toward her. "I came to pick you up."

"I have my car—" No she didn't. The blue-and-white Chevrolet he'd bought her when she'd agreed to offer midwife duties to some of Dr. Bolton's patients was nowhere in sight. "Where is my car?"

"Mick was home when I stopped to pick up Emily, and he rode here with me, took your car home so you could ride with me."

They'd met on the gravel walkway and she lifted her face for a kiss. Whether quick and soft or long and heated, she loved every one of Connor's kisses.

He laid a hand on her back and guided her toward his car.

Noting his car was empty, she asked, "Where's Emily?" Whenever she had to deliver a baby, Emily stayed with Barbara if Connor wasn't home.

"She's going to spend the night with Mother."

Jenny bit her bottom lip. She loved her daughter intensely, but she also loved spending time alone with her husband, and he had no idea how his news thrilled her right now.

She climbed in through the driver's door, and scooted over just past the steering wheel so she could sit beside him. Slanting her legs, so they weren't in the way of the shifter, she snuggled against him as he started the engine.

He backed out of the driveway, then drove along the quiet street, resting his hand on her knee between shifting gears. "Gretchen called for you today."

"Oh? What did she have to say?"

"Tina had her baby. A girl. I said we'd drive over this weekend to see them."

"Wonderful. What did she name her?"

He flashed a grin at her. "Jennifer."

"Aw, goodness." She patted the warmth in her cheeks.

"Gretchen also said that she's agreed to be on the governing board for the home, and so have Cheryl and Rachel."

"That's wonderful news. They'll make sure all the new regulations are followed."

"She said there's still room if you want to be on the board."

Jenny had considered that when she'd heard they were forming a board to oversee the changes, but she didn't want to be away from her husband and daughter, not even once a month. "No, I'll help them when needed," she said, fully satisfied with her decision.

"I'll drive you to the meetings, if that's a worry for you."

"I know you would, but I like things as they are right now. Delivering babies for Dr. Bolton's patients and taking care of you and Emily."

"If you change your mind, just know I'm fine with it."

"I know." She kissed his cheek. "You are a wonderful husband, and father."

"I had to run downtown today and stopped at the department store. Guess what I found?"

Knowing him, it could be just about anything, but the way he was grinning, she'd bet it was something he'd been on the lookout for, which also could be just about anything. "Do I get a hint?"

He hooted.

She laughed. "An owl?"

"Yes. A stuffed one, of course."

"Of course."

"Emily loved it, however, she informed Uncle Mick that he needs to practice his hoots. He's not nearly as good as I am."

"Well, don't let it go to your head," she said, recalling what Riley had said at Mick's wedding. "Your head is already bigger than your brother's."

"You're still laughing about that," he said, laughing himself.

"Don't worry, you're also more handsome than he is."

He winked at her, then asked, "We have the night to ourselves. Would you like to see a movie, or go out to eat?"

"No. Let's just go home."

"Tired?"

"No. I feel great. I just want to be home alone with you."

Waggling an eyebrow, he sped up.

She was fine with that, and fine with the fact that once home, they didn't even bother making it all the way upstairs. Stripped bare, they made love in the living room, and then, with the doors securely locked and the curtains pulled, she made him supper. Completely naked. He was naked too, and their meal became slightly burned when a particular bout of petting had her too needy to do anything but turn off the stove until her husband finished what he'd started.

Afterward, they washed the dishes, collected the clothes spewed across the living room and made their way upstairs.

"Where are you going?" he asked when she walked past their bedroom.

"Just down the hall."

"Why?"

Walking, she curled a finger over her shoulder for him to follow her to the bedroom that was never used. Her parents used the one near Emily's room when they came for their monthly visits.

Once in the room, she stood, with her hands on her hips and scanned the room.

"What are we looking for?" he asked.

"The best place to put a crib."

He turned her around to face him. "Say that again."

Her best efforts to hide her smile failed. "The best place to put a crib."

His face lit up and those cornflower eyes danced with happiness. "When?"

Overjoyed, as she had been since Dr. Bolton had confirmed her suspicions yesterday, she said, "About seven months from now."

His shout echoed off the ceiling, and the walls, and the floor. He picked her up, swung her around, kissed her. When he set her back on her feet, he dropped to his knees and kissed her stomach. "I love you, baby. As much as I love your mommy and sister."

Laughing, she slid down onto her knees so they were face to face. "Do you hope it's a boy?"

He held her gaze for a very long time. "I hope this baby looks as much like you as Emily does."

She shook her head. "I hope it has cornflower-blue eyes, just like its daddy."

He laughed. "I bet Emily will hope it knows how to hoot."

With her heart once again beyond full, Jenny said, "Between the two of you, it will learn quickly. I have no doubt."

She had no doubt that her life was perfect, either.

* * * * *